OUTDONE

TINA BROOKS MCKINNEY

Taboo Publishing

Copyright © 2014 Tina Brooks McKinney

All rights reserved.

ISBN: 0-9821089-5-8
ISBN-13:978-0-9821089-5-6

DEDICATION

God has given me a gift, and I am compelled to share it with you. This book is dedicated to all those people who have given me support throughout my writing career. Even when I had had enough and wanted to give up, your kind words kept me going. I can only hope that I will continue to entertain you. Special thanks to my family whose support I could not live without.

As some of you know, I've branched out to publish my own books. I was sick and tired of working so hard only to get robbed by my former publisher. Believe me, it was a difficult decision to make. I do miss the ease of which my books were readily available in stores. What I do not miss is begging for my royalty check, or trying to understand why those figures didn't compute. Or being lied to repeatedly. I'm done with that. So rather than sign their stupid agreement and forfeit any future payments, I'm doing it myself.

And in case you're wondering if I just called someone out, I did! Tell the truth and shame the devil. (I didn't coin that phrase but I sure do like it.)

ACKNOWLEDGMENTS

The best and the worst part of every book that I have written is the acknowledgments. I say that it is the best because I get a chance to publicly acknowledge some of the people who have shown me unconditional love and support. It is the worst as well because I invariably forget to mention someone's name. It most cases it is not intentional. I cannot possibly list all the people who have touched my heart, so if your name is not listed, please know that I'm an old bat and if I don't write it down, I'm subject to have a temporary lapse in memory.

To my best friend and husband, William McKinney, you show me every day the meaning of true love. My children Shannan and Estrell Young, my parents Ivor and Judy Brooks, you all are the fuel that keeps me going.

Theresa Gonsalves, this chick here has become my shero! She shows me love in every way and doesn't co-sign my crap. Without you, I would have given up a long time ago, and I truly do thank you for believing in me and reading my work and calling me on my crap!

My road dogs, Sharon Jordan, Joyce Dickerson, sisters from another mother, thanks for putting up with my crazy behind. My best friends Angela Simpson, Valerie Chapman, and Andrea Tanner, you already know. Barbara Morgan, Kim Moss Floyd, Patrice Harlson, Muriel Bloomfield-Murry, Detris and Candice Hamm, Marvin and Sabrina Meadows, Dee Ford, Stacy Tumbling, Tra Curry, Linda Coleman, Antionette Gates, Sheila Goss, Rose of Savvy Book Club, Ricardo Mosby, Princilla Johnson, Sydney Molare', Donna Johnson, Terrance Bethea, Sharon Russ, of Words of Inspiration, Bernice Bagley, Stephanie Heard, Mississippi Readers, all of you have touched my heart.

1 COJO MILLS

Normally, I'm the last person to give up in a fight. I'm the one who wants to have the last say, or in some cases the last punch. However, in this fight with my new husband's mother, there would be no winners. Either way, we all lost. I lost out on a potential mother figure now that my own mom had moved away, and Merlin lost the only person who had shown him love other than me.

I didn't want him to have to make a choice. I knew he had enough love in his heart for both of us, but after the way she showed her ass at our wedding, I understood his decision to disassociate himself from his stepmother. He didn't seem at all upset about it either, which really surprised me given his loving persona.

"What's got your face all frowned up, wife? We just got married and I can't get a smile?"

"Honey, don't mind me. My mind was a million miles away."

"You're bored with me already?"

"Stop playing. I could never be bored with you. Do you even know how long I've been waiting to get my husband alone?" I leaned over and kissed Merlin on his cheek. I would have done more, but I didn't want to interfere with his driving.

"Well, you got me, for life. How do you like them apples?"

"I think I like it very much, and I plan to wear it well."

"That's good to know because it's too late to trade me in on another model. I've got the paperwork that says you're mine."

"Like property? Oh no, sweetheart. We ain't rolling like that. We're mated for life because we belong together."

"Okay, I'll take that but I still got paperwork." Merlin laughed wholeheartedly. I loved to hear his laugh.

"Then the same goes for me; I've got papers on you too buddy, so don't go getting any bright ideas."

"About what? You made me the happiest man alive today. Your mom really went all out with the reception, too. I think everyone had a good time after…"

Merlin didn't have to finish his sentence because I already knew what he was going to say. A feeling of sadness came over me. My wedding day would always be paled by Gina's behavior. "I know you don't want to talk about this, but don't you think you should go by the rectory and see about getting Gina home?"

"You're right, I don't want to talk about it. Not tonight."

"But babe, her car is there. What if she gets up and decides to drive it somewhere? Or if she wants to act the fool in the rectory?"

"You don't believe God can handle it? I thought we were supposed to bring him our problems and drop them in his lap."

"I doubt it was meant literally. Like in give us your weak and hungry. That's a liberty speech, not God's creed, at least I don't think it is."

"I disagree with you there. God is a fixer and Gina needs fixing."

"What about the rest of the rectory? Do you plan on punishing them in the process?" I was getting a little irritated with the conversation. I didn't want our marriage to be riddled with regrets. If handled correctly, we might be able to salvage something of a relationship with his mother. I didn't see that happening if we just left her in the church like we didn't give a damn.

"Cojo, what do you want me to do? She has already ruined our wedding day. Do we let her screw up our night too?"

I could tell he was frustrated and so was I. "We've got the rest of our lives together. So I don't mind giving Gina a few more hours of it if it will make things better between the three of us.

"You would go with me to check on her?" He seemed genuinely surprised.

"Of course I would. I would never ask you to do something that I wasn't willing to do myself. Wrong or not, she's still the only mother you've known, and it's our duty to check on her."

"Cojo Mills, you are an amazing woman, and I am so happy to call you my wife."

"I'm sure you would do the same thing for me if the show were on the other foot."

"I'm not so sure about that. The whole thing in the church was very intense. I thought I was going to have to punch my mother out."

"You wouldn't do that! I know you better than that. Is there someone you could call who would come and sit with her?"

"I would call my dad if I thought he actually gave a shit about her. She has this one friend named Tabatha who has been around forever, but I really don't want to embarrass Gina any more than she's feeling right now. Tabatha would ride her ass bareback."

"Ouch, would she be that hard on her?"

"Absolutely. Tabatha believes in tough love. She's there when you need her, but she doesn't tolerate a lot of foolishness, and she doesn't cosign either. Those two fight like star-crossed lovers but they really care for each other.

We pulled up in front of the rectory, and Merlin made a big production of turning off the car without making a move to get out. I could tell he really didn't want to go in.

"Do you think she's still here? I don't see her car."

Merlin's face brightened with a smile. "You're right. It was parked right here when we left."

"You don't think she tried to drive or fought with the priest? Do you?

"With Gina, I never know what to think. Just when I think she couldn't possibly do something worse, she does."

"Should I go inside just to make sure everybody is still alive in there?" My joke was in extremely bad taste.

"As far as I know, she hasn't killed anyone yet. Knowing her, she's at the house having cocktail hour." Merlin turned on the car, and we drove in silence to Gina's house. Luckily, we didn't have any concrete plans for our first night as husband and wife. If we were going to be able to enjoy it, Merlin had to see this through.

I started to open the door, but Merlin stopped me.

"I love that you want to do this with me, but I think I should do this alone. Heaven knows what I will be walking into."

"Okay, I understand." I was secretly relieved. I didn't want a repeat of the last time that I had been in their house.

"I won't be long. I promise."

"Take your time, baby. I know how important this is."

"Did I tell you that I loved you today?"

"I think it was somewhere in those vows."

"Be right back."

2 MERLIN MILLS

My hand was shaking when I put my key in the door for what I hoped would be the last time. As I turned the key, I called out. "Gina, are you home?" She should have been there since her car was.

There was no answer, so I stepped all the way into the living room. I held my breath when I looked around the room. Praying that if Gina was in there that she would at least be dressed. I couldn't stand to see her naked again. Not because she didn't have a nice body, but because no son should see their mom like that. Even though Gina wasn't my biological mother, she was there for me when my own mom wasn't.

"Gina," I called again as I walked into the kitchen. Gina's purse and most of its contents were on the floor in the hallway. I cleared the first floor and didn't see her anywhere.

"I'm coming up, Gina," I yelled as I started walking up the stairs. Given the fact that she didn't answer, I wasn't very hopeful about finding her coherent when I got up the steps. I briefly stepped into my old room and snatches of memories pulled at me. Some of the worst times in my life were spent in that room, but there were also a few good memories too. When Gina first took us into her home, things were good. She provided the stability and love that was missing from my life. Back then, it was my home, but over the years it became just somewhere I slept at night. I had to turn my back on those memories.

The door to Gina's room was closed, which was unusual since she should have been the only person in the house. I knocked on the door softly and waited for a few seconds for her to acknowledge it. My anticipation of a conflict worked my nerves. I firmly knocked on the door again. When she didn't answer, I opened the door.

Gina was sitting on the bed looking directly at me. I gulped. "I knocked," I said weakly. Something about her stare had me feeling weak in the knees. Almost as if I were a kid again about to be whipped for something I didn't do.

"I heard you."

"Then why didn't you answer?" I didn't bother to keep the irritation out of my voice.

"Maybe I wanted you to go away. Did you ever think about that, genius?" She was wearing the same get-up that she was wearing at the church. Her robe was still vomit-stained, and the smell was overpowering.

"I just came by to check up on you. Now that I know you're alive, I'll be going. My wife is in the car..." I was disappointed that Gina didn't offer an apology for the way she had acted at my wedding. She was clutching a glass, so I realized that a rational conversation was not about to happen.

"How dare you bring that tramp over here!"

"She's not a tramp and I would appreciate it if you would give her the respect that she deserves."

"Don't you tell me how to act. I raised your ungrateful ass!"

Her words hurt me to the core. I had never once taken for granted anything that she'd ever done for me. I had bent over backwards just to show her how much I appreciated what she'd done, but she was the ungrateful one, not me. I knew that ninety percent of what she was feeling came from the alcohol, and the other ten percent was how she really felt. That ten percent was what hurt the most.

"I'm sorry you feel that way. I tried to be a good son. Never caused you any trouble. I worked hard in school even while holding down a job since I was old enough to work. I even gave you money when you came up short. Obviously that wasn't enough for you. It's too bad too because I used to love you, but I'm done now."

"What do you mean you're done? You can't just quit your family? I made you the man you are today."

"I'm glad you're finally recognizing that I am a man. So that's why I'm telling you, as a man, that I will not tolerate any more disrespect from you with regards to my wife. I won't put up with it, and if it means that I have to cut you out of my life completely, I'm prepared to do that."

"Who the fuck do you think you're talking to?" Gina attempted to stand up and she swayed as if she were standing on a small row boat in rough waters.

Instinctively, I reached for her but snatched my hand back. "Respectfully speaking, I'm talking to you. I'm going now. I have a wife who is waiting on me."

"What has that ratchet whore done to you? Gave you your first taste of pussy and made you lose your damn mind? Or did she use some of that backwoods voodoo to make you think you couldn't live without her?" Gina chuckled as if she had said something profoundly funny.

"There is no reasoning with a drunk, and that is just what you are. If anybody should be questioned, it's you. So why don't you do us both a favor—sleep this shit off." I turned and walked away. I was half past not caring about her stupid ass anymore.

"Don't you walk away from me, boy," Gina shouted as she attempted to follow me down the stairs. My heart rose up in my throat, but I would not look back. I had done everything that I knew how to do, and I couldn't take it anymore. I opened the door with an aching heart, hoping that she would save her own dignity and stay inside. I looked around as I rushed to the car like the very devil himself was chasing me.

Cojo rolled down her window. "Is everything okay?" Her face was wrinkled with concern.

"It's fine." I said between clenched teeth. I had just opened the door when Gina stumbled outside. She took all four steps in one stride. I was momentarily stunned by it. She was such a short woman it should not have been possible for her to do this without falling down. Especially in her inebriated condition.

"You bitch," Gina yelled as she charged the car like a lunatic.

"Honey, put the window up and lock the door," I instructed Cojo as calmly as I could. I didn't know what I would do if she tried to put her hands on my wife.

"Get in the car," Cojo shouted.

"I'm coming."

"She's trying to steal you away from me," Gina yelled as she beat her hands on the roof of the car. Her small fists were putting dents in my roof.

"Back away from the car, Gina." I was doing my best not to go off on her like she was going off on me.

"Punk ass nigger."

As much as I wanted to snap at her, I couldn't. I heard the window come down.

"Merlin, get in the car...please," Cojo whispered.

Gina was trying to get her hand in the crack of the window before Cojo put it back up. She was lucky she didn't get clipped.

"Go in the house, Gina," I said as I got into the car and slammed the door.

Gina ran around to the driver's side and started pleading with me. "Ronald, don't leave me."

"I'm not Ronald," I patiently answered. At that moment, I hated my father for what he had done to Gina. She was such a beautiful woman when she wasn't tearing herself down.

"Honey, let's go." Cojo pleaded, with tears streaming down her face. This was about the third or fourth time I had seen her cry in one day. It was tearing me apart too.

"She's in the way. Maybe I should get her in the house first."

"You can't reason with her now. Just drive away."

Cojo was right. Gina had moved to the front of the car and was pounding on the hood. I put the car in reverse and backed up enough to get around her. I half expected Gina to run after my car. Instead, she fell to her knees in a puddle of her own piss. It was the most heartbreaking scene I had ever witnessed.

"God help her," Cojo whispered.

"I told her, and I'm telling you—I'm done. I can't go through that with her again. She can't respect you or me, so I don't need her in my life."

"Merlin, you can't just dismiss her from your life. She's sick. It's not her fault."

"Please don't fight me on this. It's hard enough without that. Until she gets some help, I don't have anything for her. My primary concern is you. I ain't got time for anything else."

"Okay, babe. I'm done too."

3 COJO MILLS

Five Years Later

Lazily, I stretched my arms over my head and allowed a hearty yawn to follow as I wrapped a towel around my body. Droplets of water dripped from the ends of my hair onto my shoulders. I didn't care about the cool splashes of water that spotted my back. Sexual satisfaction made the small stuff seem trivial, and I was indeed satisfied. Merlin made it home safely from his short deployment in Iraq, and he'd just worked his magic on me!

"Umph, umph, umph. There ought to be a law against feeling this good." I danced as I grabbed a washcloth from the cabinet over the toilet and used it to wipe a clear spot on the mirror. My dark brown eyes twinkled back at me. A satisfied smile tugged at the corners of my mouth. While I'd managed to cover most of my head with my shower cap, I noticed that the cap was haphazardly skewed in the back, which allowed the ends of my hair to get wet.

"Oh fucking well." I giggled as I turned away from the mirror. I wasn't about to let something so minuscule as wet ends ruin my luxurious mood. I picked up a bottle of lotion and sat down on the side of the tub to begin my moisturizing ritual. I liked to apply lotion while my body was still damp and my pores were open. I rested my slender leg against the sink as I applied the lotion. I could not get the image of my husband's face nestled between my thighs out of my mind.

"He ate my pussy like he was starved," I spoke to my reflection in the mirror. "I guess that old saying was true: absence does make the heart grow fonder." Rubbing the lotion between my hands, I used long strokes to deeply massage my sore muscles.

He beat on my pussy so bad I wanted to call up random strangers and tell them about it. Merlin twisted my body like a pretzel. I was so engrossed in getting mine, I didn't complain about the complicated positions he put me in. In fact, I welcomed the abuse; it had been a long time coming.

Simply said, he fucked the shit out of me. If this was the way he was going to act after a six-month deployment, I was ready for an all-out war.

Merlin enlisted in the army before he graduated from high school because he wanted to be able to be a better provider for our family. We had one year together before he was actually deployed. Enlisting in the army was the last thing either of us wanted, but good paying jobs were difficult to come by. Unemployment was so high, there were college graduates competing with high school students for jobs in fast food restaurants.

Although I managed to keep my job with the state, furlough days and layoffs were a constant threat. The military offered career opportunities for Merlin that he wouldn't have had without the benefit of a college degree. According to his recruiter, after his mandatory stint of four years he could attend college for free.

I allowed a small squeal of delight to escape my lips as I jumped up from my seat on the tub. I was about to go find my husband and find out if he had anything left in his guns. With my feet back on the floor, I went into our bedroom to find something sexy to put on.

As I entered our room, my breath got caught in my lungs. Merlin was standing naked from the waist up in front of the mirror. He was flexing his newly-defined muscles. I marveled at how panty-dropping he was. I felt like the luckiest woman in the world just for being his wife. His bald head glistened in the mirror, and his coppery skin was so luminous it appeared to light up the room.

My pussy dripped in anticipation of another go-around. His eyes met mine in the mirror, and my body seemed to glide over to him. The muscles in his chest flexed, drawing my eyes to them. My hand reached out to touch him as I closed my eyes in anticipation. A shiver passed through my body as my hand touched his heated skin.

"Umm, you ready for round two?" I suggestively said as I traced my name on his chest. The temperature in the room seemed to change, as if a strong arctic blast froze my hand to his chest. The chill caused my lids to snap open.

Merlin's seductive eyes turned stony as he stepped away from me. "Round two?" His voiced seemed to rumble deep within his chest. His nostrils flared, which caused me to take a step back as well. This wasn't a look I was familiar with.

My fingers sought the edges of my towel that I had almost flung to the floor in wild abandon only moments before. "What's the matter?" I stammered.

Merlin's whole demeanor was different and it threw me off.

"You said round two. What do you mean?" Merlin pulled an undershirt from the drawer and held it in his hands.

I caught onto his game. Merlin wanted me to beg for his dick. He wanted me to profess how much I enjoyed our last lovemaking session. I coyly smiled at him and took a step closer feeling brazen. "Oh, you don't remember ripping off my clothes and fucking the brakes off me on the living room floor?"

"Cojo."

There was a warning in his tone that I failed to pay attention to as I continued to sexually tantalize him.

"You don't remember sucking my pussy lips and teasing my clit with your tongue?" I closed my eyes and started gyrating my hips to a song that played only in my head. I allowed my towel to fall to the floor as I danced for him.

"Cojo."

Once again, I ignored the menace in his voice. I was caught up in the moment. I was eager to feel his hands on my body again. "You said my pussy was the sweetest nectar that you had ever tasted...umm." My fingers trailed down my stomach and I finger-fucked myself. "Wanna taste?" I held my finger up for him to taste. My eyes still closed.

The sound of his fist connecting with my jaw reverberated throughout the room. His punch lifted me off the floor, and my arms flailed around uselessly as I sailed through the air. I was so surprised by the blow that I didn't feel the pain until my body collided with our bedroom wall. Stunned, I struggled to get to my feet. My jaw throbbed with ferocious intensity. I went through a range of emotions simultaneously. Shocked that he hit me. Fear that he might do it again, and anger at his nerve.

"Have you lost your hobbit-ass mind? What the fuck is wrong with you?" I demanded, while holding my jaw. I was beyond pissed. If there was one thing that I would not tolerate in a relationship, was a man putting his hands on me. My own father didn't hit me, so I damn sure wasn't going to let my husband do it.

"No. What the fuck is wrong with *you*?" He grabbed a shirt from the dresser and yanked it over his head.

"Is that the shit they taught you in Iraq? Because if it is, then you need to take that shit right back where you got it from." I probably should have taken the time to monitor my words, but I was so heated I couldn't think straight.

Merlin stared at me as if this was the first time that he had ever lain eyes on me. His look sent a chill up my spine, and for a moment, I didn't even recognize my own husband.

"One hour ago we were making love, and now you want to hit me? Where do they do that at?" I rubbed my jaw for emphasis and winced in pain. My entire body hurt, but my physical pain was nothing compared to the mental anguish I was going through. Never in my wildest dreams would I believe that Merlin would put his hands on me.

"I've only been home ten minutes."

What the hell did he just say? I froze. "Huh?" Obviously, I was the one suffering from delusions. There was no way he could've said what I thought he said.

"I said, I've only been home for ten minutes. Who the hell were you fucking an hour ago?" His chest swelled before my eyes as fear replaced the anger in my heart.

Something was very wrong with this picture, and I was having a difficult time trying to figure out what it was. "I…uh…I don't understand." Merlin was standing next to the door, and I needed to placate him enough so I could go through it.

"Neither do I." He took a step toward me and I backed up farther into the corner.

I needed a moment to think. One of us had obviously lost his mind, and I was quite sure it wasn't me. "This isn't funny, Merlin."

"Do I look like I'm laughing to you?" His nostrils were flaring again, and his hands were balled up in tight fists.

I looked around for a weapon. There was no way I was going to allow him to hit me again. Frantically, my eyes searched my corner of the room. The closest thing I could find to a weapon was a pair of high-heeled shoes. I inched my way nearer to the closet as he took a step closer.

"Do I?" He beat his fists against his thighs as his eyes narrowed. Gone was the lust and longing that I saw in his eyes when we were rolling around the floor naked.

"Merlin, stop it. Something is wrong."

"Ha, ain't that the understatement of the year! I come home after getting my ass kicked for six months to find my wife acting like a fucking tramp!"

"Merlin, please." Tears began to flow down my face. I knew there had to be a logical explanation for why he was acting this way. I'd heard about post-traumatic stress, and I wondered if this bullshit was one of the symptoms.

"Please, my ass. I ought to kill your whoring ass. Who was it?"

There was no reasoning with Merlin while he was in this state. I dove for the closet, but he swooped me up before I could hit the floor. I had never been so afraid in my entire life. My body trembled uncontrollably as his fingers tightened around my arms. He lifted me over his head and I screamed.

"Hey, bro, what's up?"

My head jerked toward the door at a man who looked like the spitting image of my husband. Merlin paused as his fingers dug into my skin.

"Gavin?"

Merlin's voice sounded tense to me. I felt the floor rush up to greet me as Merlin dropped me like a useless dumbbell he had become weary of.

"Yeah, man. What's up with you?" The stranger took a step into the room holding an apple, which he bit into with a flourish. He smiled a shit-eating grin and shrugged his shoulders.

Merlin's face could have been carved in granite. "How did you get in here?"

I sat up, wincing in pain. Neither of the men were paying any attention to me as I tried to comprehend what was playing out in front of me.

"You're still leaving the key under the mat just like you did when we were kids."

I had regained my voice and indignation. "Merlin, who is this man?" I was reaching for my towel to cover my nakedness. I knew it was a stupid question even before it had left my lips, but rational thinking wasn't something I was capable of at the moment. Both men stared at me as if I had just stepped off the short yellow bus.

Merlin's shoulders slumped as he moaned. "Man, please tell me you didn't just fuck my wife." The fire had gone out of Merlin's body as my eyes bucked at the inference in his words.

"Wife? When the fuck did you get married?" The stranger laughed as if he said something funny.

"Aw, man…shit." Merlin's face was pinched, and for a moment, I forgot how I was feeling.

"Hell, man, I didn't know. She came through the door looking all good and shit. It just happened. She ran up on me, wrapped those chocolate legs around my waist—it was a wrap." He shook his head as if he were sorry, but his smile indicated otherwise.

I gasped. A feeling of dread came over me. Merlin had a twin brother? *How come he didn't tell me? Where the fuck had he been all this time?* Too many questions and too few answers were racing through my mind. I stood up, but the room was spinning. I stumbled over to the bed to sit down, but Merlin pushed me to the floor. His eyes were filled with what looked like murderous rage to me.

"She was my wife—dammit," Merlin yelled as he punched the wall for emphasis leaving an imprint of his fist in it.

Was? Did this fool just say was? This nightmare was growing by epic proportions. "Wait just a fucking minute," I said as I angrily got to my feet. I marched over to the evil twin and slapped him across the face. I was hoping to wipe away his smile, but it didn't work.

His grin twisted into a scary smirk. "Aw, don't be like that, baby. You weren't acting like that a little while ago. Don't front now." He mocked me, and it took everything I had not to head-butt the motherfucker.

"You bastard!"

"That is true. Our dad never got around to marrying our moms." He chuckled, which only made me madder.

I wanted Merlin to punch his brother like he'd punched me, but he just sat on the bed and stared at his feet. I whirled back around and faced his brother. "How come you didn't tell me who you were?" Outdone, I placed my hands on my hips for want of a better place to put them. My fingers were itching to hit him again, but my hand was still stinging from the first slap.

"How come you didn't know my dick from his? I think that is a better question to be asking yourself."

I leaned back as if he had struck me. His words were piercing like a knife.

"I … uh." I heard the wail come from my husband's mouth seconds before his body collided with mine. He rushed me like a linebacker.

"You bitch! I could kill you for this," he yelled as his fingers found their way around my throat.

I struggled to pry his fingers off of me as his grip got tighter. He was going to kill me and there wasn't a damn thing I could do about it. I tried to communicate with him with my eyes and let him know how sorry I was, but Merlin wasn't looking at me. It was as if he were lost in another realm.

"I'm sorry," I gasped as he abruptly dropped his hands.

Salty tears poured from his eyes and dripped into my open mouth as I struggled to breathe.

I choked, "I'm so sorry. I didn't know."

He pushed me one final time before he rolled off of me.

4 MERLIN MILLS

I brushed by my brother without a glance. I headed for the bar in our living room. I needed a drink in the worst way. Gavin attempted to grab my arm, but I batted his hand away. I wasn't ready to deal with his ass just yet. I needed to wrap my mind around what had just happened. In my entire life, I had never put my hands on a female. I was deeply ashamed of myself.

I grabbed a glass from the hanging rack and filled it to the brim with Absolut. I didn't even bother going into the kitchen to get some ice. I just turned up the glass and drank the whole thing. The liquor burned all the way down my throat and landed in a fiery ball in my stomach. It didn't even compete with the pain that I felt in my heart. I quickly refilled my glass, but this time instead of guzzling it, I sipped at it. I walked over to the sofa and took a seat.

I could still hear Cojo sobbing in our bedroom. However, I couldn't force myself to get up and comfort her. As far as I was concerned, she had betrayed me even if it was done by mistake. "Lord, if it were anybody else but my damn brother…" I openly cried, and I didn't bother to wipe away the tears that rolled from my eyes.

Gavin snickered. "You talking to yourself, bro?" He walked into the living room with a satisfied smile on his face.

It was all I could do not to hop over the sofa and hit him dead in the mouth. Hitting him wouldn't change a damn thing. He would have still fucked my wife. "Not now, Gavin," I said between clenched teeth.

"If not now, then when? We haven't seen each other in years. Don't you want to catch up on old times and kick it with your brother?"

"Naw, nigger. I don't need the recap; I was there. Living through that shit once was enough."

"Ain't no need to get all salty. I thought you would be happy to see me?" Gavin chuckled.

"And why would you think that? There ain't been no love between us in years."

"I know. That's why I thought I would slide through and check you out seeing as you never did come through and check on me. Why is that? How come you never came to see me?"

He had to be kidding. Why would I visit him after what he did? "Damn, man, haven't you done enough already?"

"What did I do?" He looked at me with his big round eyes, which looked so much like mine that it just made my stomach hurt.

"Fuck you." I didn't want to talk to him. I didn't want to talk to anyone. I just wanted to be left alone to wallow in my misery. I could not believe he had come back into my life and tainted the only thing that belonged to me. I wished they would have left him in prison forever. Seven years just wasn't long enough for what happened.

"Damn, dude, are you crying?"

I threw back my head and finished off the rest of my drink.

Gavin said, "Hey, can I get some of that?"

My brother had some big-ass balls. Any other man would have gotten the hell out of dodge as soon as he found out that he had fucked another man's wife. He was lucky I wasn't wearing my service revolver. I do believe I would have shot first and asked the questions that I needed answers to later. "Gavin, I'm about ten seconds from killing you. You need to get the fuck up out of my house."

"Shit, I said I was sorry. What the hell do you expect me to do, kiss your ass?"

I could feel the rage building inside of me. I just wanted to be left alone – why was that so difficult to comprehend? "Stop playing, Gavin. This ain't no joke and I am way past my breaking point, so I'm asking you nicely to leave it alone."

"Or what? I ain't scared of your punk ass. You won't be putting your hands on me like you did your wife."

I could not believe he was still goading me. I felt like I was a child all over again. "Not now, Gavin," I warned. I was burning on a slow fuse, and I knew that if he actually touched me, I would spend the rest of my life behind bars like he should have done. In the end, I had to ask myself was he worth prison, and the answer was no.

Gavin had always been the bane of my existence, and even though I loved him, most times I couldn't stand him. As a child he was always getting into trouble, and I wound up getting punished for it.

"You can't keep trying to fuck up my life. I put that shit behind me." I snatched my glass and went back to the bar to refill it. I tilted the glass up to my lips, anticipating the burn.

Cojo was still crying in our bedroom although her cries were muted to me. While my head knew it was not her fault that my brother had deceived her, my heart wasn't trying to hear it. Putting my feet up on the coffee table, I picked up the remote, hoping to drown out the sounds coming from my bedroom.

Gavin came over to me and kicked my feet off the coffee table.

"Fuck off, Gavin. I ain't in the mood," I warned.

"Stop acting like a punk, man. This ain't the first time that we've smashed the same pussy. Remember Kim?"

I didn't smash Kim; I just let him think that I did.

I pointed toward my bedroom. "That pussy belongs to my wife." It took everything in me not to bash him upside the head with my glass.

"My bad. But I still don't see why you're getting so upset. How was I supposed to know that you were married? It's not like I got a phone call or even a damn letter from you."

My head jerked up. I just stared at him. I could not believe that he was taking this so lightly. "What are you doing here, Gavin?"

"Damn, I've been in the joint all those years, and that's all you have to say to me? Can't a brother come see about his kin?"

Not visiting Gavin was a conscious decision that I made a long time ago. I needed the time to forgive him for all the wrongs he'd done. Any other day, I might have been happy to see him, but he had ruined our reunion when he stuck his dick in my wife. "How did you find me?"

"Mom. She gave me your address when I showed up at her house. Funny thing is, she didn't have no love for me either. She didn't even tell me she moved. I found that out the hard way." Gavin let out a wicked laugh, but I failed to see any humor in the situation.

"Remind me to thank her if I ever speak to her again." I went and got the bottle and carried it back to the sofa with me. This day was turning from sugar to shit. Gavin and my mother in one day – it was too much.

"What? So you mad now?" Gavin pushed his foot against the table, knocking over the bottle and spilling my precious booze on the table.

"Why shouldn't I be?" I sulked.

"Man, I said I was sorry," Gavin replied as if that was supposed to fix everything.

"No, you didn't. You said 'my bad'."

"Same difference." Gavin picked up the bottle and turned it up to his lips.

"I see prison hasn't changed you much. You're still a selfish bastard, thinking only of yourself." I reached up and snatched the bottle back from him and wiped off the lip.

"Bro, you need to lighten up. If you keep treating me like this, I might develop a complex."

"Fuck you. That's the problem with you now. Everybody babied your ass and you thought people owed you something for nothing."

"Negro, please; ain't nobody babied me. It was your ass that was always running around trying to suck on Gina's tit."

"I'm not going to argue with you. Tell me what you want and get out of my house."

"Oh, it's like that?"

I threw my hands up in the air in frustration. Gavin was a superior manipulator so I couldn't let him get into my head. Whenever I went against him, I came out on the shorter end of the stick.

"Gavin, I am in no mood for your games."

"I need a place to crash." Gavin reached for the bottle again, but I quickly moved it out of his reach.

"Get your own bottle," I said, pointing to the bar in the dining room.

"I like yours better," Gavin said as he faked a left and moved right and snatched the bottle out of my hand. Although he was laughing when he said it, he had never spoken truer words. He always liked what I had, but the biggest part of the problem was he always got it. I buried my head in my hands. I wasn't ready to have this fight with my brother. In the state I was in, I would kill him.

"You can't stay here," I spoke into my hands. There was no way that I was going to allow him to stay with me after what he had done to my wife.

"Why not?"

I fought the urge to scream at him because I knew it wouldn't do any good. Gavin was the type of guy that got off on getting somebody else rattled—especially me.

"Hello, you just fucked my wife!"

"Oh, yeah. I did do that, didn't I?" He started laughing.

Before I could stop myself, I lunged at him, but Gavin pushed me aside before I could wrap my hands around his neck.

"Stop playing." He brushed himself off as if I had somehow soiled him with my touch.

Cojo's sobs got louder when she opened our bedroom door. She was holding a rag to the right side of her face with one hand, and her suitcase with the other. For a moment, I forgot about being mad at my brother.

"Where the fuck do you think you're going?"

She looked at me as if I had just bumped my head. "None of your business." She walked into the kitchen with me close on her heels.

"Cojo, I asked you a question." She had no friends whom I knew of that she was close to.

"And I gave you an answer." She continued looking around the table as if I weren't standing there.

It was bad enough that she'd admitted to screwing my brother, but my ego couldn't take her clowning me in front of him too. I reached out to grab her arm and she yanked it away from me.

"Don't you dare touch me!" She pulled down the rag and allowed me to see what I'd done to her in my rage.

My heart clenched as I looked at her swollen jaw. My anger dissolved immediately. I forgot about the macho image I was trying to maintain. "Ah, damn, baby, I'm sorry." I took a step forward. I wanted to take her in my arms and comfort her.

"You damn right you're sorry. You're lucky I don't have your ass locked up."

I took a step back. I didn't take too kindly to being threatened with the law even when I deserved it. I swallowed the lump of fear in my throat. "I understand how you feel. There is no excuse for what I've done."

She stopped searching the table and looked right through me.

"Tell it to my lawyer."

If she was trying to hurt me, she was doing a damn good job. Despite what happened here today, I didn't want a divorce, and I didn't want her to leave me. "Baby, please, can we just sit down and talk about this?"

"Oh, now you want to talk after you tried to bash my brains in? I don't think so."

"Babe, I really am sorry. Something inside me just snapped."

She just stared at me. I knew that if she left me, she would never come back. She would go home to her mother, and since she didn't like me anyway, it would be a wrap for us.

"I think I need some time by myself to think." Her voice was barely over a whisper, so I had to lean in close to hear her.

"Can't you do your thinking here?"

"No, the sight of you sickens me."

I was about to respond when Gavin walked into the kitchen.

"Yo bro, I know you ain't begging that bitch to stay."

Cojo and I both turned around and glared at Gavin. I had forgotten he was even there.

"You…rat…bastard," Cojo yelled. She grabbed a knife from the dish rack and was heading straight for my brother.

I screamed, "Cojo, no." There were so many times in my life where I wanted to kill my brother. I couldn't let her mess up her life for the likes of him.

Gavin was backing out the kitchen with his hands up in the air. He was smiling as if this were all a big joke. I grabbed her arm but, once again, she snatched it away from me.

"I told you to keep your hands off of me." She wielded the knife at me.

"I wasn't going to hurt you. I just didn't want you to do something you would regret the rest of your life."

"What? You think I care about that fucker? After what he did to me?"

"Baby, please. Put the knife down, Cojo," I pleaded.

"Punk ass," Gavin replied.

I could not believe he was still egging her on instead of keeping his mouth shut and letting me diffuse the situation. "Shut up, Gavin. You're not helping matters any."

Acting like Billy Bad Ass, he turned his back and walked away, almost daring Cojo to put him out of his misery.

She whirled around and faced me. "I'll stay, but that motherfucker has to go!" She lowered the knife, but she didn't put it in the sink, so we were not out of the woods yet.

"Baby, he just got out of prison and he doesn't have any place to go."

"And? Give me one good reason why I should give a fuck about that."

I knew exactly how she felt. I wanted to be rid of him too. I just needed to get him on the other side of my door.

"Look, stay right here and let me handle him."

She pulled out one of the bar stools and sat down on it as I walked back into the living room.

"Gavin, you're not going to be able to stay here."

"You letting that bitch tell you how to treat your own family? We haven't talked in over five years. Is this the way you're going to do your own brother?" He hawked up a bunch of saliva in his mouth as if he were going to expel it on the carpet, then thought better of it.

"Negro, please. We haven't talked or seen each other in years. We might be brothers but we're not family, and I don't want you here."

Gavin raised his eyebrows as if he hadn't heard me correctly. There was no way that I was going to side with him over my wife.

"I guess I got to go back to Mom's and tell her you wouldn't help me out." Gavin got up off the sofa and walked toward the door. This was a trick he used when we were little. Gina was real big on us looking out for each other. The only problem with that was it was rarely reciprocated.

I looked around the room for his bags, but I didn't see any.

"I could give two fucks what you tell our mother, we're not exactly on speaking terms either."

"This is messed up and you know it. I thought you would be happy to see me."

I slammed my hand on the coffee table in anger. He had manipulated me all my life. I was done. I pulled out my wallet to give him a few bucks to be rid of him. Counting out two hundred dollars, I folded up the bills in my hand. "Here, take this." Giving him the money was more to ease my conscience than to help him.

"You changed your mind?" He turned around all smiles. "Thank God I don't have to wait on another cab. I'm broke as it is."

"Naw, just take this. Maybe you can get you a hotel room until we can figure out something else."

"Shit, I don't want your money. I came over here because I wanted to spend some time with my only brother. Keep that shit." He pushed away my hand as if I offended him.

"Man, take the money. You can get a room and not have to worry about going by Mom's. We can get together in a day or so when things settle down some."

"Whatever." He snatched the money out of my hand and went out the door. He didn't say bye or kiss his ass.

This was the story of my life with my brother. He would do some jacked up shit and I ended up feeling guilty about it. Part of me wanted to run after him and allow him to stay, but the other part of me really didn't want him around. I had blocked him out of my life for good reason, but my stubborn heart didn't get the message.

5 GINA MEADOWS

"Tabatha, I need to talk with you. Pick up the phone." I hated leaving messages on answering machines, but I had called my best friend Tabatha three times and each time she didn't answer. I really needed to get her opinion before I let Gavin back into my life.

She picked up just as I was ready to hang up, sounding all out of breath. "Gina Meadows, why you blowing up my phone? This had better be important."

A part of me wanted to get mad, but the other part of me didn't have time for that.

"Every time I call it's important. You didn't know? I need some advice."

"I should have known that your ass wasn't just contacting me because you missed me."

It had been a few months since I had talked to Tabatha, and even though it might not seem like it, I did miss her influence in my life. Of course, I was not about to tell her that. She was nosey enough without that little bit of information.

"Girl, it's Gavin. He's out of prison."

"Did you expect him to be in there forever? I kept telling you to deal with him while he was locked up."

"Well, that's a moot issue now. He showed up on my doorstep and I don't know what to do."

"What do you mean you don't know what to do? Shut the fucking door in his face. That boy is bad news and you know it. After all the shit he did, I'd be scared to have him around me."

"Tabatha, he is my son."

"He's the son of a fool and you don't owe that man anything."

"Since you have never had children, I'm sure you wouldn't understand the bond we have. Even if his father was an asshole, I still owe his child."

"I have a news flash for you; you haven't had a child either. Gavin is probably twenty-two years old. The debt you feel you owe him has been paid. And in case you didn't know, you can't raise no man."

There was some truth in Tabatha's words. I didn't have to continue caring for the child of a man who had dogged me all these years, but I still loved Ronald, and while we continued to see each other, I sort of felt obligated to do for his child. "You have a point. He just showed up at my door acting as if I owed him something."

"I don't see why. As hateful as you were to him and Merlin, yours would be the last door I would knock on."

"I was not hateful." She was being downright hurtful.

"Bitch, please. Ever since you gave up your own child, you have been a hateful witch to those boys. And you're still a hateful bitch behind that shit. It's a good thing I know why you do the things you do, or I would have stopped fooling with your ass too."

"Tabatha, I didn't call you for all of that."

"The truth hurts. Why you think you and Merlin haven't spoken in all these years? If you'd done that shit to me, I wouldn't be bothered with your cantankerous butt either."

"I've got to go, Tabatha."

"Don't you hang that phone up on me. I've been waiting on this day for a long time, and you are not going to deprive me of it."

"What day?" I was perplexed.

"The day that I climbed back in your ass for being a shitty friend."

"Honestly, Tabatha, your timing couldn't be worse. I'm in the middle of a damn crisis and you want to talk about friendship?"

"I kind of think they're related. See, you made me care for those children you raised. You made me participate in their lives when I couldn't give a shit. But when stuff went south, I was the very last person you called, and sometimes I didn't get that call at all, and I just had to find out about it by my damn self."

"You should be thanking me I didn't worry your ass about every little detail of their lives. I thought I was being a good friend."

"You are a damn liar. You kept it from me because you assumed I would point the finger back to you."

"I don't know what you're going on about; I already told you I've got bigger fish to fry."

"How come I haven't heard from you, Gina?"

"Last I checked, the phone worked both ways."

"Bitch, please; I called you numerous times and you never answer your phone."

"Well, I ..."

"There is no excuse, Gina. Like I said, you're a terrible friend. If I treated you like you've treated me, you would have stopped being my friend a long time ago. Hell, it's been almost two years since I've heard from your ass, and the minute I do it's because you have a damn problem. Tell me why I should give a fuck about that?"

As much as I wanted to get mad I couldn't, because she spoke the truth. With each passing day, it was more and more difficult to pick up the phone to check on my friend. I avoided her because I didn't want to answer any of her questions. "What do you want me to say?"

"I just want you to answer one question."

I sighed. "What is it?"

"Why was it so easy for you to flush our friendship down the toilet?"

"That wasn't my intent. I promise you. Even though I haven't called you, I still consider you to be my best friend."

"You've got a funny way of showing it."

"I know; I suck. I get to feeling sorry for myself, and I tend to shut down. It doesn't mean that I don't care about you."

"Friendships are a two-way street, Gina. You can't have me over here caring about you, and you being over there caring only about yourself. Everybody has problems, it's a part of life."

"I get that, but since my problems are all of my own making, how can I expect anybody to understand them? Don't you think I get tired about moaning about it? So, I keep it to myself."

"Like when Merlin got married?"

I felt as if I couldn't breathe. I couldn't even speak for a few seconds. "How did—"

"It wasn't because you or Merlin told me. I honestly don't know who I was madder at—you or him. Do you know how that made me feel when I found out? You don't even have to answer that because you won't know since you are a lousy friend."

"What do you want me to say, dammit! I fucked up. I fucked up bad, and I couldn't tell you because I didn't want to hear I told you so."

"I didn't have to say that to you because you already knew. Tell me how many times have I dragged your nose in your shit?"

"You never did that."

"Exactly. Then you should have had no problem telling me about it. Didn't you think I would want to attend?"

"I wasn't even going to go my damn self so why I invite you?"

"But you went, didn't you?"

"I went and made a damn fool of myself. Merlin won't even speak to me."

"Oh. I didn't know that part. Please tell me you weren't the one who stood up and objected."

"Trust me, it was worse than that. My drunk ass thought it was Ronald up there instead of Merlin. I don't remember driving to the church at all, but I do remember tearing Cujo's dress and throwing up on her."

"Oh, shit. Wait, Cujo? Cujo is a damn dog from a horror flick."

"I do regret acting a fool at the wedding, but throwing up on Cujo was priceless."

"Wow. I can't believe you even said that out loud.

"Ain't no point in lying about it. She's obviously keeping him away from me."

"So how did Gavin find you? Didn't you move?"

"For someone who hasn't talked to me in a long time, you sure do know a lot about my life. Are you stalking me?"

"Are you high? I'm a thirsty real estate agent. I read the paper every day looking for leads. I knew our friendship was over the moment you put your house on the market and didn't call me."

"I don't want our friendship to be over. I've missed you terribly. I didn't list my house with you because you know everything that's wrong with it. I was actually doing you a favor by not listing it with you. Your clients would hate you because of it."

"You should have trusted me enough to spin it. I could have worked it, but we'll never know, will we? I found out about Merlin's wedding from the paper, too. There was a small announcement listed near the obituaries."

"You have every reason to hate me," I said, crying.

"Yeah, I do. Call me stupid if you want – in spite of everything, I still care about you."

"Can you come over? I really need your advice before Gavin gets back."

"Sure, I'll be there in about fifteen minutes."

"Okay, see you soon."

6 GAVIN MILLS

After struggling with the unfamiliar door, I finally managed to get it open and tossed my keys on the kitchen counter. I was so deep in thought, I didn't even see Gina draped over the living room sofa.

"How did it go?" She gaped at me with liquor-colored lenses.

"All right." I wasn't ready to discuss my visit with Merlin just yet. I still had some thinking to do. Something had changed about him, and I had to decipher what it was before I proceeded.

"Just all right? Was he there?" she demanded as if her next breath depended on my answer.

"Uh, yeah, he was there." I took off my jacket and was about to head back to my room, but it was obvious my mother wasn't ready for this conversation to be over.

"What did he have to say for himself?"

"He paid for my cab fare." I slung my jacket over my shoulder and turned toward my door.

"Don't you walk away from me, boy, while I'm talking to you."

My skin bristled as I digested the comment. It really pissed me off that Gina insisted on calling me a boy, despite the fact I was already in my twenties. I bit my tongue to keep from telling her exactly how I felt, because Gina could be a vengeful bitch. She would kick me out of her house and not even bat an eye, so I trod carefully. "Sorry, I didn't realize you had something else you wanted to discuss."

I lifted her feet off the sofa and sat down with her tiny feet on my lap. Gently, I massaged her toes. I knew this was one way to bring out her other half, the half that I once loved. Growing up with a Gemini woman was a stone-cold trip. You never knew who you were talking to until you felt the backside of her hand upside your head.

"Umph," she snorted as she scratched under her armpits. She was pretty disgusting. The last thing I wanted to do in this world was to rub her crusty feet. If I had more money in my pocket than the measly two hundred dollars my brother gave me, I would've treated her to a pedicure which she desperately needed.

I looked around the room, and it felt as if I had stepped back in time. The sofa that we were sitting on was the same one that graced our living room when Merlin and I were younger. It was still encased in plastic, which had yellowed over the years. Part of me just wanted to take off the plastic and let the sofa breathe.

"Was Merlin's trick there?"

"Are you talking about his wife?" I knew exactly who she was referring to, but I refused to go there with her.

Gina had yet to share with me what she had against sexy-ass Cojo. Until she did, I was going to tread carefully.

"I said exactly what I meant and you know it." Gina folded her arms across her ample chest. For a minute, my gaze lingered. The size of her breasts never ceased to amaze me. For such a tiny woman, she had the biggest natural breasts that I'd ever seen. I suppose that was why I had always been attracted to busty women. They could be dumb as a box of rocks, but if they had a set of knockers, yowee, I was in lust.

"Yeah, she was there." I kept right on massaging my mother's toes, hoping that she would give up her inquisition. For a brief second, I felt a tinge of jealousy because my mother was more interested in what my brother was doing at his house than in me. After all, it had been seven years since we had seen each other, and the first words out of her mouth when she opened the door were about whether I had stayed in contact with him. Shrugging, I pushed away those ugly thoughts and tried not to dwell on them.

"Why are you being so damned secretive?" She pulled her feet off my lap and sat up on the sofa, giving me a brief glimpse of the imprint of her vagina pressed against the pink leggings she wore. It made me think of Cojo.

My fingers felt nasty. Part of me wanted to rush to the bathroom and wash my hands, but I knew that would send her into a tizzy, and I didn't need the bullshit. All I wanted to do was go to my room and take a nap. Merlin's wife wore me the fuck out, and I needed to re-energize. "I ain't being secretive. It's just nothing that I want to talk about right now. I'm tired. The trip here was three hours. I need a bath and a bed, in that order." I was hoping my little plea for sympathy would get me off the hook for a few hours, but my mother wasn't having it.

"You've got all night to sleep. I want to know what your brother is up to."

"He ain't up to nothing. How come you didn't tell me that he enlisted in the army?"

"He did what?" She jumped up off the sofa and started pacing the room. She grabbed a cigarette from the pack on the coffee table and struck a match to the end.

The acrid smoke filled the room. I stifled the urge to cough. I hated cigarette smoke, and I felt like she lit it just to torment me. As an asthmatic, I tried to stay away from it because it forced me to use my inhaler. "Must you smoke that thing while I'm in the room?"

"Negro, please; this is my damn house. If you don't like it, you can get the fuck out."

I just shook my head. Some things never change. She had been telling me to get the fuck out it seemed for my entire life. I stood up.

"Where the fuck do you think you're going? I wanna hear about your brother and the service."

"I'll tell you, Mother, but I cannot stay in the room if you insist on smoking." I held my breath just in case she told me to get the hell out of her house.

"Fine, I'll put it out. Now tell me." She snubbed her cigarette into the ashtray, and flopped back against the cushions of the sofa as if I had stolen her lollipop.

"He just got home from Iraq. From what I gathered, he's been gone for about six months."

"My baby has been gone for six months, and he didn't even bother to tell me?"

Gina was a fucking trip. She chose the damnedest times to claim us as her children. Most of the time, she ignored the shit out of us and complained about not having her own child.

"I don't know nothing about it. None of y'all wrote to me and told me shit. If I hadn't of shown up when I did, I guess I wouldn't have known either."

She frowned. "Did you ask him why he made such a foolish move?"

"No, I didn't. I'm going to take a shower." I was done talking about Merlin. Something was different about their relationship as well, so I wanted to talk less and listen more.

"Yeah, take your ass to bed. Maybe when you wake up you won't be in such a stank mood."

If she thought my mood was stank, it was obvious that she hadn't checked herself out in the last thirteen years. "Are there towels in the bathroom?"

"Yeah, in the closet, and don't go messing up my fancy ones on the wall. And make sure you put the toilet seat down when you use it. If I dunk my ass one time, your black ass is out of here."

"Yes, *Mother*," I emphasized the word. If she'd told me once, she'd told me three thousand times about letting down the seat, and I was sick of hearing it. I gently closed the bathroom door, even though I wanted to slam it. For the umpteenth time, I wondered if I had made a mistake by coming back.

After a seven-year bid with the Federal Bureau of Corrections in Edgefield, South Carolina, I didn't have a lot of options. Although I got my GED while in prison, I had no real work experience and my cash flow was nonexistent. My plan was to come home, regroup, and try to get on my feet in familiar surroundings; however, I had forgotten how dysfunctional home really was, and I was beginning to wonder if the security of a roof over my head was worth the mental torture that living with Gina brought.

Taking off my clothes, I filled the tub, hoping to revive my spirits. It had been a long time since I'd been able to take a bath, and I planned on enjoying every minute of it. I stepped in. I immediately began to relax, and the things that I had been stressing over moments before no longer seemed important. I hadn't realized until that moment how much prison had changed me. Just being able to close the bathroom door was a luxury that had been taken from me. I grabbed a yellow bar of Dial and smelled it. "Ah, I feel like I've died and gone to heaven." Anything that didn't smell like prison-issued lye was heaven-sent to me because I didn't have money to buy anything better while I was in. That prison soap made your skin itch something terrible. The smell followed you around for hours. I inhaled deeply, fully appreciating something so simple as a bar of soap.

I lathered my washcloth thoroughly and reveled in the feeling of the bubbles gliding over my skin. I was feeling so good I wanted to break out with a song, but since I couldn't carry a tune in a bucket, I decided to leave that alone.

As my hand glided over my dick, I froze. My thoughts went back to Cojo, and I began to stiffen. A slow smile slid across my face as I remembered her fat pussy lips and the way they wrapped around my dick and sucked me in. She was quite a handful, and just what the doctor ordered after my imprisonment. "I'm gonna have to hit that again."

Gina banged on the door like she was a CO. "Gavin, don't you be in my tub jacking off and shit."

Her timing sucked. I rinsed off the remaining soap on my body, then stepped out of the tub. I looked down at my clothes in disgust. I didn't feel like putting them back on. I stuck my head out the door. "Mother, do you still have any of my old clothes?"

"Hell, no. I know you didn't think I would be carting that stuff around with me when I moved," she hollered back.

My heart sank because I would have no choice but to put on my dirty clothes again or walk around in the buff. "I just asked."

"Call your trifling brother and see if he can bring you over some clothes. I sure would like to see him."

Wow, that was actually a good idea, and I was surprised that I didn't think of it myself. Wrapping a towel around my waist, I padded out to the living room to make the call. "What's his number?"

"Hell, you were just over to his apartment; why didn't you get the number while you were there?"

Sometimes I just wanted to strangle her. "He wasn't all that happy to see me and I forgot. Things were happening kind of fast. Don't you have the number?"

She got up off the sofa and went into her bedroom. I could hear her grumbling, but I pretended not to notice. She came back a few minutes later carrying a small phonebook. After flipping through several pages, she finally called out the number.

The phone rang three times before Merlin came on the line. "Hello, Gina. It's been a long time."

I hung up the phone. The last thing I wanted was for Merlin to know I was staying with Gina instead of the hotel that he'd given me money for.

"Why did you do that?" Gina demanded. She was practically salivating at the mouth.

Thinking fast, I blurted out. "His wife answered."

"Well, I don't blame you then. I hate her."

I kept my hand on the receiver just in case Merlin decided to call back. If he did, I would have to make up something to say that would explain my presence.

"So what are you going to do now?"

"Can I wash my clothes here? I'll stop by Merlin's in the morning to see about getting some other clothes."

"I guess, but don't be making this no habit. Ain't nothing in this apartment free. I don't have money to be wasting it on extra water and shit." She lit up a cigarette.

"Okay, Mother, I get it. Just give me a few weeks to get on my feet and I'll be out of your hair."

"Humph. I'll believe it when I see it. I've heard it all before. I should call you 'just can't do right'."

There was a hint of sadness mixed with sarcasm in her voice and it hurt. She blamed me for my shortcomings, but I blamed her. If she'd been more loving and nurturing, maybe things wouldn't have turned out as they did. As it was, she pitted me against my brother from as far back as I could remember. I wanted to say all those things and more, but I was forced to suck it up until I could do better.

I placed my clothes in the washer and went into the spare bedroom to take a nap. Gina was still on the sofa watching television as I gently closed the door behind me.

7 GAVIN MILLS

I lie across the bed and sleep claimed me. Almost immediately, I fell into the same dream that had haunted me since the fateful day I tried to steal something else from my brother and ended up in prison. In retrospect, the time served wasn't worth the effort I put into it.

I had made a date with this cute little honey named Cheryl, who thought the sun rose and set in Merlin's ass. I flirted with her online pretending to be Merlin. One day, I asked her out and she accepted.

For me, it wasn't just about a chance to get my dick wet. I didn't have any trouble getting the girls. But Cheryl was of a different caliber of girl than I was used to. She wasn't drawn to my bad-boy persona. She didn't even know I had one. She was attracted to Merlin's physical prowess and his mental agility. I wanted to know what it felt like to be corny for a change, cracking stupid jokes and generally cutting up.

The other thing that motivated me to go out with Cheryl was Merlin's new car. For years, I thought he was a sucker for working. He started when he was younger, washing cars for change. He gradually moved on to cutting grass and shit. As far as I was concerned, they couldn't pay me enough money to get my hands dirty. What I failed to realize was that Merlin put his money to work for him and was able to buy a car before anyone else in our class. This instantly changed his dateable statistics. I was jealous of his rankings, and because he would never let me touch his precious car, dating Cheryl gave me the perfect excuse to take it for a drive.

Things might have turned out differently if Merlin's cheap ass had put gas in his car. When it ran out of gas, Cheryl and I had to walk. Her screams when I pushed her in front of a moving car woke me up at night.

Slowly, I came back to the present after reliving my first murder.

My mother stood over me. "Didn't you hear me calling you? I need to wash some clothes, so you need to get yours out of the way." She walked out of the room without another word.

I was glad that she snatched me away from the memory which changed my life, but at the same time, I was kind of pissed that she didn't put my clothes in the dryer herself. She walked right past the dryer to get to my room. I guess that would have been too much like right.

I retied the towel around my waist and went to finish drying my clothes. Having to stay in Gina's good graces put me in a precarious position. I couldn't allow my true feelings about her to show in my actions. Although I still loved her, I couldn't get over the fact that she didn't visit me one time while I was locked up. She didn't even send me a card telling me that she'd moved.

It was a fluke that I even found her. When I got out of jail, the first place I went to was our old house only to find it boarded up. Lucky for me, our former neighbor had the forwarding address. Following her was my only option, but I hadn't counted on the changes that had taken place while I was gone.

Finding out Merlin was married was a big surprise to me. When Gina first told me, I had to go over there to see it for myself. While I expected his wife to be good-looking, I was not prepared for the firecracker that ran into my arms and fucked the dog shit out of me.

Thinking of Cojo caused my towel to rise. I looked around to make sure Gina wasn't lurking around. If she saw me standing there with my dick hard, she would lose her damn mind. I quickly put a dryer sheet in the machine and closed the door, rushing back to my room.

Merlin's reaction to my sleeping with his wife was startling. Instead of beating the shit out of me, he took out his anger on his wife. I truly didn't expect that. I was prepared to go toe to toe with him for his wife's honor. The fact that he didn't demand it had me questioning what kind of relationship they really had.

The other thing that was puzzling me was Merlin's relationship with Gina. He had always been the favored child. How was it that they weren't even speaking now? That above everything else was enough to get me to go back to Merlin's house this morning. I had to find out what had been going on while I was gone. If I got to sample some more of Cojo's good stuff, that could only be an added bonus to me.

♥♥♥

"Where do you think you're going?"

I froze with my hand on the doorknob. "Really? Are we going to do this?"

"Do what?"

"Are you going to question me every time I go out the door?"

"I'll question you if I feel like it. After all, it is my door."

"You don't have to keep reminding me. I know exactly where I am." It wasn't even ten o'clock in the morning and Gina had already started drinking.

"And don't you forget it. I didn't have to open up my door to your ass either. Just because you're Ronald's son doesn't mean I have to take care of your trifling ass for the rest of my life."

"Did you fix us breakfast or are you already having yours?"

Gina opened her mouth but closed it with a snap. She chomped down so hard she could have broken a few of her teeth in the process.

"Oops, my bad. I see you're doing a liquid diet." I probably shouldn't have provoked her, but she was getting on my nerves.

"The hell you say. This is my damn house. I can do what I want in it. And if you don't want this to be your last day in it, I suggest you shut the hell up about it."

"I'm sorry, Gina. I'm going over to Merlin's to see if I can get some other clothes to wear."

Gina sat up on the sofa and put down her glass. "Ask him if he wants to come over for lunch."

"Damn, he gets lunch and I get nothing?" Even though I knew that she always preferred my brother to me, it still hurt to have her show it so blatantly.

"Get the fuck out of here. I let you sleep here, didn't I?"

"Yeah, I guess you did."

I opened and closed the door behind me quickly. If she had something else hurtful to say I didn't want to hear it. If she thought I was going to invite my brother to lunch, she sent the wrong messenger.

8 MERLIN MILLS

My heart was heavy as I closed the door on my brother. Some homecoming this turned out to be. I had tackled the hardest part, which was leaving, so coming home from my stint in Iraq should have been the reward. To think I survived bullets flying over my head only to get shot in the heart by my brother.

"Cojo?" I thought she would still be sitting in the living room but she wasn't. I fought against a rising surge of panic.

"I'm here."

I followed her voice to the kitchen. She was lying on the floor in the corner. She was my queen, and I had reduced her to this. I rushed forward and gathered her up in my arms. She didn't fight me as I lifted her from the floor and carried her into our bedroom. As I walked, I left a trail of kisses over her face. My heart was beating double-time – I couldn't believe that I used my hands against the only person in the entire world who loved me unconditionally.

"Baby, I am so sorry."

She started to struggle against me, but that only made me hold her tighter.

"Let me go." She was fighting me now as if she wanted to hurt me, but I couldn't let her go.

"Please, baby, let me explain." I didn't know what I was going to say to her that would make things better, but I had to try.

"You promised—" she wailed.

"I know, sweetie, and it will never happen again. I lost my head for a minute and couldn't see what I had before me." She didn't have to finish her sentence because I already knew what she was referring to, and she was right. I did break my promise. When she pushed me this time, she appeared to have the strength of ten men. I fell off the bed.

"Fuck that. I will not be your punching bag. You violated me and our marriage. I'm leaving you."

The three words sounded amplified to my ears. "Baby, you don't mean that. Just give me a chance to explain." I got up from the floor as she scrambled over to the far side of our king-sized bed. She warily eyed me like a cat on the defensive.

"I said exactly what I meant. You desecrated our marriage vows. I just need to think about how I'm going to get away from you." A long wail followed her sentence.

Deep in my heart, I knew that she still loved me; I just had to find a way to bring it to the forefront. "Can I talk to you while you're trying to figure this out?"

"Do I have a choice?"

She had every right to be mad at me, but her attitude still hurt my feelings. "Yes, you have a choice, but I'm begging you to please listen to what I have to say. I don't want our whole marriage to go down the drain behind this stupid shit."

She turned around and glared at me. Her icy eyes burning a hole in my heart. My entire demeanor changed when I got a good look at what I had done to her face. I wanted to whup my own ass.

"Oh God, baby, I'm sorry. I swear to you I never meant to hurt you. If you want to pick up a pan and beat my ass, then do it. I deserve it. I love you more than life itself. I am so sorry. Seeing you like this…I don't know if I can even forgive myself." I couldn't explain it but I felt a shift in temperature in the room. I allowed my hands to fall in my lap.

"You went crazy. I didn't know you," she said watching me closely.

"I know and none of that has anything to do with you. Please believe that." I was crying on the inside for all the pain that I'd caused her. Real men didn't hit women. It went against everything that I believed.

"I need to understand why." Her voice was barely a whisper, but it resounded in my head like a cannon.

"From the first day that I can remember, I had to watch over my twin brother, Gavin. However, nothing I did was ever good enough for him. He always wanted what I had and he would do just about anything to get it."

"You know what? I thought I was going to be able to do this, but I can't. Just looking at you makes me sick to my stomach. I have to leave." Cojo got up to go back into the living room, but I stopped her.

I felt panic rushing through my blood like a drug. "Sweetheart, I know you can't understand this right now, but we can work through it." I was determined to get through to her no matter how painful it was for both of us.

"That's easy for you to say because you don't have a swollen jaw." She yanked her arm away from my fingers.

Although I wanted to reach for her again, I didn't want to cause her further pain. The bottom line was there was no excuse in this world that would make this better. She began pacing the room like a wounded, frightened animal.

"Baby, would you just sit down."

"I can't do this…I just can't do this."

I understood Cojo's anguish because I broke a promise that I made to her when we first started dating in high school never to put my hands on her in anger. I honestly didn't know what came over me. Cojo walked out of our bedroom carrying a small suitcase, and my heart practically stopped beating. This was definitely not the way I had planned on spending our reunion night.

"Cojo, where are you going?" I rushed to her side, but I didn't make the mistake of touching her.

"I don't know, but I need some time to think."

"Baby, please don't do this."

"I have to. I can't look at you without wanting to bash you in the face." Her voice was trembling and it tore at my heart.

My mind was going sixty miles a minute, trying to think of something to say that would change things. "Hit me then if it would make you feel better, baby. Here, use this." I picked up the lamp that was sitting on the end table and pushed it into her hands. I bowed my head and prayed that I would be able to withstand the pain. The base of the lamp was all metal. I closed my eyes and braced myself for the impact. Several seconds passed and I felt nothing. I opened one eye and peeked up at her. I didn't know if she was waiting to catch me on the upswing or not. "What are you waiting for? Knock my lights out." I remembered hearing the same line in a movie, and it almost caused me to smile.

She put the lamp down on the table and shook her head. "This ain't no cartoon, boy! If I whacked you with that I would be rotting in prison, or worse, electrocuted. Besides, I don't believe in violence. I thought you felt the same way too, but obviously I was wrong." She kept throwing little verbal jabs that felt like actual punches.

A single tear leaked from my right eye. "Baby, please. Don't do this." I knew that I'd said that before, but I didn't know what else to say.

Her eyes were uncertain when she looked at me, but I was comforted in the fact she didn't immediately turn away from me.

She wrung her hands. "I just need some time to think."

My mind raced. What was there to think about? I fucked up, plain and simple. I was sorry, and we would get past it. I could not understand why she needed to make things more complicated than they already were. "You have to know that I will never put my hands on you again." I spoke with conviction from my heart, but her look was skeptical.

"Yesterday I believed that." She started walking backward toward the door.

"No, baby, I can't let you leave." I started in her direction.

"Are you going to hit me again?" Her voice was shaking.

Her words stopped my feet and pierced my heart. Another tear followed the path of the first, and it started a flood of despair that I couldn't control.

"Oh God, I'm so sorry. I never wanted this to happen. You have to believe me."

She started crying too. I wanted to take her in my arms and tell her that everything would be okay, but now I was beginning to have my own doubts.

"I don't want you to leave. If you can't stand to look at me right now, I'll go. Perhaps in a few days we can sit down and talk about this rationally." I said what I thought would make things better, but in my heart, I didn't want to go. Secretly, I hoped she would say it was unnecessary for either of us to leave, and we would work on patching things up together. It didn't play out.

She put down her bag and waited rather impatiently as I repacked my things to leave. For the first time in my life, I prayed and packed. I prayed Cojo would change her mind and that we could get things back on the right track before I had to leave again. I only had a two-week furlough, and I didn't want to spend the entire time fighting. As I was flinging things into my duffel bag, I thought about where I was going to go.

There was no way I was ever going to my mother's house. Therefore, I either had to check into a hotel or try to catch up with my homeboy, Braxton, to see if I could play on his sympathy. In fact, that was probably my only solution, because I didn't want to blow the money I'd managed to save while I was away on a stupid hotel. Times were too hard to be foolish with money.

"I didn't get the chance to tell you I'm being redeployed to Iraq. I have to leave in two weeks. I really wanted to house hunt while I was home so we could stop renting this apartment." I realized I sounded like I was begging, and I didn't care. I knew that my timing sucked, but I felt like I was running out of time.

"Oh my God. You just whupped my ass for something that wasn't my fault, and now you're asking me to go house hunting with you. Am I hearing you correctly?"

"Baby—"

"Stop calling me baby! That shit ended when you raised your hand to me. You ruined everything."

There was nothing I could really say to change the way she felt. "You're right. I'm sorry—"

"I should have known this wasn't going to work out especially when your mother showed her ass at my wedding. That was a big ass sign and I ignored it."

I was in begging mode, so I would have agreed to anything that would have kept me from walking out the door and kept her from reliving our wedding day. Leaving was an expense hadn't calculated, and would mess up my three-year plan. "Fine. I'll go, but can I call you later?" I didn't know what I would have done if she told me no, but I said it anyway.

"Yeah, but understand that I need time."

It was a small concession on her part, but I was thankful she was even open to dialogue with me.

I said, "I know you can't feel it right now, but I believe we can fix this."

Cojo followed me as I backed up to the door. I prayed that she wouldn't let me leave, but it wasn't so.

"Before you go, give me your key?" She held her hand out.

My heart skidded. "Huh?" I wasn't ready for that one.

She wasn't content with me just leaving. She wanted to make sure I didn't bounce back into her world without permission. Part of me wanted to object, but the other part of me knew that I had created this mess. I slipped the keys off my ring. I didn't like it, but I was willing to do anything to save my marriage.

"Can I take you out to dinner tomorrow?"

She pointed at her eye and said, "Yeah, right. Exactly how do you expect me to explain this?"

She had a good point, but I wasn't ready to be derailed. "Do you think I can bring the fixings and prepare a meal for you here?"

I saw a hint of a smile on her lips. I hoped she could see I wanted to make this right.

"We'll see."

It wasn't the answer I was hoping for, but it would have to do. "Do you have a preference?"

"My preference would have been for this not to have happened at all."

"Darling, if I could take things back, then trust me, I would. But it is what it is, and I'm going to do my damnedest to make things better between us again." I wanted some assurances from her that my efforts would not be in vain, but I guess I was asking for too much.

She just stared at me until I was uncomfortable. As much as I didn't want to go, I knew that I had to. Opening the door, I paused. There was so much I wanted to say, but every time I looked at Cojo, the words stopped short of my lips.

"I love you." I waited for a few seconds just to see if she would respond.

She didn't.

I was walking away from the best thing that had ever happened in my life.

9 COJO MILLS

I collapsed onto the sofa as the door closed behind Merlin. My body shook uncontrollably as I fought the urge to run to the door and beg him to come back. Vivid images from the last two hours of my life flitted through my mind. It was a nightmare that I didn't want to relive, but I couldn't turn it off if I wanted to.

I blamed Merlin for hitting me, but I bore some of the responsibility myself. How come I didn't know I was sleeping with a stranger? The thought made me cringe. I thought I knew everything about my husband, and now I felt as if I didn't know him at all. Why didn't I know he had a twin brother? I needed answers to stop the feelings of guilt that kept trying to invade my body.

I buried my head in the sofa as fresh tears washed my eyes. They burned my face, but I couldn't stop them even if I wanted to. I cried for what we had and what we'd apparently lost. Although I still loved my husband, I didn't think I would ever be able to look at him the same way again.

Rising from the sofa, I went into the kitchen to get some ice for my jaw. It was swollen and throbbing. As I passed the telephone, it rang. My heart skipped a beat as I debated about whether to answer it or not. Part of me hoped it was Merlin calling, but the other half of me wasn't ready to speak with him, even if it was on the phone.

My curiosity won. "Hello?" My voice was barely above a whisper. I cleared my throat and tried it again. "Hello." My hands gripped the kitchen counter tightly as my knees wobbled.

"Hey, girl, y'all fucking yet?" My friend Tiffany wickedly laughed.

"Huh?" I was holding my breath. When I finally exhaled, I saw tiny stars before my eyes.

"Don't play dumb, girl. Your told me your man was due home today. What's up? Did I interrupt y'all's flow for a second? You might want to give your man a chance to rest."

Over the phone I could hear music blasting in the background and what sounded like glasses rattling. "Where are you?"

"At Taboo Two. It's ladies night and you know I'm a sucker for them free drinks."

"Oh."

"Damn, what's wrong with you? Merlin did make it home, didn't he?"

"Yeah, he was here." I debated how much I was willing to share with my inquisitive friend. I loved her and all, but I wasn't ready to tell anyone about the assault that had taken place and my role in it.

"Whoa, hold up. What do you mean *was*?"

Shit, I didn't mean to say that. Now she would be all over me like white on rice. "Girl, stop tripping. We're cool. Just chillin'." I hoped she couldn't hear the thumping of my heart. If Tiffany knew what really went down, she would have been over here before I could hang up the phone, even if she were on the other side of town.

"What's up, boo? You don't sound right."

"Uh…girl, I'm sleepy. This brother wore me out."

"Hey! That's what I'm talking about. Six months is a long time to go without a dick. If it were me, I'd be sleepy too." She started giggling.

I couldn't tell if she was happy for me or if her ass was already drunk from the free liquor. "You've got to get a man first."

Tiffany was a player. She had a different man every day of the week. And so far, it was working for her. She didn't want for anything. If one man didn't do her right, she always had a backup waiting to fulfill her needs.

She said, "Hell, don't hate the player, hate the game."

I concluded she was drunk, because the Tiffany I knew would have cussed me out for insinuating she was pimping the game.

"Okay, since you interrupted my beauty rest, was there another reason for your call?" I needed to get her off the phone before I started crying again. She gave me a temporary reprieve, but I felt depression sneaking up on me.

"I told you why I called. I just wanted to hear you answer the phone panting and moaning. Give the dick a chance to breathe, it will last longer."

"You're sick."

"I love you too."

I chuckled because if things had worked out differently, she might have interrupted some of the greatest sex I had ever had.

"So let me holler at Merlin the magician."

Panic set in. What was I going to tell her? *Why must she ask for him at a time like this?* "Girl, bye. I worked the nigga over. He's out cold."

"That's what I'm talking 'bout. All right then, I'll get at you later. You two have fun."

"Thanks. You be careful out there."

"I'm cool. I've got two or three niggahs ready to take me home. I'm good."

"If that was supposed to make me feel better, it didn't. Don't go hopping into cars with folks you don't know. I don't want to turn on the television in the morning and hear about you."

"You worry too much. Go back to that sleeping dick in your bed and leave the grown-up stuff to me." She laughed as she hung up the phone.

Part of me wanted to shout it out that I wasn't okay, but it was too late. I was alone with my thoughts once again.

"Shit. Why didn't I tell her what happened?" Even as I said the words out loud, I knew why I had kept my silence. If I had told Tiffany what transpired here tonight, she would have arranged to have Merlin killed or seriously fucked up, and she would have never forgiven me if I decided to speak to him again. I didn't want my marriage to end. Even though I didn't understand why Merlin took his frustration out on me instead of his brother, I knew he loved me. I just had to find out why he reacted the way he did.

Taking the ice from the freezer, I made my way back into our bedroom. I tried to ignore the physical reminders of what had happened in that room. The biggest of which was my dresser mirror. My reflection mocked me. Before I could stop myself, I hurled the ice pack at the mirror and it shattered into a million pieces. The shards of glass littering the floor were like the pieces of my life—all broke up.

I buckled onto our bed as all the fight drained out of me. I'd never felt so lost in my life, and I didn't know how I was going to be able to go on if I didn't manage to salvage something of my relationship.

Lord, I can't give up now. I wasn't trying to convince God, I was trying to convince myself. I always thought I would never allow a man to put his hands on me, but this had to be an exception to the rule. I told myself it was different because he was provoked and not a random beating just for the hell of it.

"That shit doesn't even sound right to me," I whispered. Regardless of the reasons, the fact remained that even though Merlin was upset, taking his anger out on me was not the answer, since I was clearly as much of a victim as he was. I buried my face into my pillow, trying to hide from the pain.

10 COJO MILLS

The sound of the phone ringing roused me from a troubled sleep. I inched across the bed to silence the ringing instrument. "Hello?" My voice was hoarse and raspy. I felt dehydrated from all the crying. My eyes burned as they sought out the clock: 9:27 p.m.

The voice on the other end of the phone remained silent.

"Hello." I was irritated because whoever it was, wasn't speaking.

"Cojo ."

It was Merlin. My heart clenched as our fight replayed in my mind.

"Yes." I was still hurt, but I also loved my husband.

"Are you okay?" He was breathing heavily over the phone.

I wondered where he was and what he was doing, but I refused to ask. "Yeah." He couldn't possibly want an honest answer to his question. I waited to hear what else was on his mind.

"Sweetheart, I'm so sorry."

Bitterness struggled to erupt from my mouth, but I fought hard to hold it in. I didn't want to fight with him, but didn't know what to say.

"Are you still there?" he asked.

"Yeah." Unwanted tears fell from my eyes. I tried to hold them in, but that only made me cry harder.

"Are you crying?" His voice broke, and I could tell he was about to get emotional too.

"I'm okay." I gulped back the sobs that kept trying to escape my throat.

"I didn't call to get you upset. I just wanted to hear your voice and to know you were all right."

"Okay…well…I'm all right."

"I love you, Cojo."

"I love you too, Merlin."

He broke down crying then. My heart went out to him. If he felt one-tenth as bad as I did, I knew that he was hurting.

"I want to come home."

I heard the pleading in his voice. My heart wanted to tell him to hurry up, but my brain needed some time.

"Not tonight," I whispered. It didn't feel right telling my husband no, but it would have been worse if I allowed him home and found I still couldn't stand the sight of him.

"Have you eaten yet?"

"No, I'm not hungry." I searched my brain for something else to say to him, but my mind was blank. I wasn't trying to make him suffer; I just needed to find some acceptance in my heart. For a few seconds, there was silence on the line.

"Well, okay then. I won't hold you any longer."

A pregnant pause filled the air.

"Okay," I said.

"Can I come see you tomorrow?"

I could hear the hopefulness in his question, and even though this wasn't the first time we had slept in separate beds since we'd been married, it was the first time that either of us had gone to sleep unhappy or sad with each other. "I guess so. I doubt if I'll feel like going in to work tomorrow. Too many questions…"

"Well, see you tomorrow."

Merlin knew I rarely missed work. He hung up the phone quickly. I wanted to call him back to assure him things would be okay, but I had no idea where he was. More importantly, I didn't know who he was with.

A tiny devil landed on my shoulder and whispered in my ear. *He's probably out fucking someone else. Serves you right for kicking him out of his own home.*

"Stop it," I yelled into our empty apartment. I felt like I was losing my mind. I got up from the bed and began pacing the room. I didn't want to start speculating on where he was, but the seed had been planted. I snatched the phone from the wall and tried to call him back. I was going to tell him to come home, even if it meant his sleeping on the sofa.

I dialed the fast access code to display the last caller, but unfortunately the number didn't come up. "Damn." I dialed his cell phone and it went to his voicemail. I didn't leave a message. I shoved the phone back onto the cradle and continued to pace the floor. The phone rang and scared the shit out of me. I snatched it before it could ring a second time. "Hello." I was ready to have my husband home.

"Put Merlin on the phone," a drunken voice demanded.

Anger replaced the fear that had just vacated my heart as I struggled to maintain my composure. My mother-in-law was the last person on the planet I wanted to speak with at this particular time. Why on earth was she calling after so many months of silence? Ignoring the fact she didn't even say hello, I answered her. "He's not here at the moment." My hand stood poised to disconnect the phone.

"Where is he?" she demanded.

I wanted to tell her it was none of her fucking business, but I held my tongue.

"Out," I replied. Over the years, I had tried a few times without Merlin's knowledge to make friends with this woman, but she made it very clear she wasn't interested in being my friend. I wasn't the one who ruined her wedding; it was the other way around.

"Now you listen here, Missy. I want to speak to my son, and I want to speak to him now."

"I'll be sure to tell him when he gets home." I hung up the phone. That simple act of defiance made me feel better. I went into the living room and curled up on the sofa and went to sleep. The bed seemed empty without Merlin in it.

11 GAVIN MILLS

Gina was standing in the doorway of my room when I looked up. Her eyes were bright red, and I could tell she was pissy drunk.

"I can't believe that bitch hung up on me," she slurred.

"What bitch?" I was standing in my underwear, and she didn't even have the decency to knock on the door or turn away when she realized that I didn't have any clothes on.

"The bitch your stupid-ass brother married."

I struggled to hide my irritation as I pulled on my socks.

My mother's tirades were nothing new to me. Once she had something in her craw, she'd go on and on about it seemingly forever. I grabbed my pants from the bottom of the bed and slid my legs into them. If she was the least bit embarrassed about seeing me damn near naked, she didn't show it.

"Why she got to be a bitch?" I zipped up my pants and reached for my shirt. Originally I'd planned on taking a nap, but I changed my mind. I wanted to get out instead to get something to eat and possibly grab a beer.

"What? Are you taking her side now?" She had this crazy look in her eyes, and I instantly regretted saying anything at all.

I should have agreed with her and kept it moving. "No, Gina. I'm not in this mess and I'm not taking sides."

"Good, because I was about to send your ass packing tonight."

I ignored her as I put on my shoes.

"Where are you going? I thought you were going to take a nap."

"I was but I'm hungry, so I was going to go out and grab me something to eat."

"I thought you said you didn't have any money." She eyed me suspiciously.

For a moment, I thought she was going to demand that I empty my pockets like she did when I was a kid. "I got enough to grab a burger and some fries."

"Humph. If I were you, I would save my money just in case you found yourself out on the street." She turned and left my room.

The veiled threat hung in the room like a stale fart. I was going to have to do something about my financial situation quick, fast, and in a hurry. "Can I make a sandwich then?"

"Yeah, but don't go making a mess. I know about you and those grilled cheese sandwiches." My mother was a real piece of work. She didn't want me to go out, but it was clear she didn't want me with her either.

"I won't. Do you want me to make you a sandwich too?" I didn't really want to fix her a sandwich, but if I didn't make the offer, I would have to hear her mouth for the next twenty-four hours.

"No, I ate already."

I wanted to ask her why she didn't bother to share her food with me, but I let it go. I learned a long time ago to pick my battles with my mother. Since I was not in a position to do any better for myself, I would just have to suck this one up.

Opening the refrigerator, I searched the practically barren box, but the only thing close to edible was a few pieces of cheese and some questionable bologna. "Dag, Ma, how long has this stuff been in here?" I brought the bologna to my nose but immediately pulled it back.

"What?"

"Never mind." My appetite had suddenly gone away. I walked back into the living room.

"You ate already?"

"Naw, I changed my mind." I sat down on the love seat across from my mother.

She didn't even look at me. She was watching *Real Housewives of Atlanta*, a reality show everyone seemed to enjoy. Even the dudes in prison watched it every week.

"You actually watch this shit?" I didn't attempt to hide my personal feelings about the show, which I thought was about a bunch of broads living off their husbands' success.

"Watch your language."

With the exception of the television, the room was silent. If I had a television in my room, I would have gone in there to watch something else, but the small room only contained a bed.

"How long have you lived here?"

My mother tore her eyes away from the tube. "Huh?"

"This apartment. When did you move in?"

She took her sweet time answering me, and I was beginning to believe that she had placed me on ignore status. "Why?

"No reason, I was just making conversation."

She settled back onto the sofa and continued to ignore me. "I ain't stupid. You're looking for an excuse from me for moving and not letting you know, but I don't have one. If you hadn't gotten your ass locked up, you would have known where I was."

I was silent for a moment. "It was an accident."

"It may have been, but it doesn't change the price of tea in China."

"What does China have to do with any fucking thing?"

"Don't you get all snippy with me. I don't have to explain anything to you."

"Gina, I am not blaming you for anything you've done. Obviously you did what you thought you had to do. I was just trying to find out where my shit is."

"Your shit, as you call it, was thrown out with the trash. I never expected to see you again, so there was no need to cart that crap around with me."

A pain settled deep in my heart. I hated my father for turning a once loving woman into a callous bitch. "I remember a time where you used to love us." I was speaking more to myself than to her.

"You stupid bastard. How the hell could you form your lips to say that to me? If I didn't love your stinking ass, I wouldn't have gone through the trouble of raising you. I made the choice to raise you instead of having my own children."

I was sick of hearing about the child she gave up. Her so-called choice didn't have anything to do with me. "Don't ever call me stupid again. I may be a bastard, but that was beyond my control." I threw my head back in defiance without thinking about the consequences.

"Excuse me? Who the hell do you think you're talking to?"

Reality struck me in the face. I was staying with this woman who made all the difference in the world to my comfort. Hell, it wasn't the best existence, but it was the only one I had at the moment. "Mother, I'm sorry. I lost my head." I practically choked on the words as they left my mouth.

"Humph. You must have. I didn't have to take your ass in. I'm done with raising you two boys. What thanks did I get? Nothing. Both of you shit on me every chance you got."

I cut a huge slice of humble pie. "I said I was sorry. You've always been there for me." She might have felt like I was lying but didn't bother to silence me. Truth be told, she was the one to sell me out when the police tried to blame Merlin for that girl Cheryl's death. She told them that it was me who had taken off in Merlin's car.

"You got that right; I've always been here for you and Merlin, but you made my life hell while you were here, and I don't intend to go through that shit again. So if you are even *thinking* about starting some trouble, you can just get your shit and go."

What shit? I didn't have anything other than the clothes on my back and she knew it. My blood started to boil as I struggled not to respond to her latest jab. "I see that I've awakened some bad memories. I'm going to bed because I don't want to take the trip back down memory lane with you. It wasn't good the first time, and I don't feel like going there again."

"Stop it. I don't base my opinions of you on the past. I'm thinking of the here and now, and you're nothing to be proud of. You were worthless when you were born. Your damn daddy did that to you. I tried to beat that shit out of you, but I know who you are—you're rotten. Not at all like your brother..." Her words trailed off as if she lost her train of thought.

"You're talking crazy, Mother." The words slipped out of my mouth. I'd spent my entire life in my brother's shadow, and it hurt to be reminded of it now. Even though I wanted to debate her on this matter, I couldn't afford to, because at the end of the day, I still needed a place to stay.

Her words hurt me to my heart, but I wouldn't allow her to see the pain she had caused me. There was a time when she was the only woman I cared about, and it hurt me that she couldn't see me for my brother. He became the object of my hatred.

"Are you saying that you never loved me?" This time I wasn't asking if she loved us, I was only concerned about me.

"Of course I loved you. What choice did I have? That doesn't change the fact that you're evil. You don't have the same thought process as your brother. For you, everything is twisted."

"And what role did you play in that? I'm a product of my environment."

"I will not take the blame for that. Your father's sperm destroyed you."

"Is that how you really feel about me?" My heart sank into my chest. I knew I had disappointed her a time or two, but I never believed that Gina had such a low opinion of me overall.

"I raised you, wasn't that enough? I can think what I want. Back then, you were a disappointment. Now you have to make your own way—I'm done."

"Why? How was I a disappointment? I was a fucking kid?"

"'Cause you were just like your damn daddy."

"Your issue should be with my father and not me!"

"You're right about that. I do have issues with your father, but your father didn't show up on my doorstep asking to move back in. You did!"

I wanted her to hurt as much as I did. "But what about your influence? Didn't you have a part of shaping me into the man I am today?"

"Are you trying to say I made you into the failure that you are?" She planted her hands on her hips, and I wanted to slap the hell out of her.

"I'm not a failure. I'll admit I wasn't the best child a parent could have, but I was never a failure."

"The proof is in the pudding then. You'll have to prove it to me because I'm not about to take your word on it. As far as I can tell, you don't have shit, you still don't want shit, and you ain't never going to be shit." She turned away as if the conversation was over.

"How you gonna say some shit like this to me and just walk away? Your ass ain't perfect either." I knew I was out of line, but she wasn't going to continue talking to me out the side of her mouth without my saying something. I didn't ask her to raise me. Hell, I didn't even ask to be born, and she was punishing me for both of those things that I didn't have any control over.

"Niggah, you must have lost your motherfucking mind. I ain't some hood chick you done met on the street, You had better show me some respect."

"I'm sorry you feel disrespected, but have you ever thought about how I feel?" The words burned as they exited my mouth.

She had only been thinking about herself for years, and I was sick and tired of that shit.

"You damn right you're sorry. I have half a mind to kick your sorry butt right out of my house, but I'm a woman and women don't treat men like that." As usual, she focused on what she wanted to hear and not what I said.

"Please forgive me." I was ready to leave before I said something that would force me to take up residence in a homeless shelter or someplace like it.

"I just need you to get out my face. Go on back in your room. I'll deal with your ass tomorrow." She held a bottle of gin around the neck like an old friend, swinging it as she spoke.

When I saw the bottle, I knew that there would be no reasoning with her, so I quickly left the room and said a silent prayer that she would go into her own room and go to sleep. Walking away without telling Gina exactly what I thought about her was probably one of the hardest things I'd done in quite a while. It left a sour taste in my mouth.

"Stankin' bitch," I retorted as I quietly shut the door to my room. I wasn't sure what I was going to do about my future, but I damn sure knew I would have to make a decision soon. I wouldn't be able to continue living under Gina's roof if this were any indication of how things were going to go.

12 COJO MILLS

I don't know what I was thinking when I agreed to allow Merlin to come by the house today. I wasn't ready to forgive or forget, and he needed to know that what happened between us was totally unacceptable. He had to know I was not going to tolerate being his punching bag no matter what—I didn't care what the circumstances were.

I loved Merlin like I'd loved no other, but I was not going to relive the horror of the last twenty-four hours for the rest of my life. I would just as soon end up alone forever before I agreed to going down that road.

As much as I wanted to believe my husband that it was an isolated incident, I needed some assurance from some people who knew him longer than I did. We had only dated for a little over a year before we married.

I picked up the phone, but embarrassment made me hang it up. There was no one in my life who I was willing to confess this trouble to. Tiffany and Braxton both went to school with Merlin long before I did, but rather than confess this rough patch to them, I was going to have to deal with this situation all by myself. Hanging up the phone was a humbling experience. It made me feel isolated, and I never thought I would feel that way again when I married Merlin, my best friend.

During my childhood, we moved a lot due to my father's job with the military. Throughout that time, I never made any lasting friendships until I met Merlin. Before I met him, it didn't really matter to me that we didn't have any real roots. Once we became involved, the thought of leaving him almost drove me insane. He was the only person I had ever opened up to.

During my senior year, my mother started getting itchy feet, and I begged her to allow us to stay until after graduation. She was reluctant at first, because she thought Merlin and I were becoming too close. However, when I convinced her that we weren't being intimate, she reconsidered.

What I did after that was shameful. Knowing how my mother felt about my having sex with Merlin, I seduced him into having it – in her bedroom. I wasn't proud of my trickery, but it helped me achieve my desired results. My mother demanded that we get married right after graduation. Up until the night before, I never regretted my treachery.

Merlin had thrown me a raft of love, but now I didn't know if this was a raft of love or of entrapment. Had I set myself up for failure by deceiving him? Questions kept ringing in my head as I tried to make heads or tails out of what had happened in our home.

Merlin was a first for me: the first man whom I had relations with; the first man who I had loved; and the only man who I wanted in my life forever. But he showed me a side of him tonight that scared the living shit out of me.

Was I wrong about giving this man my love? I couldn't figure out who I was maddest at: Merlin for not believing that I was tricked by his brother, or at Gavin for taking advantage of my enforced celibacy.

"Dear God, what have I done to deserve this?" I wailed at the ceiling. I buried my head into my pillow. I tried to burrow deep, but my head kept bopping up, because I knew in my heart I didn't do anything to deserve this pain that I was going through.

The phone interrupted my thoughts. I scurried away from it as if answering it would hurt me. I couldn't imagine who would be calling me this late. I allowed it to ring two more times before I answered.

"Hello."

Merlin said, "Babe, just in case you're wondering, I'm at a motel not far from the house."

I let his statement hang in the air. If I'd admitted to caring where he was staying, he might get the wrong impression.

"I miss you, babe. I'm so—"

"Save it, Merlin. In fact, let me get off the phone because talking to you is only making me mad. Call before you come in the morning." I hung up before I could start crying. It felt like my heart was breaking into pieces.

I threw myself on the bed and had another good cry. I remember once reading that crying was good for the soul, but I doubt they meant this type of crying. I went through a whole gambit of emotions until I got sick and tired of my damn self.

I pulled myself out of the bed and went to take a shower. In the past, showers always refreshed me. While I was bathing, I didn't think about what I was going to do next, I just went through the motions. I knew that I wouldn't be going to work tomorrow, but I had to do something with my time or I would go crazy.

I started cleaning up the mess that Merlin made in the bedroom. As I cleaned, I tried not to think about the violence I saw in my husband that I never knew existed. Without a shadow of a doubt, there was some very bad blood between the brothers. I tried to keep moving so I wouldn't dwell on the past twenty-four hours.

I changed the sheets on the bed and vacuumed the carpet, getting up the smaller pieces of glass that I was not able to see with my eyes. When I shut off the vacuum, I heard the answering machine going in the kitchen.

"Merlin, this is your mother. Pick up the phone."

I rolled my eyes. The very last person that I wanted to hear from at this moment was his meddling mother. Talking to her was bound to make me feel even worse than I felt right at the moment, so I continued to listen to her talk to the machine.

"I know you're back in town 'cause your brother told me. Now be a good boy and pick up the phone." She was speaking to the machine as if Merlin were actually standing there ignoring her ass.

"Merlin, we need to let bygones be bygones. Well, you're probably busy, but you need to stop by and see me." She hung up the phone, and I breathed a sigh of relief.

As long as she stayed her ass on her side of town instead of coming over to our house, I'd be all right.

During the time that Merlin and I had been married, she came to visit once. She was drunk, and all she did was complain. Most mothers would have been proud to see that their children were doing better than they had, but not Gina. She acted as if Merlin owed her the same creature comforts that we'd been able to obtain. I walked into the kitchen to erase the message because I was not about to allow Gina cause us any more drama.

♥♥♥

I sat down at my computer and typed a letter to Shirley Strawberry, who hosted an advice column on a popular radio station. I needed some sage advice from someone who didn't know either Merlin or I.

Dear Shirley,

I could really use your opinion and some advice on something that happened to me that has left me feeling lost and confused. My husband, whom I love dearly, was supposed to return from active duty yesterday. When he got here, we professed our love in a very physical way, if you know what I mean. There was no need for talking as he has been gone for six months. We just got busy!

The only problem is the man who I ended up getting familiar with wasn't my husband. I accidentally slept with his twin. Shirley, I didn't even know he had a twin!!

Needless to say my husband got all mad, but instead of him taking out his anger on his brother, he took it out on me. Shirley, I never thought in a million years my husband would put his hands on me. I thought he wasn't that kind of person, and now I have a black eye to prove that he is. I really love my husband, and I don't want my marriage to end, but I cannot allow him to put his hands on me. His stupid brother thinks it's all a joke. I put both of them out of the house and now I need to know what I should do.

Shirley, please tell me what I should do.

Desperate, Battered & Confused.

I debated sending my email for about two hot seconds. I really respected the opinions that Shirley gave, and sometimes her co-host Steve offered some good advice as well. I got my phone and set my alarm so I could make sure I turned on my radio to listen. There was no guarantee that she would read my letter in the morning, but I was hopeful.

♥♥♥

The dawning of a new day did nothing to improve how things played out the day before. My eye was officially black, and the other aches and pains that I had felt intensified. I didn't want to start my day feeling bitter, but I couldn't help it if I were constantly reminded of the mess. Despite the early hour, I decided to fix myself a drink.

After I called out to work, I turned on the radio to my favorite station and turned on my computer. I was looking for any type of distraction to get my mind off my troubles. I had another hour to wait for the Peach letter of the day to be read over the radio.

When someone rang the doorbell, it caught me completely off guard. I wasn't expecting anyone, so I approached the door with caution. My husband and I weren't social people, and we didn't have a bunch of friends who stopped by unannounced. I tiptoed to the door and peeked through the peephole. I was shocked to see Merlin standing there. I snatched open the door, fire burning in my eyes. "Merlin, I said in the morning, but I didn't mean the crack of dawn."

"You trying to make the same mistake twice?" Gavin was grinning at me like we shared some kind of special connection. These brothers looked so much alike I couldn't tell them apart.

I stumbled back from the door, and he took this as an invitation to come inside. He turned and shut the door behind him.

"What are you doing here?" I was very nervous about being alone with Gavin again after our last little encounter. Something happened between my legs that I needed to ignore.

"Merlin told me to come by and pick out a few outfits to wear until I can get my shit together."

"Merlin isn't here."

"I gathered that." He walked over and took a seat on the sofa as if he had every right to be in my house and in my presence.

Any other time I might have found his cockiness appealing, but something about Gavin rubbed me the wrong way. It was like fingernails scratching against a chalkboard. "I don't remember asking you to come in."

He sat up from his lounging position with a sinister smirk on his face. "But you didn't ask me to leave either, right?"

I wanted to slap that silly smirk right off his face. I could tell that Gavin was used to having his way with women, but he had come against the wrong sister this time. We may have wound up in a compromising position once before, but that shit would never happen again, despite the excretions that were soaking my panties.

I walked over to the phone to call Merlin. I was not about to play this little game with Merlin's brother. Keeping my eye on Gavin, I dialed Merlin's number.

He answered on the first ring. "Baby, I'm so glad you called. I've been up all night, and I just can't get it together. I've been so worried about us."

I still wasn't ready to have that conversation with my husband, but I needed his help to get his brother out of my house. "Merlin, your brother is here." I cut right to the chase so there would be no confusion as to the reason for the call.

"He's what?" Merlin shouted into the phone.

"He's here, in the living room. He said you told him to come over today to pick up some clothes?"

"Shit, I forgot about it. He caked me last night after we last talked. I'll be right there."

I felt better knowing that Merlin was on the way. I hung up the phone, and this time it was me that had a smirk on my face.

"What? You had to call the troops? If I didn't know better, sis, I might think you didn't like me or something."

I had to fight back the urge to fling my crystal vase at his head. I could tell he liked to get a rise out of people, and I refused to allow him to see me upset again. "I could care less what you think. My husband will be here soon."

"Damn, do you want me to wait outside?" He was trying to be funny.

"As far as I'm concerned, you can sit out on the curb with the rest of the garbage." I didn't try to censor my remark because there was just something about Gavin that brought out the worst in me.

"Ouch, that hurt. I know you're still mad about yesterday, but can't we just put it behind us?"

I was outdone. I could not believe he would sit right in my face and say some stupid-ass shit to me after what he did.

The devil whispered in my ear: *But you liked it.*

"I'm not going to even dignify your question with a response." I left him sitting in the living room. I went into the kitchen to make myself something to eat. I wasn't really hungry, but I was trying to dispel the nervous energy I felt. Regardless of how much I disliked my husband's brother, I had to give it to him: he knew how to get down in the bedroom. So keeping my distance from him was a very good idea.

I pulled some bacon from the refrigerator and placed several slices on the microwave rack. It wasn't until I had turned on the microwave that I realized I had cooked more than I intended to fix. It was too late to turn it off, so I went ahead with every intention of making breakfast for my husband.

"You fixin' some for me, too?" Gavin called from the living room.

"When donkeys fly."

"Come on, sis, is that any way to treat your family?" Gavin had snuck up behind me. He was standing so close, I could feel his breath on my neck. Electricity flowed through me and nestled between my legs. I grabbed a knife from the dish rack. I was prepared to cut him if I had to.

"Whoa, babe, it's not that serious." With his hands in the air, Gavin backed out of the kitchen.

"Either you wait for your brother in the living room or wait outside. The choice is yours." I punctuated my words with the tip of the knife.

"Damn, if I didn't know you already had some, I would swear you needed some dick in your life." He rushed out the room before I had a chance to throw the steak knife I was holding tightly in my left hand. I instantly recollected how he had pinned my legs over his shoulder and gave me every inch of his business. The smell of burnt bacon and the ding of the timer brought me back to reality. Gavin just didn't know how close he had come to being a casualty.

Grabbing a hand towel, I removed my breakfast from the microwave and tossed it in the trash. I turned on the vent to get rid of the smell and opened the window to allow some fresh air into the apartment. I had just finished washing the rack when the doorbell rang. Drying my hands on a towel, I went to answer the door, but to my chagrin, Gavin had beaten me to it.

"What's up, bro? You lose your key?"

I could see a vein pulsating at the base of Merlin's neck, and I knew I had to do something to diffuse the situation. Walking past Gavin, I gave Merlin a big long kiss on his lips. I could feel his body relax against mine.

Merlin closed the door behind him. "How long are you here for?"

"Dag, what is up with y'all? I said I was sorry about yesterday. It was an honest mistake."

Merlin tried to step past me to get to his brother, but I grabbed his hand and pulled him back. The last thing we needed was a repeat of the day before. A physical altercation wouldn't do anything to resolve the nasty situation.

Merlin said, "Whatever, dude. I'm going to get you a few things so you can be on your way."

Gavin frowned; his nostrils flared. "Well, I missed your ass too."

My head swung between the brothers. If I hadn't seen it with my own eyes, I would not have believed that two men could look so much alike. Even their mannerisms were identical. It was as if their egg was split in half. I tore my eyes away from Gavin, who was trying to stare a hole in me.

Not wanting to get into another conversation with Gavin, I followed Merlin into the bedroom as he went through his clothes that I hadn't managed to snatch from their hangers and chuck to the floor.

Merlin looked up when I walked into the room. "I guess I deserve this too," he said as his eyes surveyed the mess.

For a moment, I felt ashamed of my childish actions. Throwing his clothes on the floor or even setting them on fire, which was my first inclination, would not make the situation any better.

"Merlin, I've been thinking. Yes, this is a fucked-up situation, but you're not entirely at fault. I have to share in some of the blame." I could see the hope dancing in Merlin's eyes.

"I blame myself for not knowing he wasn't you. If we're going to get through this, you have to promise me you will never, ever, put your hands on me again."

"Baby, I swear to you on everything I hold near and dear to my heart, that I will never do anything to hurt you ever again." He took a step toward me, but I instinctively backed away.

"Not so fast. I'm not finished."

He pulled back.

"We are going to have to get some counseling before this thing festers and gets even uglier than it already is."

"I'm cool with that, but I'm only here for two weeks, minus a day now. If you think it will help, I'm willing to do whatever you say."

I walked toward my husband with my arms outstretched. Even though I was afraid of the decision I had made, I knew I wasn't ready to give up on my man and what we had built together.

Merlin wrapped his arms around me, and we clung to each other. We were so in tune with each other, we forgot about Gavin in the other room. I was startled when I heard the refrigerator door shut, and I pushed away from Merlin's embrace.

I was instantly mad again. "Your brother doesn't have any manners."

"Don't remind me. When he leaves, I'll tell you all about him."

"You definitely need to do that, because I find it strange that we've been together all this time, and you never mentioned that you even *had* an identical twin. Is there anything else I should know about you?"

"Naw, that's it. Let me get this fool some clothes so he can get up out of here."

I left Merlin digging in the closet while I went into the bathroom to wash my face. It was bad enough I had to see myself looking like a boxer; I didn't need anyone else looking at me.

13 GAVIN MILLS

Merlin's untimely arrival irritated the shit out of me. I anticipated her being alone, and I was a little hopeful that we would get the chance to sample each other again. As much as I tried to get the image of her naked body out of my mind, she kept swirling around my dreams all night long.

I speculated on how long they'd been together and just how tight their relationship was. If their connection were broken, I wouldn't be opposed to stepping in and helping Merlin if he were having problems getting the job done in the bedroom.

"Damn, did y'all forget I was here?" I yelled into the bedroom. When they didn't immediately respond, I decided to help myself to some of the breakfast Cojo was making before Merlin interrupted us. The smell lingered in the air but I didn't see any bacon. I didn't care that it was burnt. My ass was hungry, and I would rather eat up their food than to spend the money that my brother had given me.

"Hold your damn horses," my brother yelled back.

I was going to have to check his ass sooner or later. He must have forgotten how badly I used to tear that ass up when we were growing up. I didn't care that he went to the army and came home a little swollen. I could still take his ass because I could out-think him. Merlin was a sensitive guy, and he fought with his heart more than his mind. I, however, was a fighter through and through. I had no problem getting mine by any means necessary and he would do well to remember that.

Cojo had already thrown the bacon in the trash, so I couldn't munch on it. I pulled open the meat drawer and saw that she still had a half a pack of bacon in there, so I proceeded to cook it all up. As far as I was concerned, we were family.

"What the hell do you think you're doing?" Cojo demanded. She startled me and I almost dropped the bacon I was holding.

"Damn, girl, why you wanna creep up on a brother like that?"

"You have no business in my damn kitchen."

"Hell, I didn't think you would mind. I told you earlier I was hungry. Why don't you bring your fine ass in here and cook me up something so I don't get your kitchen all messed up?" I winked at her.

Cojo scowled at me. "Merlin, you had better come and get your brother before I have to hurt him." She snatched the bacon out of my hand and threw it in the trash.

I wanted to hit her ass so bad I was shaking. "Girl, you'd better stop playing with me. Shit, I ain't your husband."

"You damn right you're not."

"You're kind of feisty. I like it, but don't get ahead of yourself or you might not like the consequences."

"What, is that a threat? Am I supposed to be scared of you or something?"

"Naw, I don't have to threaten you. I offer promises."

Before I could say anything further, Merlin came into the room carrying a small duffel bag which he thrust toward me hitting me in the chest.

"This should hold you." He tossed me a set of car keys. "You remember my old Malibu? You always liked it. It's in the lot; it's yours. We can get the registration taken care of later. I've given you money, clothes and transportation. I'm done fucking with you, Gavin.

"Thanks, bro, good looking out." I wasn't paying my brother the least bit of attention. He was trying to act like he had a set of balls in front of his woman.

We stood around the kitchen staring at one another until I decided it was time to make my exit. I was definitely going to have to come back so I could whisper in Cojo's ear. Right now, she was playing all hard to get. I was willing to bet I could get her to change her mind about spending some time with me.

I said, "Well, I hate to break up this party. I'm gonna bounce."

"Good," Cojo replied.

I waited for a few beats to see if Merlin was going to check his bitch or if he would suggest our getting together later, but the invitation didn't come. I turned and left the kitchen, working my way to the door with both of them hot on my heels. It was a very uncomfortable moment for all of us.

Cojo stepped up from behind Merlin and opened the door. She was playing the victim role very well as I stepped through the doorway. Once I had cleared the path, the door slammed behind me. All I could hear from the apartment was the sound of the locks being engaged.

"Damn, that was cold," I muttered to myself. I stood there for a few seconds, pondering what I was going to do next. I didn't want to go back to my mother's, but I had very few options outside of that. It had been a long time since I'd been home, and even when I did live in Atlanta, I had lost touch with all of my associates.

I tossed the bag over my shoulder and found Merlin's car in the parking lot. It started on the first try, so I assumed Merlin kept it up with regular maintenance. As I pulled out of the apartment complex, I looked back just in time to see the window flicker shut. I felt a twinge of guilt about the whole situation, but I quickly forgot it as I made my way to McDonald's to get something to eat. My plan was to fill up on a few of their Dollar Menu items and go back to my mother's to crash.

I turned on the radio as they were reading the Peach Letter for the day. Magic 107.5 was popular even in the joint. A syndicated show, we would crowd around the radio to hear the letter of the day.

I turned up the volume when Shirley started reading the letter. After hearing the first sentence, I knew who wrote it. I started laughing so hard I had to pull over. Since I didn't have a driver's license, I didn't want to risk violating my parole and getting caught.

Today's letter is from someone who signed their letter as Desperate, Battered and Confused. Since Steve isn't in today, Tommy is going to give us the male perspective. Dear Shirley...

I was stunned that Cojo had the balls to put what happened to her out for the world to comment on. It was a gutsy move although a silly one. Especially since she had already decided to forgive my brother for whipping her ass. It would have been different if she kicked his ass out on the curb as she threatened to do me.

Shirley said: I can't believe I'm saying this, but I wish Steve were here to handle this one. She has a lot of information in here, but there are two things I just can't get past. One is the fact that she has a black eye, and the second is her claiming to have slept with her brother-in-law by accident. How is that even possible? I mean, at some point, even twins are different.

Tommy interjected: What I want to know is when did she figure it out? Was it before or after the don't stop, get it get it? You know how you women are, you know when something ain't right down there?

Shirley: Tommy, stop; you know this is a serious letter, and we should be offering some kind of advice to this woman.

Tommy: Who said I wasn't being serious? You know what your problem is, Shirley? You are reading this letter to see what she said. You need to be reading it to see what she didn't say.

Shirley: I have no clue what you are talking about. What did I miss?

Tommy: I sure wish my uncle was here to see this. I have stumped the master. So let me break it down to you, O blind one. She told us in the letter what she did and what her husband did, but she neglected to say what the brother did. That is what is missing from the letter. Now, Shirley; put yourself in this lady's shoes, and if you were so upset because a brother stole something from you, wouldn't you be calling him out?

Shirley: I don't believe you, Tommy. I think you might actually have a point. She didn't mention anything about being mad at the brother.

Tommy: And there you have it. I think you all should let me read these letters from now on. The reason why she ain't mad at the brother was because he did something the other brother couldn't do. And maybe the reason why the husband went after her was because he knew it too. Now it's time for us to take a break. Call in if you would like for me to solve something else. I think I have finally found my purpose.

I was smiling when I went inside McDonald's. Tommy did have a point. I knew there was something between Cojo and I, and I wasn't going to rest until I found out what it meant.

14 MERLIN MILLS

As soon as Cojo and I were alone, I began to feel nervous. We were both aware of the issues between us, and it seemed as if neither wanted to be the first one to address it. I felt out of place in my own home, and it was making me crazy. I paced around the living room trying to work up the nerve to speak to my wife. She had moved away from the window and was standing behind the sofa. She appeared as nervous as I was.

I walked over and took a seat on the sofa in a non-threatening way and asked her to sit with me. I waited until she looked comfortable before I began.

"It's not easy for me to talk about my issues with my brother." It wasn't much of a beginning but I was trying.

Cojo just stared at me for a few seconds. "You can start with why you felt it was necessary to keep the fact you have a brother a secret."

"Honey, it wasn't that I was trying to keep him a secret. It's been so long since I thought about him that I just forgot him. By the time you started going to our school he was already gone. He was like a bad dream; no one talked about him."

"How does one go about forgetting such an important part of his life? You have to make me understand that, because I've always wanted a sibling, so I damn sure wouldn't forget about them."

"You would try to forget too if you had someone in your life who caused you so much pain. Gavin was a major pain in my ass when we were growing up."

"Most siblings are."

"No, you don't understand. I'm not explaining it right. It was more than just being a pain in the ass. He did things, terrible things, and used to blame me for them."

"What kind of things?" She cocked her head to the side as if she were trying to figure out if I was telling the truth.

"Now that I'm talking about him again, it sounds trivial even to me. But back then, it was drama city."

"Well, you're going to have to make me understand because I feel as if you lied to me, and I don't like it."

"I'm telling you, baby, it was more of an error of omission than a lie. I needed to close the part of my life that involved Gavin." I got up and started pacing the room again. I knew that I had to make her understand if we were going to have any chance to stay together. "Gavin used to talk to this girl who had a crush on me. He talked her into going out with him." Just thinking about it made me feel queasy.

"And?" Cojo had a hint of attitude in her voice, but I tried not to let it bother me as I continued the story.

"Well, I guess I'm not saying this right. He tricked her into going out because she thought she was going out with me."

"Oh, so you got mad? That's not enough to forget your brother even existed."

"I was told he pursued her for weeks, and he used my computer to do it. Hell, I didn't even know she liked me until after the fact."

"Did y'all go to school together?"

"No, she went to another school. She was a cheerleader who sometimes flirted with me, so I guess that's why he was able to trick her."

"That's messed up, but why wouldn't he just talk to her on his own since you didn't even know her?"

"To be honest, I have no idea why he sucked me into the whole mess, but it was ugly, especially when the police got there."

"Wait, this isn't making any sense. What did the police have to do with it?"

"I don't know if it was part of his plan, but he took my car and went to pick her up. He ended up running out of gas and they had to walk. Somehow or another she wound up getting hit by a car. The police thought I had something to do with it because my computer records showed we were corresponding, and according to her mother, she left with a boy named Merlin." I paused. "Gavin told the police I caused her to get hit. He always blamed me for stuff he did."

"Oh my God. How terrible – was she okay?"

I didn't want to admit that I believed Gavin pushed the young lady into the street. "She died, and the only reason Gavin went to prison and not me is because Braxton and Gina stepped up and told the police it wasn't me, and that Gavin had stolen my car."

Cojo nodded. "That's kind of jacked up, but it still isn't a reason to disown him." She folded her arms across her chest as if my explanations weren't enough.

"Baby, it's so much deeper than this one incident. Our relationship was always troubled. He always wanted what I had. If he couldn't steal it, he would fuck it up so it was taken from me. He competed with me for everything. Most of the time, I didn't even know the competition was going on until I lost whatever it was I wanted."

"That's not so unusual between siblings, is it?"

"Maybe not, but things changed when he killed that girl. He was willing to let them send me to jail for something I didn't do. That was when I had to accept the fact that my own brother hated me."

"Hate? That's a pretty strong word. You know words have power."

"Cojo, he caused me to get arrested for something I didn't do. They came down to my job in the middle of the day and handcuffed me. They took me off the clock and kept me there overnight, and I wound up losing the very first job I ever had as a result of his fuck-up. And let's not forget that the girl's brothers kicked the shit out of me because I couldn't convince them that I didn't have anything to do with her death."

"That's unfortunate, but it's not enough to forget or ignore your family."

"That's easy for you to say when you haven't lived the life I have. It's different when it happens to you."

She said, "I get it that siblings fight. I get it. I get it that they sometimes feel jealous. I truly do, but because I haven't lived through that, I can't help but to feel envious."

"I'm telling you, he was and is a rare breed. To this day, I don't know if he ever found love in his heart for me. I had to divorce him from my life in order for me to go on."

"Why?"

"Because I loved him too much to allow him to continue to hurt me, and it was clear to me that he didn't give a damn about me."

"Why do you say that?" She cocked her head to the side, and for a split second I began to believe that he had gotten to her enough to turn her heart against me.

"It wasn't one action; it was the summation of all his attacks that made me close my heart to him. He didn't leave me much choice."

"Then I truly don't understand why you took your anger out on me instead of him."

"I was wrong for that. I can't explain it. You were the only thing I ever had that he didn't ruin. He hadn't touched…"

I wanted Cojo to take me in her arms and tell me everything would be all right. Instead, she leaned back on the sofa, appearing to be deep in thought. On one hand, I should have been thanking my lucky stars that she hadn't sent me packing, but on the other, I missed my wife. I had yet to show her how very much I missed her after our forced separation.

A red-winged devil landed on my shoulder and started whispering in my ear. *She don't need you like you need her because her needs were already met by your brother.*

I silently groaned at the dramatization that played out in my mind. Thoughts like these could surely ruin my happily ever after.

15 COJO MILLS

Merlin paced and talked. "Sweetie, I don't know what else I can say except that this was an isolated incident, and that I will never put my hands on you again. After today, I'm done with my brother so he won't be an issue again."

"Family means everything to me. You turned on me yesterday without finding out what the circumstances were. That is what bothers me most, because you are my family, and the most important person in my world. I would never do that to you."

"I know, sweetheart, and I am deeply sorry. I acted on impulse without thinking. Haven't you ever felt like that before?"

I was tired of talking. I would never fully understand what drove Merlin to keep such a big secret from me. Someone needed to take the first step to mending our relationship. I wanted to hold my husband in my arms and have him make sweet love to me, but I didn't know how to say it to him. This whole situation was very confusing to me because I never had a problem communicating with Merlin before. In fact, most times I didn't have to tell him what I wanted—he knew. The silence that followed was irritating, and neither of us was strong enough to change it.

Finally, Merlin took my hand. "I love you, and I want us to work on saving our marriage."

No sweeter words could have been spoken to me. I was hoping my husband believed enough in our marriage to make it work. I wasn't deluding myself by thinking that he wouldn't have his moments when he remembered I had slept with his brother, but I believed that our love would prevail.

"I have faith in us." There was nothing left to say as I melted into his arms. All the pain and anguish of the last twenty-four hours were put aside. I got to enjoy the feel of my husband's arms around me, and I was excited about what would happen next. My clit came alive, yet not how it had when Gavin showed up at my door the previous morning.

"Are you sure?" Merlin pushed me away from his chest and tilted my chin so he could look me in the eyes.

I felt so much love for him in that moment it was difficult to speak. After all that we had been through, he still thought enough about me to ask me if I was sure.

"I've never been so sure of something in my life." The lines that had etched his face moments before dissolved, and he stood before me looking like a twelve-year-old child.

My heart swelled again with love. This was my soul mate and I loved him. He picked me up and carried me into our bedroom and gently laid me down on the bed. He stretched my arms out, a clear indication that he didn't want me to do anything.

"I've been waiting for this moment for six months," his voice was a low growl, and it turned me on just listening to him.

I tried to keep my eyes open and focused on him, but my mind wandered as he started to strip for me. Since I'd been with both brothers, I couldn't help but notice that they were both gifted in the drawers. Even though I'd been with my husband before, it had been awhile, and Gavin was freshly painted into my mind. Merlin wore his desert fatigues and a tan wifebeater that showed off his pecs, but I wasn't craving his pecs; I needed him to bring on the dick in spectacular style. I needed him to erase the thought of his brother from both my mind and body!

"You're taking too long," I said. I needed him to fill my body so my mind could stop the doubts that were flowing through it. I wanted to make sure that he was still able to fulfill me after I'd had a taste of the forbidden.

"Baby, I don't want to rush it. You know it's been a long time since I've been able to look at a woman, let alone touch my wife. I need to savor the moment, or else I'll no doubt explode before we get started." His arms were raised over his head as he was taking off his shirt, but he halted and his shoulders shook as if he were trying to ward off bad memories.

I could tell in that moment he was remembering what I was trying so desperately to forget. That's when I knew that I had to take matters into my own hands to get our relationship back on track.

As he stood there frozen in time, I slipped out of my clothing. At first, I was going at this with my mind, but now my heart got into it. I didn't want to give up on my marriage or the man whom I had grown to love. "Open your eyes," my voice was sultry and commanding.

"Damn." He couldn't say anything else, but he didn't need to. His dick fought against the confines of his shorts and told a story that his lips didn't have to.

"I love you," I whispered as I turned over and got on my knees. Even though I would have gotten more enjoyment from a frontal assault, I knew he needed to be in control of the dick slinging. I pointed my ass in his direction and prepared myself for the punishment. Mere seconds passed before I felt the head of his dick pressing against my hole. He wasn't going for the pussy; he was pushing into my ass without lube or chaser. Instinctively I tightened up. I wanted to stop him, but I resigned myself to taking it. He had to discipline me somehow, and this was going to be my punishment. It would be rough for a few strokes, but eventually I would feel the groove.

That's what I told myself, but in reality – it hurt like hell. I couldn't produce enough lube to make the fucking even remotely enjoyable. He actually chased me around the bed before he found release. Not wanting to lose the sexual bond that we'd formed, I slipped into the bathroom and wet a washcloth. I washed my ass and spent a considerable amount of time washing his dick with the warmed washcloth. When I finished, I replaced the warm cloth with my mouth.

"Ah…shit, baby, what are you trying to do?" He stood on his tiptoes as if that would stop him from coming in my mouth..

I took a moment to allow his dick to slide out of my mouth to answer. "I just want you to know how much I missed you."

Once again he tightened up, but as my lips sought his dick again, he had no choice but to give in to the feeling.

He said while I deep throated him, "Baby, I thought of you every night. I love you so much." He palmed the back of my head.

Even though I had him in a compromising position, I knew in my heart he was telling the truth. I could just feel it.

"Can I cum inside of you?" His voice was low, but I was close enough to hear it, and it was like music to my ears.

"All day and every day." I relinquished my hold on his dick and flipped over so he could sink his shaft deep inside of me.

He climbed on board and let me have five great pumps before he ejaculated. Normally I would have felt cheated, but tonight it was all I needed to get off my damn self. We came together, but my mind was making comparisons. *Is he better than Gavin?* I was treading on dangerous ground and I knew it, but I couldn't control my thoughts any more than I could control the weather.

"Damn, baby, that was good." Merlin sighed. He ran his hand down my back and rested it on my ass.

It was good for me too, but it wasn't great like what I had the day before with his brother. I couldn't get Gavin's crooked dick out of my head. "Yes, it was." I felt as if I should say more, but I couldn't figure out what else to say.

Merlin snuggled closer, and I wondered what was going through his brain. Was he doubting himself as well? I tried to fall into a comfortable nod, but I could not escape the thoughts racing through my brain. As much as I hated to admit it, the chemistry between Gavin and I was unlike anything I had ever experienced before, and part of me wanted more. Gavin was only the second man I'd slept with in my life, and he was truly fucking with my mind. If I had to choose between the two sexually, I would have chosen Gavin even though I knew he was trouble. Scary or not he was exciting.

16 GAVIN MILLS

Going back home is never easy, especially if you didn't have your shit together and the person you came home to didn't want you.

"I hope you know this is only a temporary thing," Gina said.

"I know. You don't have to keep reminding me." I was trying to slip past her and go to my room, but she wasn't through making me feel like crap.

"Did you look for a job today?" She stood there with her hands on her hips like she was about to climb in my ass if I didn't give her the answer that she wanted.

"I went to the library and put in a few applications online."

Her eyes widened in apparent shock. I know that she didn't expect that response from me, and I tried to hide the smile that threatened to creep up on my face. I was lying my ass off, but she didn't need to know all that. I just needed to keep her off my back for a little while.

"Humph. Online, huh? Ain't nothing like a face-to-face interview."

"I'm going to do that, Mother, but I had to make an appointment first. I just can't show up all unannounced."

"Why not? That's the way that I found my job."

"And that was like a hundred years ago."

Her mouth twisted into an evil frown. I could have worded it a little differently, but I knew times had changed since she last looked for work.

"Are you trying to get smart with me, boy?"

I bristled because my days of being a boy were over. I was twenty-five years old and didn't appreciate her trying to treat me like I was still a teenager. I wanted to tell her exactly how I felt about her evil ass, but I still needed a free place to stay until I found my next hustle. Working nine to five was not for me. Although I had my GED, I didn't have any work experience unless you counted my time working in the kitchen at the jail. Experience or no experience, I was not about to sling fries at some burger joint.

I needed to find something that would allow me to get some quick money so I could get the hell out of her house. My mind went back to Cojo. If I could turn her out, there was a good chance that she would allow me to kick it with her. She looked like she was handling her business and doing it well. I was sure that I could sweet-talk myself into her life if I could just get rid of my brother.

Gina snapped her fingers to bring me out of the daze. "Are you going to answer me?"

"Huh?" I had stopped listening to her a long time ago and had no idea what she'd said to me.

"I asked if you were getting smart. I'm not going to have you living in my house disrespecting me."

I sighed. "I wasn't trying to be smart. I was just saying that things have changed. Nowadays, everybody is using the Internet to conduct business. I'm surprised that you aren't up on that."

"I don't need that shit in my house. That's just another way for the government to spy on you."

"For crying out loud. There are so many benefits from having a computer. You could do all your shopping online and pay your bills."

"Shop for what? I have everything that I need. And I pay my bills through the mail or in person. It's been working for me all this time, I don't see why I should change it."

I looked around her sparsely furnished apartment and stifled a snort. "You might even find a man on the Internet."

"I don't need no man. And if I did, I damn sure wouldn't be looking for him on the Internet. Online dating is for those thirsty bitches."

I didn't agree with her statement because I thought some dick was definitely in order for her. I was of the opinion that if she got broke off in the right way, she would have an immediate attitude adjustment. "Those are only examples of the things you can do on the Internet. You might even look into starting a hobby."

"Hobby? What do I need a hobby for? What's wrong with my life the way it is?"

This conversation was going absolutely nowhere. Gina was in complete denial about her miserable life and there was nothing that I could say to change her opinions. If she wanted to keep on deluding herself, there was nothing that I could say or do to change it. I just wanted her to get out of my way so I could go into my room and start plotting on how I could work my way into Cojo's life. "So, what do you know about Cojo?"

"Cojo? Why the hell are you asking about her?" She turned away and walked over to the sofa and sat down. She twisted up her nose as if she smelt something bad. It was clear from her facial expression that she seriously disliked my brother's wife.

"She's in the family now, so I wanted to know something about her."

"Humph. She ain't in my family."

"Why don't you like her?" This conversation was about to get interesting to me, so I walked over to the love seat and sat down directly across from my Gina.

"I don't have any opinion about her at all. She's a non-motherfucking-factor." I could tell she was lying her ass off. She switched on the television, clearly done with our conversation. Her constant companion, a glass of amber liquid, was sitting on the end table.

If I were smarter, I should have used that opportunity to go to my room, but I had to open up my stupid-ass mouth and push the envelope. I had got the focus off of my not having a job and onto something else. But by pressing her to talk about something she didn't want to talk about, I brought the focus back to me. "So you're going to just ignore me?"

She turned off the television and gave me her full attention. "I know what this is about. You need to stop lusting after your brother's wife and find your sorry ass a job. You're doing the same shit that landed your ass in prison. Obviously, you haven't learned shit."

Damn, she busted me out big time. I thought I was being all slick, and she saw right through my mess. I stood up. "I ain't lusting after anybody. All I did was ask a damn question." I started to stomp off.

"Who the hell do you think you're talking to? You ain't gonna come up in my house and talk to me any kind of way." She was working on a major neck snapping attitude, and I wanted to kick my own ass for not following my first instincts.

As much as I didn't want to, I knew that I was going to have to apologize. "I'm sorry, Mother. I wasn't trying to be disrespectful."

"Umph."

This time I didn't hesitate to get the hell out of the room. I didn't know how much longer I would be able to hold my thoughts and feelings inside. Being back home, I was finding it hard to remember why I missed the place in the first place. Gina was like a stranger to me, and my brother didn't want to have anything to do with me. Part of me wanted to ask her about my dad and if he was still sniffing around, but I wasn't a glutton for punishment.

17 MERLIN MILLS

Falling asleep should have been a no-brainer. My wife and I had just made love, and we were fighting to salvage our marriage. Everything should have been right with the world, but I still had the little man riding my shoulder, talking in my ear. He had a lot to say too, and most of it I didn't want to hear. I was certain to fail if I continued to listen to him. He ragged me on my performance in bed. I didn't last two hot minutes. I tried to tell myself it was because of my long abstinence and my overstuffed balls. It sounded good in my head, but my heart knew the deal.

Damn, should I start calling you 'two'? the devil man asked.

Two? I thought.

Yeah, as in two-minute brother. You busted your nut before she could even catch up.

It's been a long time.

Do you really believe that?

She got hers.

How do you know she wasn't faking it? You know women are good at it. Stroking our egos, and we're dumb enough to believe it.

Cojo wouldn't fake an orgasm.

Are you sure about that, buddy?

The seeds of doubt were planted, and as I lie there waiting for sleep to take me away, I watered those seeds. Dealing with my brother always made me feel this way. The fact that he had actually been intimate with my wife wreaked havoc with my head. I didn't want to lose the only woman I cared about to him.

The devil said, *Gavin tapped that ass for real. You just played with the pussy.*

"Will you just shut up," I mumbled aloud.

Cojo lifted her head from her pillow and peeked at me. "What?" She wiped at her eyes, trying to clear the crust from them.

"Nothing, sweetie, go back to sleep. I had a bad dream."

She snuggled closer to me. The smell of her sex was like an alluring drug. My dick rose to attention. I wanted some more, and this time I vowed to last longer than two minutes.

I palmed her grapefruit-sized breast in my right hand, kneading her nipple. It became hard as a raisin in seconds. That was one of the things that I loved about my wife. Her body responded to my touch. A low purr escaped her lips as she gently pressed her ass against my dick. Even though she was drowsy, she still responded to my touch, and that made me feel better.

"Can I lick your pussy?" I whispered in her ear. My dick throbbed in anticipation.

She'd never said no in the past, so I didn't expect her to tonight. She flung her legs open wide as I slipped down under the sheets to meet her at her V.

This was the first time that I had ever suggested oral sex after we'd already had sex. Cojo liked to have her vagina smelling fresh, but there was nothing wrong with what I was smelling. I smelled the essence of our love, and I was ready to taste the fruits of our passion.

"Don't you want me to spruce up?"

"No, I want it just like it is."

As I lowered my head and took the first taste, she moaned.

"Damn baby, what's come over you?"

She did not want to hear my answer to that question because it would have really hurt her feelings. I wanted to make sure I erased all memory of my brother from her pussy. My dick might have been lacking, but my lips were killa.

"I told you...I missed you." I flicked her clit with my tongue again. That was an understatement. Being stuck for six months with a bunch of dudes was no damn joke. I could have done like some of my boys and taken advantage of the women who were also stationed in the Green Zone in Iraq, but I chose to remain faithful to my wife. That was another reason why it hurt me to find out that Cojo had slept with my brother. I nestled my face between her thighs and inhaled deeply. This was my wife, and the woman who I chose to spend the rest of my life with. I needed to have her juices all over my face.

You still drinking behind your brother? Little man whispered in my ear.

"Shut the hell up." I shook my head to get the tiny voice out of my head.

"What's going on, baby?" Cojo raised up on her elbows to see who the hell I was speaking to.

I felt like the village idiot. "Your pussy is talking to me and I was telling her to be patient. We have nothing but time." I thought I was being clever on the fly coming up with a plausible lie on demand. But I also felt guilty for lying about my true feelings.

The little man started talking to me again: *You must be doing something different than he did. Why else would she question you? Has she ever questioned you before?*

This little private conversation was working against my erection and my desire to have my wife again.

"I'm just tripping. I've been dreaming about when I would be with you again for so long, my mind is on overload, not to mention my dick."

"Oh, baby, that's so sweet."

Why did it sound like she was placating me for my early ejaculation when I know she came too? These were the thoughts that I needed to erase from my mind if we were going to continue to have a happy and loving relationship. I couldn't keep those doubts in my head, or they would destroy me. "I'm good, baby. I just have something on my mind."

I threw the covers off my side of the bed and swung my legs over the side, no longer interested in sucking on her pussy.

"Where you going, baby?"

"Going to get something to drink. Go back to sleep."

"Can you bring me some, too?"

Damn, I was hoping that I could take my time and get myself together before I had to come back in the room with her. "Sure. Can I get you something else while I'm in the kitchen?"

"No, just some water will be fine."

I walked into the kitchen with a heavy heart. Part of me wanted to punish my wife with my lovemaking, but it backfired on me. The shit got so good that I couldn't control myself.

I pulled two glasses out of the cabinet. I really wanted a stiff drink, but she would question my drinking so late at night, especially since neither of us really ate that much. I was going to have to suck this up until I could get some time alone.

I carried the glasses back in the bedroom, and to my surprise Cojo was fast asleep. I could have cried I was so relieved. Turning softly on my bare feet, I left the bedroom and crept back into the kitchen. I poured out the water and went to the bar and fixed myself a generous drink. I sat down on the sofa and gazed at the television. I didn't dare turn it on for fear that it would wake my wife.

"Lord, what am I going to do?" I whispered as a tear rolled down my face. I glanced around our apartment. It wasn't bad. Before I left it felt like my home, but now I felt as if I didn't belong. I felt like I was a stranger just visiting, even though I knew where everything belonged. I put my feet up on the coffee table as I sipped from my glass. I felt the beginnings of a headache coming on, and I was too tired to go and get some aspirin. Another tear slid down my face.

Just a few days ago I was behind enemy lines, and now I'm crying like a little punk because I shot my load off too quickly. I was so fucked up in the head, it didn't occur to me that this was a natural reaction after being deprived of sex for so long. It was almost like the first time, especially when I was used to having sex on the regular.

I heard a car pull into the parking lot. Its headlights briefly lit up the living room. I wondered who was coming home so late, so I got up to peek out the curtains. I couldn't see the car because of a huge maple tree blocking my view.

Even though it was dark outside, I could see enough details to tell it was a man. He wore dark clothing and kept his head turned so I couldn't make out his facial features. Something about the man was familiar. He walked toward our breezeway, and for a moment I lost visual contact with him. I moved from the window to the door. I wanted to see what apartment he was going to enter. Much to my surprise, the man was walking straight to our apartment. He put his ear to our door and stood there.

I was stunned. Wearing nothing more than my drawers, I yanked open the door. "May I help you, motherfucker?"

The man raised his head and grinned broadly. "Hey, bro," he said as he looked me up and down.

"Gavin, what the fuck are you doing here, and why do you have your ear pressed against our door?"

"Uh…"

My blood pressure escalated. He was about to spoon-feed me some bullshit just like he used to do when we were kids.

"Uh…hell," I bellowed. Something just wasn't right about his sudden interest in me and what was going on in my life. We hadn't been close in so many years, why now?

"I…uh…I was just in the neighborhood, and I was only making sure everything was okay with you since I haven't heard from you." He had a sheepish grin on his face.

If I wasn't standing there in my underwear, I would have socked him dead in his face. "Do you know what the fuck time it is?" My fingers balled into a fist, itching to slug him just once.

"Naw, man. What time is it?" He was playing stupid on me, and it was making me madder by the second.

I looked past him to see if anyone was watching the spectacle we were causing in the hallway. "Negro, you playing games with me? First you popped up this morning, now you show up after midnight. What's up with that?"

"I ain't playin', bro; I just wanted to make sure my brother and his wife were okay, so now that I've done that, I guess I'll be getting on home."

The need to touch him was so tempting, but I didn't want to start any shit while I was standing in my drawers.

Cojo crept out of the bedroom. "Merlin?"

I quickly turned around. I had forgotten she was asleep in the next room as my voice got louder. Cojo was nude as a newborn, and I was providing Gavin a show by holding the door open. I swung back around to look at Gavin. His eyes widened as he took in all her splendid glory. "Baby, go back in the room and put some clothes on. I'll be there in a minute."

She jumped back as she realized that we weren't alone. "Oh God!" she screeched as she ran back to our room and shut the door.

Gavin seeing my wife naked was becoming old hat and getting on my damn nerves.

"That's one fine woman you got there. Glad to see you handling your business."

I snorted in disgust at his pitiful concerned act. "I'm going back to my wife." I started to close the door to my brother's leering eyes.

"Before I go, just answer one question for me." He put his hands up to stop me from closing the door.

"What is it?" The sight of him was pissing me off.

"Why are you out here in the living room drinking when you could be snuggled up with that dime piece of a wife?"

Damn, he must have seen me peeping through the curtains. That was it. I made up my mind to shut this shit down once and for all. "Do you have that cell phone on you that I threw in with the clothes?"

He pointed his thumb toward the parking lot. "It's in the car."

"Good. I'll call you in twenty minutes."

Gavin grinned as if I had made his day. "Oh, yeah? For what? I thought you were going back to your sexy wife."

"I'm tired of drinking alone. Figured we could have a few drinks together."

♥♥♥

I marched into our bedroom and started getting dressed.

"Where are you going?" Cojo said.

"Out. I need to handle something." I put on my Atlanta ball cap.

"Out where?"

"Not right now, Cojo. What I'm about to do won't take long." I grabbed my car keys from the dresser and left.

"What was Gavin doing here?"

"Damn it, I said not now." I knew I shouldn't use that tone of voice with her, but I was so angry I wasn't even thinking straight.

18 MERLIN MILLS

I jumped in my car and sped out of the parking lot with my tires screeching against the asphalt. I called Gavin when I reached the first stop sign.

In the middle of the first ring, he said, "I see you're still Mr. Punctual."

"You remember that bar, Central Station, in East Point?"

"Yeah, I used to sneak in there a few times back in the day."

"Meet me there." My mind was telling me to turn around and go back home, but my heart had its foot on the gas pedal.

Are the drinks on you? Bars don't agree with my budget."

Some people never change. Gavin always wanted to freeload off people, getting by without any effort on his part. The motherfucker just took, took, took.

I pretended to laugh. "Sure, everything is on me. Ain't that the way it's always been?"

♥♥♥

I was pretty fucked up when Gavin finally pulled up in the parking lot. I had bought me a pint of gin and had just about killed the entire bottle.

He walked up to me. "What's up, fam?" Gavin had a familiar smirk on his face, and it was enough to ignite my short fuse.

I launched my body from the side of the building and slammed into my brother, dragging him to the ground. I punched him in the nose and blood went everywhere.

"Man, what the fuck is your problem?" Gavin struggled to get to his feet, but I clung to him like body odor.

"You're my fucking problem. Why the hell do you keep popping up at my house like a bill collector? I told you I wasn't fucking with you."

"You tripping, man. I told you I was just in the neighborhood."

"I'm not stupid, man." I punched him in his jaw as hard as I could.

I rattled his head and appeared to have stunned him. We had a tit for tat tussle in the parking lot.

He said, "Man, you better stop fucking with me."

Gavin was still trying to recover when I head-butted him. I had learned a lot in the military, and I poured all of my aggression onto him.

"I won't tell you this again. Stay the fuck away from me and my wife."

"You're bugging!" Gavin finally regrouped and was able to pull free of me. He used someone's car to pull himself to his feet.

I quickly got up and circled my prey, coming in low. I wasn't ready for our scuffle to end. I have a lifetime of pent-up anger at him that I was ready to disperse. My brother had caused me a lot of pain throughout my life, and I was past done being his whipping boy.

He rubbed his hand over his jaw and shrugged his shoulders, trying to pretend I didn't hurt him at all. "You got a nice right cross. They teach you that in the service?"

I didn't come there to talk. I wanted to let my hands speak for me. I rushed him again, but this time Gavin stepped out of the way and I charged by him.

"Are we fighting over a bitch? Pussies come and go...brothers are for life."

"That woman you refer to as a bitch happens to be my wife. Now I'm going to tell you one last time, stay the fuck away from her." I swung again and managed to hit him in the arm. I could tell that he was finally getting mad, but I didn't give a fuck.

"Ain't nobody thinking about her." He attempted to punch me in the chest, but I quickly deflected the blow and delivered one of my own. He said, "Now I'm going to pretend like you didn't bust my nose because you're my family. But make no mistake about it, you're weak. You've always been the weak one, and I'll use that to my advantage and beat shit down your leg."

"This is your last warning. You're not welcome at my house." I stepped back.

Gavin opened his trunk, changed his shirt, then got into his car. We were making so much noise in the parking lot, I was surprised someone hadn't called the cops yet.

"You heard what I said," I warned him.

"Whatever, motherfucker," Gavin said as he rolled down the window and spat at my feet.

I wanted to reach through the window and drag his ass out, but when I reached for him, his car tire ran over my foot. I winced as I grabbed my injured limb. Gavin pulled off as I danced around on the gravel, trying to make the pain go away.

"Bitch ass," I shouted to his departing car.

♥♥♥

Cojo snatched the front door open when I approached it. She covered her mouth and her eyes widened. "Oh my God, Merlin, where did all that blood come from?"

"Leave it alone, Cojo." I limped past her.

"I smell alcohol; have you been drinking?"

"What part of 'leave it alone' is confusing to you?" I slammed the bathroom door shut and locked it. My buzz was wearing off, and I had a major headache. I also felt bad for fighting with my brother.

♥♥♥

Cojo was still standing in the living room when I came out of the bathroom. I tried to walk by her, but she wasn't having it.

"Are you going to tell me what happened, or are you about to go back to your motel room?

I stopped short. I wasn't used to Cojo using that type of tone with me. Ours was such a loving relationship, which was truly being tested.

"Gavin and I had a disagreement."

"Oh, Merlin. We both know violence is not the answer to anything."

"It might not be the answer, but it sure felt good. I'm not about to have the man sniffing around here. There ain't nothing in this house that belongs to him."

Cojo opened her mouth to say something but must have changed her mind. She went into the bedroom and closed the door behind her, leaving no doubt in my mind where I would be sleeping for the night. I went and retrieved my empty glass and filled it again.

The little man was sitting on the edge of the sofa waiting for me. *"You know she was taking his side, don't you?"*

I slugged my drink back and poured another. I planned on drowning the little man out. He would either grow bored talking to himself or I would pass out. Either option worked good for me.

19 GAVIN MILLS

I didn't have anyone to blame for that disaster of a visit but myself. I wasn't thinking with my head when I went over there, I was thinking with my dick. I slammed my hand against the steering wheel. I had left his house looking stupid, but the image of Cojo naked was burned in my brain; even the fight with my brother wasn't enough to keep me away. I had to have her again—there were no ifs, ands, or buts about it. I was going to have to devise a way to get Merlin out of the house so I could at least talk to Cojo and see if she felt the same way I did.

If creeping was the only way that I would see her again, I didn't mind. I was like my daddy—I wasn't the marrying kind. I was a fuck them or leave them type of guy. This thing with Cojo was far from over.

I didn't really want to go home, but I knew that I had to do something before I broke down Cojo's door or did something else foolish. I didn't quite understand why I was so attracted to her. Maybe it was the forbidden fruit aspect of it. Although she was beautiful, it was more to it than that.

Merlin's stupid ass don't even know what to do with that little freak. Shit, there ain't no way I would have been out trying to pick a fight, instead of in that bedroom tearing that shit up. My dick started to rise as I thought about her round, soft ass and the way that it had filled my hands.

I was sexually frustrated in a way that I hadn't been since I was a teenager, and the thought of going back to my mother's house to beat my meat wasn't the least bit appealing. Knowing her ass, she would knock on the damn door right before I shot my load into my pillowcase. Then I would want to beat her ass for adding to my already blue balls.

I decided to drive down Cleveland Avenue to see if I could find some hoes on the stroll. It had been a while since I'd been in Atlanta so I didn't really know where to go to find me some free pussy. Since I had a little money in my pocket, I was willing to pay for a piece of ass. I was hoping to find some hot young thang who wouldn't mind stretching out on the back seat of my car or sucking my dick as I drove around the block.

I rubbed my dick in anticipation. It was late, however, and most young girls were probably in the house, but I was too aroused to go home frustrated.

I spotted a young honey walking down the street like she had just lost her best friend. "Bingo." I slowed my car down as I came up on the girl. I rolled down my window. Her shirt was clinging to her skin, and I could see sweat rings under her arms as she drifted under the street lamp. She appeared to have been out there for some time because she walked like each step hurt. I drove even slower. I expected her to notice me and solicit her goodies, but she must have been lost in thought because she didn't even look up.

I pulled up next to her at the curb. "Excuse me, miss. I'm a little lost. I'm trying to get back to I-20. Can you help me?"

"Huh?" Her head snapped up and she looked all around as if she was unaware of her surroundings. She was young, very young—just like I liked them.

"I'm sorry. I didn't mean to startle you, but I was wondering if you could help me find the highway."

She stood still for a few seconds before she took a hesitant step toward the car. She didn't come too close, but she came close enough so that I didn't have to speak as loud.

I didn't expect her to be scared, especially since she was on a well-known hoe stroll. As she got closer, I was able to get a better look at her face and her perky breasts, which strained against her soaked shirt.

"I'm sorry, I really don't know. I'm not from around here." She backed up a step.

"Oh, okay." I started to pull off because she was giving me a bad vibe.

She looked around again and yelled out to me, "Wait."

I put on the brakes and tried to hide the smile that spread across my face. It was hot as hell outside, so I knew she would prefer being in a car with me to humping down the street in her high-ass heels. My dick throbbed as I watched the indecision play across her pretty face.

"Yes?" I kept my tone even so as not to run her off. I didn't want her to know how badly I needed her. The way I was feeling, she could have been bat-shit ugly with one tooth in her head and it wouldn't matter. As long as she looked clean and had a pussy, I was game. I always kept a condom or two in my wallet, so I wasn't worried about anything else.

"Can I trouble you for a ride?"

"Uh …" I didn't want to appear eager so I hesitated.

"Please? I had a fight with my boyfriend, and I want to get out of this neighborhood before he comes looking for me." She took two steps closer to the car and my dick thumped against my zipper.

"I'm sorry, sweetheart, but I don't want no trouble. I'm just trying to find my way home." I sat up straight in my seat as she leaned into the car.

"I won't be no trouble, but I've been walking for a long time and my feet are killing me." Her breasts seemed to be mere inches from my mouth.

"I hear what you're saying, but what if your man comes running up on me and wants to start something? I can't take that chance, I'm new to Atlanta. I'm stationed at Fort McPherson Army base, so I can't afford to get in any mess.

"Please, mister, I promise it will be okay."

I didn't say anything for several seconds. My eyes scanned the streets and my rearview mirror. I even turned around to look out the back window to make it seem like I was worried. In all reality, I wished a motherfucker would try to come between me and this pussy. I was ready for a real fight after my altercation with Merlin.

"Get in." I leaned over and opened the passenger side door.

She ran as fast as her heels would allow to get to the other side of the car. Her face was twisted up in a grimace that wasn't appealing at all. She plopped into the seat and shut the door. "Thank you," she said as she glanced over her shoulder.

"Put your seatbelt on." I pulled back onto the street, happy with this turn of events.

She was fumbling around with the seatbelt so I reached over to help her. She jumped at my close proximity.

"Relax, ma, I was just trying to help you. I would hate to get a ticket for something so trivial as a seatbelt violation."

She visibly relaxed and allowed me to pull out her seatbelt. Once she was settled, I picked up speed.

"The highway can't be far from here. Where do you live?" For a second I thought she didn't hear me, because she didn't answer. "My name is Merlin Mills, what's yours?" Old habits die hard I thought as Merlin's name rolled off my lips.

"That's interesting. Never met a black man by the name of Merlin." She took off her shoes and started massaging her feet.

"I smell stinky feet," I said jokingly.

"My feet don't stink." She attempted to put her shoes back on.

"Hey, don't do that, I was just kidding. You don't have to put them back on if you don't want to."

She still hadn't volunteered her name, but I wasn't going to press her until she was ready to talk. In all honesty, I couldn't give two fucks about her name. All I wanted from her was some head and some of that young pussy. I could almost smell it, like it was some expensive perfume she wore.

"So what was the fight about?" I didn't know if she was going to answer the question, but I put it out there. Perhaps if I came across as an older brother, she would start to trust me.

"How old are you?" She was very good at evading questions.

"Twenty-one." I was really twenty-five, but that was on a need-to-know basis, and she didn't need to know.

"You don't look twenty-one."

"How old do I look?" If she said thirty, I was going to put her out at the next corner, pussy or not. I waited for a few heartbeats with my foot hovering over the brake.

"I would have said eighteen." She giggled as she said it, and my ego inflated like a helium balloon. She sat back in the seat as if she had known me all of her life.

I started to feel more confident that I was going to get what I wanted. She was still massaging her foot.

"If you put one of your feet on my lap, I'll massage it for you."

She looked at me with this quizzical expression on her face, and I was afraid that I had scared her away, but she hesitantly handed me her right foot. It rested on my thigh, and I firmly massaged it while keeping my other hand on the wheel. Instead of giving me her left leg, she handed me her right, folding her other leg underneath her. Her legs were spread like a sexy check mark lying upside down. I was incredibly turned on by her limber legs.

"Mm, that feels so good," she murmured as her head rested against the window.

I looked over at her and her eyes were closed. I smiled. Things were going a lot better than I thought they would. She had to be young because no experienced woman would allow herself to be in this situation. She didn't know me from Adam, but she was wide open for me.

"Thanks, it's what I used to do before I joined the army." The lies were just rolling off my tongue.

"What you used to do? What's that supposed to mean?" She raised her head up off the window. She was tall, at least five feet six, and probably weighed about 135 pounds.

"By profession I'm a masseuse. The army is a temporary hustle. I set up in hair salons and fitness clubs to help people relax."

"Oh, that's nice. I never met a masseuse before."

We traveled for a few more miles without conversation. I kept a firm pressure on her right foot, and she continued to moan softly.

"How's your other foot?"

"It still hurts."

"Put that one up here too, and I'll work on it."

If she were paying attention, she would have realized that we were driving around in a big circle. I knew exactly where I was, and I was in no hurry to get to the highway. In fact, we were now driving down the same street that I had picked her up on.

She placed both of her feet on my lap. She could have removed the right foot, but she didn't. She must have liked the way my hands felt on her. As I massaged her left foot, her moans got louder.

"You're good. I would pay money for a full-body massage."

I started trying to calculate how much money I had left in my pocket. I was ready to get a hotel room so I could show her just how good I could make her feel. Inside and out.

"Thanks, it's a job I enjoy."

"Do you do men too?"

"That would be a no. I do this job because I enjoy it, and there is nothing enjoyable to me about rubbing on another man."

She giggled again, this time louder. "You're funny. I like you, Merlin. You have the hands of a magician." She laughed at her own joke.

"If you only knew." I was growing tired of waiting. As much as I enjoyed touching her feet, I needed more.

She said, "We went to a frat party with some of his friends."

Her voice was so low as if she were talking to herself and not me. I wanted to tell her to get to the point so we could get to fucking, but I kept my peace, as painful as it was to do.

"He got to drinking and paying more attention to his boys than me, and I was ready to go home. He called me a few ugly names and told me that if I wanted to leave I knew where the door was."

"Wow, how long had you been dating this jerk?"

"For about seven months. I don't know what got into him tonight. He was acting like a stranger."

"I'm sorry that happened to you."

"Angie, my name is Angie Simpson."

"Nice to meet you, Angie." I continued to rub her feet. I was still trying to figure out how I was going to get this little honey in either the back seat or to a cheap hotel room.

"You can stop driving around in circles now and take me home."

Well, I'll be damned.

20 GAVIN MILLS

I thought I was going to have to trick my way into Angie's panties, but she flipped the script on me. As soon as the door closed, she turned into a lioness. She was so aggressive, she almost scared me for a minute. Now I don't see nothing wrong with a forceful woman, but damn, hold the fuck up for a minute. She gripped my dick like it was made of plastic instead of sensitive flesh.

"Hold up, honey, this joint is still attached."

She looked at me like she was about to punk me or put my ass out, but I didn't want to get this close to pussy and not get any so I smiled.

"I'm just saying, take your time. I ain't going nowhere." I squeezed her ass trying to take control.

"I'm not trying to rush you and shit, but this is my parent's house. If you want some of this, we've got to hit it and quit it." She didn't have to say it to me twice after she explained the situation.

I moved in close and pulled her to me. I damn near smothered her with my lips as I tongued her down. Now that we were on the same page, I felt the same sense of urgency that she felt. I began grabbing at her clothes. I wanted her naked in the worst way, and I assumed she felt the same way too because she also began pawing at my clothes.

Since my clothing was limited, I winced when I heard a button pop off and roll on the floor. I would make sure to remember to grab the button before I left so I could sew it back on later. I gently pushed her away from me so I could take off my own clothes. She stood there for a moment, but when she saw that I was removing my shirt, she started taking off her own clothes as well.

We were in the living room, and from the looks of it, this was where it was about to go down.

"I like it rough, daddy." She bent over the sofa and exposed her apple bottom to my eager dick.

I was already excited when I saw her shapely ass, but when she said she liked it rough, I damn near blew my load into the air. What exactly did she mean by *rough?* Did she want me to spank her ass or did she want me to choke her as I came? I was perfectly willing and able to handle it either way. "Where you want it?" Visions of nasty acts danced in my head. It was rare to find someone as young as Angie who was into the really nasty things. Normally, they didn't acquire the really kinky taste until they were at least thirty-five.

"I want you to ram that big dick so far up my ass that it comes out my mouth."

I was outdone and my knees grew weak. My prayers had been answered. I felt like Angie was a kindred soul, and I was about to give it to her. I could not believe that her dude slept on this shit. "Did you let the other dude hit it like this?" I normally didn't like to discuss other men while I was about to get my groove on, but this whole night was just like a dream to me. I could not believe that things were turning out just as I had planned them.

"Are you just going to talk, or are you going to show me what you are working with?" She wagged her naked ass at me.

This chick had man-sized balls. If I wasn't careful, she could very well turn me out. I brought it to her hard, and I stifled the moan that escaped from my lips. She was tight, but access was easy. I was surprised at how receptive she was, and it only excited me more.

"Harder."

Damn, I felt like I had died and gone to heaven. This bitch was allowing me to give it to her like I was grilling her pussy.

"Fuck my asshole harder goddammit!"

"Oh, you think you can take all of this?" I boasted. I was feeling quite good about myself at this point. Not only was I in those panties, I was dick deep in that ass.

"Stop talking and keep fuckin'," her voice was rasping and deep.

If I didn't know better, I would have thought that Reagan from the *Exorcist* had entered the room. I dug deeper, hoping to give her what she was looking for, and to achieve my own release as well.

She matched me thrust for thrust. "Yeah, just like that, baby. Fuck me like you mean it."

The pressure was on, and her nasty talking was taking me to another level. I wasn't used to having a woman talk trash to me and it was messing with my head. She had me thinking I was invincible when I really wasn't.

"If you want me to give it to you right, you may want to shut the fuck up." As soon as those words left my mouth, I knew I'd screwed up. Her ass clamped down on my dick like a vice as she pushed my dick out in the cold. "Damn, baby, I didn't mean it the way it sounded. All that talk, you know, was killing the moment."

"I know what you mean, your smartass mouth ruined it for me too. I guess we're both shit out of luck. Lucky for me, I got me a battery operated dick that doesn't talk back." She started to get off the sofa which really pissed me off.

"Bitch, get your ass back on the couch." I was heated.

"Bitch? Oh, I got your bitch." She reached under the sofa and brought out a baseball bat. At first, I thought she was playing around or something until she hit me across the shoulders with it, rattling my neck. Talk about an error in judgment, this bitch was crazy. She cracked me over my arm, and it felt like she broke it.

"Are you crazy?" I was about to call her a bitch again, but I stopped myself. As frantic as things had become, I was still turned on and I wanted to calm her sexy ass down enough so I could bust my nut. Even though my arms hurt like hell, I still had an erection. "Damn, baby, I like your attitude. Back that ass up on my dick." I raised up on my knees and scooted to the middle of the sofa. I was about to take this shit to another level. If things went my way, I would have her screaming for her momma.

Obviously I wasn't the only one turned on by her aggressive behavior. Angie backed her shapely ass up in the air, and I plunged into her pussy as if I were trying to break through to the other side. "That's right, fuck me," she yelled.

That was it for me. I came and I was through. My dick shriveled and escaped her pussy. I never felt so dejected in my life. I couldn't hang with her young ass.

"Don't tell me you're done? I'm not having that. You're gonna fuck me longer than that. I'm just getting started."

I was not in the mood for any more of her smartass remarks, and I damn sure wasn't going to let her hit me with that bat again.

"Come again?" I was giving her a chance to change her attitude before I choked the shit out of her.

"What? Are you hard of hearing all of a sudden? I said are you going to give me some dick or not? I don't have all night."

That was it, lights out on the young pussy. I snatched her neck and held on until the fire left her eyes and her lips closed in blessed silence. I continued to squeeze her neck as I jacked off. I rammed my dick inside of her and busted the biggest nut that I had ever experienced. It was so good, I almost wanted Angie to wake up to ask her if it was good for her too.

As I tossed her limp body to the floor, I got angry. Who did she think she was talking to? I put on my shoes and proceeded to kick her about the face and ribs. With each kick, I felt victorious. She wouldn't be giving anyone else any lip. I was making sure of that.

Fear about what I had done didn't descend on me until the last little soldier had made its way into her pussy. Each soldier a part of a DNA chain that could send me to prison for life. At the very least, I should have used a condom, but it was too late to think about that now.

"I've got to kill this bitch and get rid of the evidence," I said out loud. It wasn't my fault that she got a little mouthy and wound up dead. I searched around the room for my pants that I had discarded earlier. Most women didn't understand that their wicked mouth brought on most of their problems.

Why did she have to start talking about my performance as if I hadn't been doing a damn thing? If she had been able to keep control of her pie hole, she would be alive right now and basking in my arms. Once I secured my clothing, I looked around the room to decide the best way to cover my tracks. I didn't touch much in the room, but I couldn't chance a smear of a fingerprint here and there, so I decided to torch the house.

I left Angie's crumpled body on the floor between the sofa and coffee table as I went in search of something that would help me reduce this house to rubble. Time was not on my side. I had no idea how long her parents would be gone. The only thing I knew was that if I were caught in the house, I would be facing life for real this time.

I found what I was looking for in the carport. A full can of gasoline was sitting next to the push mower. I was surprised that they would leave it out in the open, especially since gas prices were so high, but that was their problem, not mine. I picked up the can and raced back to the living room splashing gas as I went. I wanted the focus of the fire to be downstairs so that all evidence of me being in the home would be destroyed. I even poured a liberal amount of gas on the stairs. Once I emptied the entire can, I struck a match and threw it and the can into the living room and ran out the house.

The explosion was minor, but the effect was immediate. I watched tiny plumes of fire etch its way through the house. I jumped into my car and sped away, hoping that there were no nosey neighbors witnessing my speedy departure.

♥♥♥

I really didn't think the whole fire thing through. I knew I wanted to get rid of evidence, but I had no idea the fire would spread so quickly. The entire first floor was in flames by the time I was halfway down the block. My curiosity got the better of me, so I drove back and parked my car on the side of the road to watch.

My dick got hard as I watched those flames leap from the downstairs windows to the upper floors. It was such a rush! I pulled off as the first fire truck pulled onto the street. I wasn't about to be one of those idiots who stayed at the scene and wound up getting arrested because they had no real reason to be there.

I could still smell Angie's scent on my hands. When I got home, I would have to sneak past my mother because I reeked of sex and gasoline. It was difficult to believe that a random fuck led to murder, but I had no regrets. She had no business trying to clown me after I'd served it up to her. She wasn't appreciative, so the bitch deserved to die. My mind floated back to when I had sex with my brother's wife. She didn't complain, so why did I have to hear that shit from some random chick? *Fuck that, I don't think so!*

♥♥♥

As I parked my car at my mother's house, I checked the car to make sure the cunt hadn't left any telltale evidence. I looked around, making sure that I wasn't being observed as I got out of the car. It would be just my luck to get away and get caught by some damn bullshit. After a few minutes, I was comfortable that I had gotten away with murder again.

"Bitches beware!" I was ecstatic. I was ready to go out and do that shit again, especially since it was so easy to do. That was one of the perks of being a good-looking motherfucker. Women didn't require much to give up the goodies, and I was Johnny on the spot to provide them.

As I put my key in the door, some of my high evaporated. I wasn't up for my mother's smartass mouth tonight. If she knew what I'd done, she would be careful about how she spoke to me because it wouldn't take much to put her miserable ass in the ground too.

21 ANGIE SIMPSON

I woke up and immediately started coughing. Acrid smoke burned my nose and clouded my vision. Flames were eating through the living room rapidly, and I knew if I didn't act fast the fire would devour me, too. I could hardly move my head my neck was so sore. It felt like Merlin still had his powerful fingers around my throat.

I pushed through the pain I was feeling, and started to crawl toward the door. The air down low was easier on my lungs.

The front door was covered by a wall of flames so I crawled to the kitchen, hoping for an easier exit. I froze when I saw the kitchen was equally engulfed in fire. Panic seeped into my veins as a frightened wail escaped my mouth. Through the wall of flames, I could see the back door. I tried to hold my breath while I figured out what to do, because I was on the verge of choking to death.

I was trapped. I didn't want to die. I had always heard that the three worst ways to die were drowning, suffocation, and fire. In my opinion, fire was the worst. I put my head down on the floor and gulped in air as I tried to think. I didn't have a whole lot of choice.

I quickly got to my feet and turned on the kitchen faucet. I grabbed all the towels from the drawer and stuck them in the sink. Dropping back to the floor, I draped the soaked towels over my head and shoulders. In my mind, I envisioned myself outside on the cool grass. Going through the fire was my only chance at survival. I spit into my hands and wiped the saliva over my eyes. Time was running out. Behind me was a complete wall of flames, and the floorboards were starting to fall into the living room. I felt like it was now or never. I had to make a move. My head hurt and my lungs felt like they were about to burst. With a low scream, I lunged through the wall of flames and charged the back door.

The flames burned the hair on my arms and legs. I howled in pain, but I couldn't stop moving. I pounded on the door, but it refused to open. I was certain I wasn't going to make it.

"God, please!" I shouted. I looked around for something to break the glass, and that was when I realized I was pushing the door instead of pulling it. I fumbled with the knob which was hot to the touch. It burned, but I refused to let go as I turned the knob and flung the door open, gasping for air.

The house seemed to explode behind me and pitched my body into the air. My arms flapped around helplessly as I sailed over the hedges in our neighbor's yard and landed on the grass. The force of the fall pushed most of the remaining air from my lungs.

I tried to turn over and look at the house, but I couldn't move. I managed to lift my head, but this intense ringing in my ears caused me to put it back down again. My throat was raw. I wanted to cry for help, but I couldn't.

Where the fuck were my neighbors? Any other time they would be peering out their damn windows trying to catch me cutting up, but the night that I needed them—nothing. The explosion should have brought people from blocks away, but I couldn't see anything.

I began to tremble with relief and maybe shock. I could not believe I had gotten out of the house, and I couldn't help but to feel a little bit victorious. The last thing I remembered before passing out was the fact that I didn't have on any clothes.

22 GINA MEADOWS

I sat on the couch in my favorite spot and ran my mouth on the phone to my best friend. "I didn't tell you that boy stayed out all night and didn't have the decency to call."

Tabatha said, "Now wait a minute, Gina. Why are you acting all mad? You didn't want him there in the first place and that boy, as you call him, is a grown-ass man."

"Grown or not, it is still common courtesy to call someone you're staying with and let them know that you ain't coming back. He's trifling, just like his damn father. Thinks he can come and go as he pleases, treating my house like it's a hotel and shit."

"Girl, make up your mind. First, you complain that he came back to stay with you temporarily, and now you want to fuss because he stayed out all night. Give him a break."

"Whose side are you on anyway?"

"I'm not picking sides. Right is right. If Gavin treats your house like a hotel, it's because you let him think that it was okay. I think you're miserable with your choices in life, and you want everyone around you to be miserable too. And you know what else I think? It all started when you aborted that baby."

I wanted to hang up the phone. I both hated and loved the fact that Tabatha always spoke from her heart no matter how much it hurt. "I am not miserable. Maybe a little unhappy, but that's a far cry from miserable." I was a little irritated by what she was saying, because it wasn't as if her life was perfect either. I might have loved the wrong man, but she changed men like underwear.

Even though this thought went through my head, I would never say them to my friend. "Well, let me ask you something. If you really believe that I like making folks miserable, why do you continue to hang around me?"

"Because I love your miserable ass. Now, what are you doing this weekend? A couple of friends and I are going to take a bus trip to Biloxi, and I wanted to know if you want to go?"

"Girl, I ain't got any money to be throwing away at no damn casino, and neither do you."

"Since when did you start knowing what's in my wallet? Last time I checked you weren't paying my bills." She sounded angry.

"I'm sorry, boo. I guess I am being a bitch. When are you leaving?"

"We're leaving at five o'clock on Friday evening. Are you going or not? It's an overnight trip, so I need to know now just in case I need to ask someone else to share a room with me." Her voice was laced with bitterness.

"Yes, thanks for inviting me. I'm sorry, so please don't be mad at me. Having that boy around me just has me acting.

"Yeah, whatever. Look, I've got to go. I'll pick you up around 4:15 on Friday." She hung up before I could even say goodbye.

I was really going to have to work on watching my tongue with Tabatha. The last thing I needed to do was alienate her. Whether I liked what she said at times or not was irrelevant. I wasn't always the bitch; circumstances made me this way. I used to be a loving woman who always had a smile on my face. That is until Ronald fucked me over, and I can't seem to get past the pain he caused me. I wanted him to pay for all the turmoil that he brought into my life, but he continued to ignore me, and that hurt worse than the betrayal.

I swung my legs to the floor and went into the kitchen to fix myself a drink. No matter how bitchy I felt inside, drinking was the only thing that I did which made me feel better. At least that's what I told myself as I refilled my glass. An empty glass is very convincing as to the wondrous things a full one would do. This is how I ended up drunk so many days and nights. I was always chasing that next high that would make me forget how terribly lonely I was. With the exception of work, I spent most of my time with myself, which might not have been so bad if I had learned to love myself first.

I walked passed Gavin's room and snorted in disgust. He had only been there for a few weeks and already the room smelled of him. I hated it. His bitch ass needed to get a job.

"Get up, Gavin. You ain't about to stay out all night and sleep all day."

"Aww, man. Are you serious?"

"You damn right I'm serious. Now get your black ass out of that bed and go look for a job."

"This is some bull—"

"You had better not finish that sentence unless you want to walk out of here and find these locks changed; your ass better get up." I slammed his door.

I didn't care if he got mad or not. He was going to get his lazy ass out of my house.

23 MERLIN MILLS

While Cojo was at work, I reported to the base to pick up my mobilization orders. My two-week break went by so fast it was ridiculous. Despite our earlier problems, Cojo and I had settled into a comfortable routine, and it pained me that I would have to disrupt it. Although we appeared to have put our differences behind us, we still weren't where we used to be. It seemed as if we were going out of our way to be nicer to each other, and it came off to me as being fake and pretentious.

"Communication Specialist Mills, the captain will see you now."

I jumped to attention, startled away from my thoughts. I followed the lieutenant to Captain Jamison's office and waited outside the door to be announced. I was nervous as I entered the captain's office. Rumor was she was a real bitch on wheels, and I didn't need her busting my chops about anything. I marched over to her desk, stood at attention, and gave her a salute.

Captain Jamison was a petite woman who would have turned my head if she wasn't in uniform with all the medals on her chest warning me to stay in my lane.

"At ease." She hardly looked up at me. She had a stack of files on her desk off to the corner, but she was reading one that I assumed to be mine.

I waited for what felt like fifteen minutes, but was probably more like three. That's one thing that I hated about the army. They stressed about being on time, but made you wait for everything. Being such a regimented entity, they were highly disorganized. God forbid the enemy found out just how disorderly we actually were; this country would be doomed.

I had an itch in the back of my throat, but I was so scared to cough for fear of having to hit the floor and knock off fifty pushups. Captains liked to flex like that, especially the women. She closed the file and looked me straight in the eye, which made me even more uncomfortable than when she was ignoring me.

"I said at ease."

I hadn't realized that I was still holding my shoulders straight with my arm cocked at my head. I chuckled a little bit as I lowered my arm.

The smile that slipped across her lips disappeared and was replaced with a frown. "Something funny?"

"No, ma'am." Instinctively, I pulled myself to attention again for what I was sure would be some form of punishment.

She completely threw me off guard with her next statement. "Have you enjoyed your little vacation?"

My eyes widened in surprise because she sounded like she actually cared. I thought about my response before I answered her. "I've been working out on the regular, Captain, so I don't get lazy."

This time she actually snickered.

"Good answer. I see someone has prepped you well."

I relaxed a little bit, but I didn't allow myself to get too comfortable.

"I have your mobilization package here." She lifted a fat envelope from the file that she was reading.

I couldn't read the expression on her face. I wasn't sure if she wanted me to reach out and take them. She just waved them at me.

She said, "Do you like Iraq?"

"I will go anywhere the army sends me." My responses were straight from the book and not my heart.

If she were trying to trip me up, she would have to come a little bit better than that. I was told that if I were to get too happy about an assignment, they would switch it and send me somewhere completely different. Iraq was okay, but if I had my choice, I would stay my black ass right here in Atlanta.

"Cut the shit, Specialist. This isn't a game. I'm just trying to find out where your head is at."

I started to get nervous again. No one had prepared me for this type of subterfuge. I definitely didn't want to leave Cojo alone in Atlanta now that my brother was back in town, but how could I explain it in a way to make my commanding officer understand? Although Gavin hadn't stopped by in a minute, I still wasn't ready to take any chances after his last late-night visit. I felt as if I was being put between a rock and a hard place. Should I trust the captain or was this a trap?

"No offense, Captain, but boot camp taught me that officers don't care about feelings or what we want. We are the property of the United States Army."

"See, Specialist, that's where you're wrong. There are some of us who actually care. Off the record, I allowed the army to ruin my marriage. I, like you, was married when I enlisted. I got my commission based on my college experience so it wasn't that bad, but I still had to travel and leave my husband at home. I thought we had what it took to make the marriage work. At the time, my husband and I both agreed that my enlisting was the best answer for our situation." She paused.

I waited expectantly. Her situation sounded so much like my own. I was intrigued by what she was saying, but I couldn't understand why she was sharing it with me.

After a few more seconds, she continued, "At first, things appeared to be okay. I was told that once I finished officer's training I could return to our hometown of Jacksonville, Florida, but recruiters have a tendency to tell you what you want to hear and not necessarily the truth. As a result, I stayed away too long, and when I got back, my husband had moved on both physically and emotionally. He had no problem spending the monthly stipend I sent home, but he had no desire to resume what we had because he'd fallen in love with someone else."

I saw what I thought to be tears forming in her eyes. Instinctively, I wanted to go to her and rock her in my arms, but I knew that would be the fastest way to the brig! "Captain, I can't thank you enough for your candor, and if the opportunity to speak is still on the table, I can honestly say that I do not wish to leave Atlanta at this time for personal reasons sensitive to my marriage." I debated as to whether to divulge what had happened between my brother and my wife, but the scab hadn't quite healed, so I kept my mouth shut.

She picked up my file and began reading again as if I wasn't even in the room. Her face once again became stoic. It made me nervous. While she was relaying her story to me, her face was softer. I could tell she still felt the pain of her husband's betrayal. I wanted to ask her how long ago this had happened to her, but I knew better than to question an officer. If she wanted to tell me, that was one thing, but asking questions was a big no-no.

"I'm not going to be able to keep you here indefinitely, Specialist, but I will personally see to it that you get a job on post for a while. Maybe a month or so, but don't make the same mistake that I did. When it's time to ship out, make sure everything that you value is intact."

"Thank you, Captain. I will work on it." All the worry and dread of leaving I'd carried around on my shoulders had been lifted away with the stroke of a pen; even if only temporarily.

The captain handed me my new work orders. "Your new deployment date comes from upstairs; it will arrive by mail."

My heart was so full as I exited the captain's office. I didn't know how she understood that this was what I needed, but she did. Now, maybe I could relax a bit and work on saving my marriage. I would also be around to keep an eye on my brother; at least until he got in trouble again and was run out of town. Although I should have been giving my brother the benefit of the doubt, I knew him well enough to know that his good behavior wouldn't last long.

24 COJO MILLS

It had been a wonderful week since Merlin told me he didn't have to go back to Iraq right away. I hoped the war ended before he got his letter. However, my day wasn't starting right at all. First, I woke up late and my stomach was bothering me. All morning long I kept running to the bathroom as if I had to vomit, but nothing was coming out. If I was going to get sick, I wished it would happen already and let me go about my business. By lunchtime, I'd had it.

I went to my supervisor and asked to be dismissed for the day.

"You aren't pregnant, are you?" she asked as I was leaving her office.

I was too stunned to react to her question. This thought never crossed my mind, but that could be the reason why I had been feeling so yucky lately. "Damn, she may have a point." It was always our desire to have children, so I wasn't shocked at the possibility, but the timing could have been better. I couldn't help but wonder why, after six and a half years, it might be happening now? Merlin and I were still tiptoeing around each other, but I was confident that he would accept our child with open arms. I decided to stop at Rite-Aid on my way home to get a pregnancy test.

Now that I had a plan of action, I actually started to feel better, but not well enough to stay at work. It was Friday, and I wanted to get a jump-start on my weekend. All of a sudden, I was excited. Without thinking it through, I called Merlin. "Hey, baby, I'm headed home. I'm not feeling well. My boss said I should go home and take it easy."

"Cool, I'm headed back to the house too. Is there anything that I can pick up for you?"

I wanted to tell him to get me a pregnancy test, but I decided to keep that little secret to myself until I knew for sure. "No, I just want to get some rest."

"How about I fix us some dinner and we watch some movies and call it a night."

I said, "That sounds good to me."

"Is there anything in particular that you want to see?"

"No, surprise me. You're good at picking out movies, so I know I won't be disappointed."

"All right then, I'll see you when you get home."

I hung up the phone with a smile on my face. Although we still weren't where we were before, it was better. I was just glad that Gavin had stayed clear of our house. I still couldn't believe that I didn't realize that the man I had sex with was not my husband. Merlin's mother had also stopped her string of confusing phone calls, which was okay with me too because I didn't like her ass anyway. Girls only get two special moments in life: proms and weddings. Gina fucked my wedding up to where I don't even look at my wedding pictures.

My smile slid from my face at the thought of my mother-in-law. She was such a hateful heifer and I didn't understand why. In the beginning and a few times afterward, I did everything I could to make her like me, but she was bound and determined not to. From the first day she met me, she acted as if I wore shit on my face instead of foundation. After several attempts to woo her, I gave up.

My thoughts wandered again. I stopped at Rite Aid and purchased a pregnancy test. There were so many to choose from, I just grabbed the cheapest one I could find and rushed back to the counter. I had to go to the bathroom in the worst way and didn't want to risk using a public restroom, especially with that strain of swine flu going around.

I drove home so fast I scared myself. I'd just gone to the bathroom right before I left work, but it felt as if I hadn't been all day. This was one of the reasons why I thought I might be pregnant. In addition, my breasts we sore and sensitive, and I couldn't shake the constant feeling of nausea which followed me all day long. I hadn't thrown up yet, but I came close several times.

I turned into our apartment complex doing thirty, and didn't put my foot on the brake as I rode over the speed bumps. This didn't help my breasts one bit. I winced in pain.

"Shit." I rubbed my free hand over my breasts. The pain took my mind off the fact that I had to go to the bathroom so badly. I hit the second speed bump at the same pace. I wanted to slow down, but my situation was urgent. I couldn't imagine what my car would smell like if I actually did wet myself. I pulled into the front of our building and had the door open before I'd even parked the car. I grabbed my purse and my bag from Rite Aid and dashed up the sidewalk toward my apartment. I ran as fast as my doubled-over body could go.

With keys in hand, I tried to get the key in the lock. "Dear God, please." I couldn't get the key in the hole to save my life. After several attempts, I gave up and rang the bell. A few seconds passed before Merlin answered the door. I had all but resigned to pissing on myself. At least I was at the house and wouldn't ruin the upholstery of my car.

"What, you got to go to the bathroom again?" Merlin was laughing as he stepped out of the way.

"Yeah, move." The end was in sight, and I prayed that Merlin had left the seat down in the bathroom. I was unbuttoning my pants as I raced down the hallway to our bedroom. I could have used the guest bathroom, but in my haste I forgot about it.

"Thank you, Jesus," I said as I sank onto the seat in relief. The hot piss ran into the toilet. I released a heavy sigh. I rested my head on my arms as I allowed myself to finish taking a leak. I completely forgot about the pregnancy test that I had in my bag. Had I been thinking, I could have killed two birds with one stone. However, I was quite sure that I would have to go again within the hour.

"Everything come out okay?" Merlin was outside the door and he had jokes.

"Don't you have something you need to be doing?" I didn't attempt to mask my irritation.

"Dag, I didn't mean to piss you off."

I could tell by his tone that Merlin was hurt. I didn't mean to lash out at him, but he shouldn't have been lurking outside the door. I quickly washed my hands because I needed to apologize before my behavior ruined the rest of our weekend.

"Baby, wait, I'm sorry. I told you I wasn't feeling well, and I'm sorry I took it out on you." I reached out to touch his shoulder because his back was turned to me.

He immediately melted and turned around and took me in his arms. At that moment, things felt just as they used to between us, and I fell in love all over again with my husband.

"Honey, I'm sorry. I was so excited to have you all to myself that I completely forgot you weren't feeling well." He led me to the sofa and gently pushed me down. Once I was seated, he pulled the reclining lever to elevate my feet. Then, he took off my shoes and began massaging my feet. I was outdone. Merlin was good to me, and he often did sweet things for me, but I could not recall one time that he had taken off my shoes, let alone massaged my feet.

"I'm fine now that I'm home. I just want to take a nap until dinner is ready. I'm so tired."

He reached over my head and grabbed the throw from across the sofa and draped it over me. Kissing me on the forehead, he left me and headed in the direction of the kitchen.

"I wonder what he will say if, in fact, I do end up pregnant," I mumbled to myself.

25 COJO MILLS

I took me an entire week to work up the nerve to take the pregnancy test. Every time I tried to do it, I chickened out. When I finally did it, I had mixed emotions about the results. Part of me was ecstatic. We wanted children; however, the circumstances surrounding this pregnancy made me sick.

"Shit." I was terrified about telling Merlin. If I had doubts about my child's paternity, I was sure he would too.

Thus far, he'd been respectful, and had been trying to get our relationship back on track, but I had no clue how he would react once he found out that I was pregnant, and there was a very good possibility that the child may be by his own brother. The very thought made me feel like throwing up, so I could only imagine how my husband would feel when I told him.

"Should I tell him?" I uttered the words, even though I didn't believe in the deceit that it would take to carry this out. I have always been a strong proponent for the rights of fathers, but should I risk my family for a mistake? I didn't knowingly have sex with my brother-in-law, so shouldn't I get a pass?

I also had to consider Gavin's reaction to my news. In a perfect world, he would ignore the probabilities, congratulate us and keep it moving. But the world wasn't perfect, and Gavin had it in for his brother. This situation could get ugly fast.

Up to now, Merlin hadn't come right out and asked me why I wasn't able to tell the difference between him and his brother. I knew it had to be eating at him because it was eating at me. I tried to rationalize it to myself and I couldn't. The brothers were both gifted in the dick department, but one was decidedly better than the other.

"It is what it is, and I have to face the music." This was a bitter pill to swallow, but I couldn't change what had happened. I was going to tell Merlin as soon as he made it home from the base. As much as I loved him, I would not deceive him. He had to know all of the facts. If he chose to leave me, then so be it.

♥♥♥

I sat his dinner in front of him. "Merlin, I need to talk to you, and I need for you to remain calm. Can you do that?"

"What do you mean? I'm always calm."

Flashbacks of when he was trying to kick my ass passed through my head. He paused, and I would like to believe that he saw those same images.

He started cutting his steak. "Okay. I understand what you're saying, but I'm cool. Give it to me."

"This is difficult for me to say, but I'm pretty certain that I'm pregnant." I let the elephant land in the room before I proceeded.

He knew our sexual history, and the implication I left unsaid. I waited for his response with bated breath.

Merlin looked like a runaway slave about to be punished. I felt the same way. What would I do if I were pregnant by my husband's brother? What would he do? Shit!

26 MERLIN MILLS

"Wow, pregnant. Are you sure?" I didn't know how I felt about it. My stomach was churning, and I felt slightly sick. I had suspected she was pregnant all along, so this wasn't a complete surprise. On one hand, I felt jubilant that I was about to have my first child, but the fear that the child wouldn't be mine overshadowed those emotions. I had to find a way to balance those two sentiments before I said something that would drive another wedge between me and my wife. I stuck a fork full of steak in my mouth, even though I had lost my appetite.

"I took a home test and it was positive, but I haven't been to the doctor yet."

"I see." What did she expect me to say? I felt myself getting angry, but I immediately pumped the brakes because it really wasn't her fault that this happened.

I had to keep reminding myself of this daily. I rose up from the dinner table and went to her. I opened my arms and she willingly came into them. We would make it through this storm whichever way it went.

"Baby, it's going to be okay." I wanted her to feel comfortable that I was in it for the long haul with her— even if the baby turned out to belong to my brother. I loved Cojo so much; I could not bear being without her. Whatever feelings this child brought up in me would have to be ignored if our marriage stood a chance of making it.

"Are you serious?" She had tears in her eyes.

I could tell that she wanted to say more, but I silenced her with a kiss. I was going to make this work if it killed me. She trembled in my arms and my heart swelled. I knew I was doing the right thing. I pushed her away from me slightly and put my hand on her belly. I looked directly into her eyes.

"I love you and our baby." I left it unsaid that it might not be mine because, as far as I was concerned, if it came out of my wife, it was my baby.

"Merlin, I'm sorry."

"Hush now. Let's not talk about it. In fact, we need a break. Can you get off tomorrow?"

"I think so; what are you thinking?"

"Just take off and let me handle the rest of it."

She went to the phone to call her supervisor, who was also a friend. When she hung up the phone, she was beaming. Now I had to kick my ass into gear to pull off a fantastic weekend that would prove to her that I loved her more than I loved myself.

♥♥♥

My buddy, Braxton, told me about some cabins that were located up in the North Georgia Mountains. I thought that would be the perfect getaway for a couple who were trying to rediscover the love they had for each other.

I did a Google search and found several cabins, and took all the virtual tours and picked the one that was the most lavish. The cabin had three bedrooms, a pool table, a full kitchen, an outdoor Jacuzzi, and a wraparound porch equipped with rocking chairs. Next, I went to the grocery store so that I could select the food I was going to cook for her while we were there. My plan was that she wouldn't do anything except go to the spa, shop, and whatever else that tickled her fancy.

I toyed with the idea of whitewater rafting, but decided against it because of the baby, but I did sign up for the wine tasting and grape stomping. This was the only selfish activity I scheduled. I knew she couldn't do the tasting, but she might get a kick out of squishing grapes with her bare feet. I was excited.

As I continued to put groceries in my cart, I stopped. I had this amazing urge to share my news of impending fatherhood, but I was at a loss for whom to share it with. In a situation like this, the first call should go out to a mother, but that idea instantly soured in my stomach. Knowing my mother, she would say something stupid like "Why you wanna do that shit for?" Or she might come back with some jacked-up shit like, "Are you sure it's yours?"

This was something I didn't want to dwell on. Surely God wouldn't be so cruel as to finally allow us to conceive, and in the final hour say that it wasn't mine. I was mumbling as I wandered through the aisles. Suddenly, I wanted to cancel the trip and take some sort of paternity test, because there was no way in hell I was going to raise a bastard child of my brother's.

As soon as the thought entered my mind, I felt ashamed of myself. If I was going to allow this to ruin my marriage, I didn't deserve Cojo at all. It wasn't her fault that Gavin deceived her!

27 GAVIN MILLS

I could hear the television as soon as I put my key in the door. If I didn't know better, I would have sworn that my mother was going deaf in her older years. She was watching *Dancing With The Stars,* and it was cranked up to what had to be the highest level.

My gut instinct was to yell at her to turn that shit down. This was her house though, and I wasn't paying any of the bills, so I kept my mouth shut.

I peeked around the corner to see where my mother was. I wanted to be prepared for her attack before it actually happened. I was riding on a high that could likely explode if she came at me wrong. The last thing I wanted to do was kill my mother and end up losing the only place in the world that I could stay at for free.

Gina wasn't visible when I stuck my head around the corner. That meant one of two things: she was in her bedroom knocked out, or she was passed out on the sofa. I tiptoed up to the sofa, silently praying that she wasn't on it but in her room instead. I didn't feel like hearing her mouth tonight.

I continued to creep up to the sofa. My heart dipped a little bit when I saw her sprawled over it. Based on her positioning, I assumed she more than likely fell rather than laid on the chair. She was naked from the waist down, and her legs were spread-eagled over the side. Her glass was lying on its side, its contents having soaked through the carpet leaving a nasty brown stain. The phone wasn't on the base, and an annoying message was playing asking her if she would like to make a call.

I shook my head in disgust. Heaven knows who she was trying to call before she passed out, but more than likely it was my deadbeat dad. For the life of me, I couldn't understand why she was still chasing after his ass when he made it clear that he was done with her.

I tiptoed past her to see if she had anything left to drink in the kitchen. I was still riding the high of my earlier escapade with some chick I met at Club 702, and I needed to come down if I had any intentions of getting some sleep tonight.

"Jackpot."

Mom had gone to the store and the entire counter was stacked with liquor. I claimed a bottle of Absolut and retired to my room. Normally, I wouldn't have risked taking a full bottle of her booze, but from the looks of her, she wouldn't even remember going to the store, much less what she got while there.

I turned on my small television which I had bought at a yard sale, and put it on low as I cracked open the bottle. I searched the channels until I found the news. I wanted to see what, if anything, was being said about the fire on the east side a couple of weeks back. I felt good about covering my tracks since I hadn't heard anything about it so far.

I was halfway through the bottle and still hadn't heard anything about the murder. "Shit, that's good news." I was feeling pretty invincible, even though I was drunk as a skunk. I went out into the hallway to take a piss. I stumbled into the bathroom and peed on everything but the seat.

"I'm gonna have to clean this shit up in the morning." This wasn't the bathroom that my mother used, so I felt confident that I could hold off washing the piss off the walls and the sides of the bowl until morning.

I paused when I peeked back into the living room to check on my mother. The television was still loud as hell and she hadn't moved. However, this time my focus wasn't on whether or not she was sleeping, but how good her fat pussy looked.

My mother was not a bad-looking woman. She had gained some weight over the years, but a pussy stays the same size no matter how large a woman gets. Her clit appeared to be winking at me, and my dick instantly took notice.

Now, I will admit that I was a pretty lowdown dirty dog and would do just about anything for the thrill of doing it, but delivering the package to my mother was a definite no-no. I tried to turn away, but my dick, which was still sticking out of my pants, had other plans. I crept closer. Her scent was tantalizing my nose. "Damn, did her pussy just wink at me?" I didn't even have to touch my dick. It was already throbbing.

♥♥♥

"Fuck that," the words fell out of my mouth, but those were not my words. My dick was talking through me.

She won't even know that we're there. Her ass is out like a light.

In my inebriated mind, I didn't have a choice but to follow my dick, because it was clear that it wouldn't allow me to sleep tonight unless I did.

All right, motherfucker, do what we do.

"Oh, that feels good, Ronald."

I didn't waste time. My dick was already hard, and her dumb ass thought I was my daddy. I knew that I had to get in and out before she was conscious of what really was going on. Without wasting another second, I plunged deep inside of her. Her body jerked, but she didn't open her eyes. I felt her pussy wrap around my dick.

"It's been so long, Ronald. Fuck me."

"Damn, your shit is tight, Mommy." I didn't mean to talk, but the words automatically came out my mouth. Shit, she was tighter than the hoe that I'd bagged earlier that week. I worked my dick around in circles, and even though she was unconscious, my mother kept up with me. Even in her sleep, she was following my dick. I took one of her full breasts into my mouth, and it was done—I came in my momma. I wish I could have spent more time with her, but I had taken a big enough risk as it was. I didn't want her drunk ass to realize I wasn't my dad.

I felt remorse for the first time in my life as I pulled my limp dick out of Gina. This was probably the lowest moment in my life, but when I looked up at Gina, she was smiling. That made me feel a little bit better.

28 GINA MEADOWS

I woke up the next day with a serious hangover after drinking myself into a stupor. The last thing I remembered before falling asleep was Ronald. I sat up and that was when I realized that I was practically naked.

"Oh God," I muttered as I recalled getting undressed so I could have phone sex with my so-called husband. He convinced me to get my vibrator from my nightstand and stay on the phone until I could find release.

"Shit, don't make no damn sense." I was beating myself up because once again, I put myself in the dunce chair all for the love of a man.

Ronald could talk my panties off on I-285 at twelve noon in the fast lane. That's how powerful his mack game was.

My pussy felt worn, as if I had used all ten inches of the dildo turned on high for an extended amount of time. I leaned over the sofa to see if I could find the purple bandit. That was my nickname for my high-powered lover.

As I continued to search for the only thing that had shown me love in the last two years, I lost my balance and came crashing to the floor, ass up. "Shit, that hurt." My boobs were smashed into the floor, and the dildo lay dangerously close to my mouth. A vision of sucking that dildo flashed through my mind, but in this flashback, I swallowed. "I ain't fucking with that Patron no damn more!" I pushed myself up off the floor and tried to get back on the sofa with as much dignity as my ringing head would allow. My stomach was churning; my brain felt like it was trying to leap out of my head, and my pussy felt freshly fucked. *Damn, that was some good phone sex.*

I needed to go to the bathroom in the worst way, but as I attempted to move, my stomach lurched. The last thing I wanted to do was clean up a mess of vomit. I rocked myself on the sofa, trying to push the pee back up that threatened to leave a yellowish stain on my plastic-covered, off-white sofa. "Lawd, please." The rocking wasn't helping my head, but it did seem to ease my bladder, because instead of the pee being focused in one place, I was spreading it around. My pussy felt swollen, but I attributed that to using the dildo without lubrication. Ronald convinced me that I didn't need it. "Take it like I give it—rough," is what he'd said to me, and my stupid ass did it.

My pussy was going to be sore for weeks. I had managed to rock the pee away enough to stand and go to the bathroom. I was ashamed of myself for falling for Ronald's bullshit again.

I stumbled into the bathroom, still a little woozy from the booze and the intense hangover that I was experiencing. It wasn't until my ass found its way to the toilet seat that I remembered Gavin.

With all the booze in my system, I'd completely forgotten that he was staying with me until he could get himself on his feet. My mind scrambled, trying to remember if I'd gotten naked before or after he got home. Oh shit, I couldn't remember! I broke out in a cold sweat. Even though I didn't care much for the man my son became, I still had enough decency not to want him to see me drunk and naked at the same damn time!

I jumped up from the toilet in midstream and raced to his door, trailing piss behind me. "Lawd, please don't let Gavin be in this room." I didn't pray as often as I should, but I was hoping this one time God wouldn't put my call on hold. I swung open the door without bothering to knock. I held my breath. Gavin was lying on his back across his bed. He was ass out, too!

"Damn." This was the first time that I'd gotten to see his dick since he was around six years old. I had to admit that I was impressed. He was hung just like his dad. Even in its relaxed state his dick was notable. "Like father, like son." Those words slipped out my mouth before I could catch them. It wasn't that I was into the incest thing, but in reality, Gavin wasn't my biological son. Our only connection was that I had fucked his father and raised Ronald's children like they were my own.

So was that considered incest? Obviously the booze was talking for me, because I had to stop myself from rushing the bed and taking his flaccid penis in my mouth. I stood in the doorway with drool practically dripping out my mouth as I watched my son sleep, wearing only a T-shirt with his dick swinging in the wind. A vision of that same dick pounding against my pussy filled my mind. In my head, I knew it was just a vision, but my body felt as if it had actually happened. I shuttered inside.

The doorbell rang and there I was stuck like Chuck. I froze. My eyes darted from door to bed and back again. I needed to shut the door before Gavin could see me standing there practically naked. I had to put some pants on so I could stop the doorbell from ringing again. As my head turned back again toward Gavin, I thought I saw him smile. I quietly shut the door and rushed back to the living room to find my pants.

29 MERLIN MILLS

Every minute I stood in the vestibule of my mother's apartment was torture. The news of fatherhood had me acting impulsively. I had to share the news with someone. I rang the bell again as I placed my ear to the door.

I could hear movement, so I stood back to wait for my Gina to answer the door. Each second I waited, I debated whether this was such a good idea. Gina never had a nice thing to say about my wife. She barely had a good thing to say about me. I was turning to leave when she finally opened the door.

She was disheveled, and her eyes had this wild look to them.

"Are you okay?" I felt genuine concern for her, the likes of which I hadn't felt since I was in high school.

"What are you doing here?"

If I thought she would be happy to see me, those thoughts were doused by her sour greeting. I felt like kicking myself for even thinking that stopping by her house was a good idea. I should have let sleeping dogs lie. "Hello, Mother." I hoped that I could thaw her icy exterior by calling her Mother, but that only seemed to make her more agitated.

"I asked you what you were doing here. Hell, I haven't seen you in years. What, you want to move in here now too? Did that siddity wife of yours throw you out?"

My good mood disappeared as I realized the huge error in judgment I had made. I turned around to leave. I didn't need her negative energy hanging around my neck like an albatross. "Forget it, Mother. I tried. Have a nice life." I stomped down the three steps that led to her apartment, angry at myself for making such a stupid mistake. I left a little of my joy on her stoop, but I was determined to take the rest of it back to my house.

"Wait," she hollered a little too loudly for the enclosed breezeway of her apartment complex.

I hesitated, because I didn't know whether she was preparing to strip away the rest of my joy, or if she were actually sorry for treating me the way that she had. I turned around slowly. She was patting her wild hair back in place. She attempted to straighten out her pants, which appeared to have been put on backwards.

"How are you?" Gina's voice was gentler. She almost acted like she cared.

"I'm good." There was a brief moment of awkward silence.

"Do you want to come in?"

I hesitated. Although it was my idea to go over to her house, I already regretted my decision. As if she could read my thoughts, she tried to reassure me.

"It's okay; I'll be nice."

She smiled again, and the sucker in me smiled back. I was so happy about the baby, I lost my friggin' mind. I stepped past her and entered the apartment. She closed the door behind me. For a second, I grew fearful, but I was determined to say to her what I came to say.

"For years, Mother, you've treated Gavin and I like shit." This wasn't the way that I wanted to start the conversation, but the words came out nevertheless. I heard her inhale sharply, and I saw her pull herself up as if she were ready to fight me, so I quickly finished my thought. "But now that I'm about to have a child, I can understand how you've felt all these years caring for my father's children without the benefit of a ring."

The wind was sucked from her sails and tears flooded her eyes, and mine too. I never thought about how she felt before.

I said, "For years I hated you for the way that you treated us, but I'm finally beginning to understand what that must have done to you every time you looked at us."

"What is it that you're finally understanding?" Her tone was accusing as she mocked me. She sounded like she was about to kick my ass as she did when I was a small child.

"You were acting off of emotions, Mother. I can't imagine what a thankless job it was to raise someone's children and not have any of your own." Once again, my words surprised even me. That wasn't what I intended to say to her when I came to her door. It was like something or someone planted those words in my mouth. Before I could lose my nerve, I continued. "I didn't understand it when I was a child. In fact, I didn't understand it until today when my wife told me she was having my child. You were reacting to all those years my father treated you like a second-class citizen, and now I understand. I'm not saying I agree with the way you treated us, but I finally understand, and I forgive you."

My mother remained speechless. I'm sure she didn't expect this speech from me, and was just as surprised as I was that I'd made it, but I needed to have her in my life as a positive role model for my child. But she was going to have to change her ways toward my wife if that was going to work, because she would *not* continue to abuse my wife and the mother of my child.

Gina said, "I don't know what to say."

This was the first time in a long time my mother didn't have a snappy comeback. She opened her mouth to speak but nothing came out. Part of me wanted to hug her, but I couldn't even remember the last time I was physical with her.

The tears that had flooded her eyes rolled unchecked down her cheeks. She didn't bother to wipe them away as they slid into her mouth. "I'm sorry, Merlin. All these years I've been wrong, and I couldn't see it for the pain Ronald's leaving me caused."

I didn't say anything because I knew that to be true, but I still didn't understand what she had against my wife. She sank down on the sofa and allowed her sobs to overtake her. Once again I wanted to comfort her, but I wasn't sure how she would react.

I said, "So where do we go from here?"

She looked up at me with what appeared to be hope in her eyes. "Are you willing to give me a second chance?" She was wringing her hands together.

"I will, but you've got to let up on Cojo. I can't have you disrespecting my wife and the mother of my child."

Her eyes narrowed. I thought she was about to do a Sybil on me and flip out. I took a step back just in case I was going to have to defend myself, because she was not about to go upside my head like she used to do in the old days.

"I'll try."

That wasn't good enough for me. I wanted assurances that she wouldn't hurt my baby again. "What is it with you and her? Has she ever done anything to offend you?" I was clearly perplexed about it, and I wanted to understand this too.

My mother took her time with her answer. As far as I was concerned, if she had to think this long, she didn't know the answer her damn self.

"There was never anything wrong with Cojo. I'm sorry about my behavior at your wedding. Cojo's a sweet wife and you're lucky to have her."

This wasn't the answer I expected. My mother was full of surprises today, but I guess I was too. I never had the nerve to come right out and ask her what the problem was. I just chose to ignore it hoping that it would go away in time.

I said, "Then what's been the problem? She's tried real hard to be friends with you, but you held her off."

After a painful pause, Gina said, "She had everything that I didn't."

Ah, that made sense. She was jealous of my relationship with my wife.

"When I looked at you two together I saw the woman who your father left me for."

"Mom, you are going to have to get over that or it will destroy your life." I meant those words from the bottom of my heart.

"I know. I tried, but every time I put that man out of my heart and my mind, he calls and says something that makes me fall for him all over again."

"And how long are you going to allow this to go on?"

"So, you're a therapist now?" She laughed out loud.

She might have been joking, but this was a form of therapy. She needed to face the fact that my father just wasn't going to do right, and she would either continue on that emotional roller coaster or get the fuck off.

"He's done with me." She began to sniffle.

"How about you saying you're done with him?"

She looked at me strangely as if the thought never occurred to her. "Hmm … that does sound better."

"Keep saying it enough and you'll believe it. Then, the next time he calls talking smack, you can tell him to step off." I smiled to soften the blow. I loved my father simply because he was the man who gave me life, but as far as being in my life, that didn't happen.

"When did you get so smart?" Gina stared at me.

"I've always been smart, but you were too angry to see it." I didn't say that to hurt her feelings, but the truth was the truth.

"You're right. I couldn't see what was right in my face. I'm sorry, Merlin."

"I'm sorry too, Mom. We should have had this conversation a long time ago."

"Don't fool yourself. If you had come to me with this a few years ago, I might have killed your ass." She smiled this time, and we both loosened up.

Hesitantly, I stepped forward and gently pulled her from the sofa and hugged her. At first she didn't hug me back. I felt as if I'd moved too fast, but then she threw her arms around my waist and hugged me back as if her life depended on it. It was a very special moment for both of us until she roughly pushed me back.

"Did you say you were expecting a baby?"

A wide grin crossed my face.

I guess it finally registered with her that she was about to be a grandma. "Yes, Grandma."

She punched me lightly in the shoulder. "I'm too fine to be a grandma. They are just going to have to call me Gee-Gee or Glam Ma." She looked about as happy as I felt. She started patting down her hair and posing for me, even though she looked a hot mess.

I didn't miss the distinct smell of alcohol when I hugged her either.

"Where is Cojo? I've got to go make friends with her. I don't want her to continue to hate me, because I want to be in my grandchild's life. It's my chance to do what I gave up by not having my own child."

"That's good to know. But that little reunion is going to have to wait until we get back in town. I'm taking Cojo away for the weekend to celebrate."

For a second, my mother's eyes clouded over, but they quickly cleared. "That's nice, baby."

My heart soared because she hadn't called me baby with sincerity since I was six or seven. "You could do me a favor, though."

"What's that?" She looked hopeful again.

"Keep an eye out on our mail. I'm expecting my redeployment orders, and I need to know if they come while we're away."

"How am I going to keep an eye out on your mail or apartment when I've never ever been there?"

That was a dig, but I knew she knew exactly where it was because she gave the address to Gavin. "I'll write down the address and leave an extra key so you can check the mail and leave it in the house. We'll be home on Sunday."

"Okay, that's the least I can do for all the damage I've done to our relationship over the years. I'll call you if you get anything that comes from the military."

"Thanks, Mom." My heart felt like it was about to bust. I hadn't felt this good since Cojo told me she was pregnant.

"How far along is Cojo?"

"About four weeks." I handed my mother the extra keys I had on my ring, and she placed them on the fireplace. I got lost in thought thinking about the cute little girl or the handsome son who we were going to have.

"Ain't this special." Gavin came out of the guest bedroom clapping his hands.

Rage the likes of which I hadn't felt since I kicked his ass came rushing back at me. I had no idea Gavin was crashing at my mother's house. If I had known, I would never have come over here. "What are you doing here?" I snarled.

"Oh, no forgiveness for me?" Gavin was mocking me, letting me know that he heard every word that I had said to Gina.

"Leave me alone, Gavin."

"What did I do?" He had this innocent look on his face, as if he had never done any wrong, but I knew better…much better.

"I got to go, Mom. I'll invite you over once we get back." I turned to leave. I needed to get out of there before I said or did something to that asshole brother of mine.

She walked me to the door and we shared another hug. It felt good to be back in her graces, and I had high hopes that she was going to get her life together.

"Have a safe trip," she said.

"Yo, Merlin," Gavin yelled stepping from behind my mother.

Part of me wanted to keep on walking without even acknowledging him, but I didn't want my mother to know the extent of my animosity toward my brother. "What?"

"You sure that kid is yours?" Gavin showed me his devilish grin.

30 MERLIN MILLS

How the hell did I forget that bastard was back in town? Shit, I thought he left! I was angry as hell, and almost wrecked my car trying to get away from my mother's house. I was very concerned about why Gavin was still here, which only led me to believe that he didn't have any place left to go. However, this was going to ruin any chance of my mother and Cojo getting to know each other.

Hell, Gavin would be in Mom's ear all night trying to get her to hate Cojo again. I felt as if all my efforts today had been wasted. "I'm gonna fuck that bastard up! He's screwed up my life for the last time." I banged a fist against the steering wheel as anger surged through my veins. With Gavin still in the picture, it was harder to ignore the paternity of my child—that more than anything else hurt me. Gone was the resentment that I felt against my wife, but I had to know for certain that she was carrying my child and not my brother's.

I drove around for at least an hour before I got my emotions under control. I was going to take my wife away for the weekend and leave my doubts at home. Regardless of who fathered the child, it would still be mine. Turning the car around, I headed home to my wife. With any luck, I could get a quickie in before we got on the road. I pulled out my cell phone and called Cojo.

"Where are you?" she said.

"I'm almost there, sweetheart. Are you all packed?"

"Yeah, I've been done for hours. I was beginning to think something happened to you."

"I'll explain everything when I get there. Do me a favor and pack the small cooler with ice and water, and grab a few snacks so we won't have to stop except for gas and to go to the bathroom."

"Where are we going?"

"You're going to have to wait and see, but make sure you packed some sweaters."

"Sweaters? It's eighty degrees outside."

"Humor me." I didn't know if she would need them, but it would be better to be safe than sorry. Despite how I was feeling an hour ago, I still wanted to make this a memorable weekend for my wife.

♥♥♥

The drive was approximately two hours. It had begun to rain, and I had to slow down my speed considerably. We also had to make frequent stops because Cojo just couldn't hold her water, but I didn't mind. I was enjoying the quality time we were spending. She spent her time reading and wasn't really paying attention to where we were going. When I pulled up to the cabin rental office, I could see the look of disdain on her face. I could tell she wasn't happy, and if I were honest, I wasn't either. This shack didn't look anything like the cabins I saw on the Internet.

"Be right back."

She didn't say a word. Hopefully, the cabin didn't look as bad on the inside as it did on the outside. When I got back into the car, there was a chill in the air, and it had nothing to do with the mountains. I put the address to the cabin into our GPS system and turned the car around. Cojo had even cut off the radio and her book was closed on her lap. All of a sudden, she was focused on our destination. I said a silent prayer.

The cabin was about twenty-five miles from the rental location and farther up the mountains. I had never driven in the mountains before and was a little nervous, especially since it was still raining and starting to get dark.

♥♥♥

Finally, we found the road that led to the cabins. I had to drive slower because I didn't want to run into any wild animals or into a ditch. Cojo was sitting up straight in her seat, peering into the approaching night. We traveled straight up the mountain. It was very scary. At one point as we were going down again, the road narrowed to a single lane. I don't know what I would have done if I had to back out to let another car pass.

As the GPS announced that we'd arrived at our destination, I let out a heavy sigh. I was tired and the pressure to please wore me out.

"Merlin! Are you serious?" Cojo looked at the cabin in awe.

"Yes, baby."

"We're really going to stay here?"

"Did you think I was going to make you sleep in a shack?" I handed her the key so she could check out the house while I unpacked the car. I had groceries and our suitcases in the back. I wanted to get everything inside before it got totally dark. She leapt out of the car and raced to the house.

What the fuck was I thinking about? I was no mountain man. I was a city boy, I mused. As I looked up and saw the way Cojo was acting, all my fears went right out of my head. Her reaction was enough to make anything I had to go through worth it.

♥♥♥

"Sweetie, this place is amazing! However did you find it?" Cojo twirled around the living room flapping her arms.

"I'm glad you like it, honey. Braxton told me about it." I had just brought in all of our provisions so I hadn't even had a chance to look around at our surroundings. I flopped down on the first available chair and tried to catch my breath. I didn't know if it was the mountain air or Cojo's heavy ass suitcase, but I was tired.

Cojo sat down in my lap. "It's got a pool table downstairs and a Jacuzzi. I've died and gone to heaven."

I was happy she was happy. Before I started dinner, I decided to light the fireplace. Although it was comfortable in the cabin, I thought the fire would be more romantic.

♥♥♥

I'd been fucking with the fire for a full fifteen minutes, and I was starting to get frustrated. This was just another reminder to me that I was out of my element. I was also getting spooked because there were no curtains on the first floor of the cabin, and all I could see outside was darkness. My imagination was running wild as I envisioned bears rushing the windows and glass doors.

"Honey, take a break. Let me do this," Cojo said as she patted me on the shoulder.

I wasn't annoyed at all when she volunteered to help me out. I was sick of that fucking fire and couldn't care less whether we had one or not. "Go for it. I think the wood is wet. We should have brought one of those starter logs." I got up off the floor and went into the kitchen to start dinner. I had planned a surf and turf meal for my baby. Now that we were in the cabin and most of my duties were done, it was time to relax. I fixed myself a drink. "Babe, do you want a soda or something?" I knew not to offer her booze because of the baby. If she weren't pregnant, I would have probably served her champagne. I looked into the living room to check on her since she didn't answer, but she was laid out in front of the fireplace that was giving off this hearty blaze! "Well, I'll be damned." I couldn't help but laugh, because she had that fire lit in three minutes flat.

31 GINA MEADOWS

"What the hell was that all about?" I turned on Gavin after Merlin walked out the door. I knew there was bad blood between the brothers and a lot of it was caused by me. I wasn't happy with the role that I played, but I never really saw myself until this moment.

"What?"

"Don't play dumb, boy." I knew it would piss Gavin off that I called him a boy, but I didn't care. Merlin came to me after all those years of silence and told me he forgave me, and I would be damned if I allowed my other so-called son to fuck that up.

"I'm not playing dumb. I just asked Merlin if he was sure it was his kid. After all, he's been away doing the patriotic thing; ain't no telling who his wife was keeping company with. You told me she was a little slut."

"I was wrong about that. I didn't even know her."

"So you lied on her? Why would you malign Cojo's character?" His tone was totally condescending.

"What would you know about maligning someone's character? Hell, I didn't even know you knew that word since you barely went to school."

He had me heated as no one else could do. As a child, he was always a selfish bastard who had to have everything his way. Between him and Merlin, he was the most difficult to raise.

"I didn't need school. I was also smarter than the average child."

"You were street smart, I'll give you that; just like your daddy. Always talking somebody out of shit. But you still don't have the skills to survive on your own because if you did, you wouldn't be here shacked up with me."

"I'm just down on my luck. But if you showed me half the love you give so willingly to my brother, I'm sure I could come up."

His words hurt me more than his fists ever could. I was guilty of not showing them love, but was I that bad? I don't think so. I provided a roof over their heads and food in their mouths; what more was I supposed to do?

"Why are you directing all your anger at me? I'm not your mother!" I was mad now.

"You were the only mother I knew." Spit was flying out of Gavin's mouth. All of his pent-up aggressions were coming forth, and I started to get scared thinking that he might do something to me.

"You should talk to your father about that," I said.

"I would if I ever saw his ass." He was pacing back and forth like a wild animal.

"He'll be here next week to close the deal on our new house." I turned and went into my bedroom. Part of me wanted to warn Ronald that he was going to have to deal with Gavin when he got there, but the other part felt like Ronald had made his bed, and now he had to lie in it.

"Fine. Next week, what day and time?"

"You know your father; he gets here when he gets here."

"Knowing my father, that's a laugh." He didn't smile when he said it. "I don't know that motherfucker any more than the man on the moon."

"You're going to have to have that conversation with him, not me."

He turned and walked away. I thought he was about to go into his room when he turned back around. "New house?"

Shit, I hadn't meant to say anything about that to Gavin, at least not until I knew for sure it was going to happen. "Yeah, your father says he's finally coming home."

"He's moving back to Atlanta after all these years?"

"Yes." I figured if I kept my responses to one-word answers he would let up, but I was wrong.

"So what, y'all going to be this one, big, happy family?" The sarcasm dripped from his mouth.

"I hope so." I tried to sound confident, but I'd been down this road before.

"Am I part of that family?"

I could sense the vulnerability in his voice, but I didn't have an answer to his question, since he was a grown-ass man and Ronald felt like grown-ass men should live like grown-ass men. "You can discuss that with your father when he gets here."

"Why can't I have that discussion with you? You're the one who raised me, not him."

"That's true, but when your father gets here, he will be the man in the house, not me."

"You just accepted Merlin back in your life. Why can't you accept me?"

There was no denying the pain he was feeling this time, but he didn't melt my heart completely. I remembered all too well what he was like growing up. He was a mean-spirited child, and it appeared he hadn't changed much.

"Why does it always come back to the same thing?" I was sick of all this rivalry between them. I accepted my part, but damn.

"Because I can't stand his pansy ass." This time he did go into his room and slammed the door.

I started to go after him and tell him that the only person allowed to slam doors in this house was me, but I decided not to press the issue. I grabbed my things from the sofa and went to take a shower. "I hope he stays his ass in his room until I get out of here."

32 MERLIN MILLS

After dinner, Cojo and I went downstairs to check out the hot tub. I hadn't had a chance to explore the rest of the house since I was busy preparing dinner while she took a nap. The basement was just as impressive as the main floor. Unlike the main floor, which had shiny hardwood floors, this area was carpeted. "This is nice."

"I know; you should see the upstairs, too. These people thought of everything."

"I saw the pictures on the Internet, but it looks even better in person."

She turned to me and gave me a big kiss.

"What was that for?"

"For being you."

"Think you can work your magic on that fireplace while I crank up the hot tub?"

"Sure. The instructions for the tub say it's already on. All you have to do is take the top off."

"The instructions? Where did you see the instructions?"

"There's a book on the coffee table in the living room. They also have this picture book that inventories everything in the house, down to how many knives they have in the kitchen. It says if anything is missing or moved, we will be billed for it."

"Damn, that's a good idea."

"I told you they thought of everything." She knelt down to start the fire, and I went outside to the tub.

"It's creepy out here," I yelled to Cojo.

"Stop being a wuss."

I could tell she was joking so I didn't let it get to me, but it really was creepy. The area where the tub was had a light, but other than that, you couldn't see a thing. The temperature had dropped, but it really wasn't that bad. I laid our towels on the heated towel rack and took the cover off the tub. I tested the water with my arm, and it was definitely on. "Hey, babe, we're good to go."

"Here I come."

I stripped down to my boxers and got into the tub. The warm water felt good. I looked up as my wife came out of the cabin naked as the day she was born. "You getting in naked?" Not that I minded. But still, what if someone came by?

"Of course, silly. Can't nobody see me but you." She had a point, but I wasn't about to take off my boxers.

If a bear came charging out of the woods, I would feel better having something covering my package. I just couldn't see myself trying to defend us with my shit bouncing all around.

She climbed into the tub and settled in between my legs. It felt like the water instantly heated up when she stepped into the tub, and my dick got hard as she leaned against me.

"Stop poking me in my back."

"I can't help it, babe. You have that effect on me." I just knew she was smiling even though I couldn't even see her face. The night was picture perfect.

"The next time we come we'll have the baby with us," she said.

"You like it that much to come back?"

"Who wouldn't? It has everything."

"Babe, remember when you asked where I was earlier?"

"Yeah."

"Well, I wasn't exactly truthful with you. I stopped by my mother's house."

Immediately, Cojo tensed up in my arms. I pulled her closer to my chest. I expected her to say something, but she didn't.

I said, "Having this baby means the world to me. I had to share our news. I want so much more for our child than I had. I want our child to have a family." I let my words settle in.

Cojo was still tense and felt cold to the touch, even in the warm waters of the hot tub.

"Relax, babe, it went better than I thought it would go."

"What did she say?" She was trembling.

"First, I told her I forgave her for being such a shitty mother."

"You said that?" She tried to turn and face me, but I didn't want her to, so I held her tighter.

"Yeah, I told her that now I'm about to be a father, I could understand how she took out her anger at my father on us, and I wanted to break the cycle and have her be a part of our lives."

"Umph. Well, I wish you good luck with that."

I could tell she didn't mean it, but I let it go. "I also told her that if she were going to be a part of our lives, I would not tolerate any more disrespect to you. I said you were the love of my life and the mother of my child." I felt her inhale sharply.

"And?"

"She said you were a good woman and she didn't dislike you, but she was jealous because you had all the things that she wanted." I thought about telling her about Gavin, but I refused to bring him into our lives. I was willing to forgive my mother, but Gavin was a whole other story.

"Are you serious?"

"Yeah. It was a touching moment. I think we have a chance, if you allow it."

When she tried to turn around this time, I let her.

"Merlin, that's all I've ever wanted." She gazed into my eyes.

We shared a passionate kiss, and the next thing I knew, I was naked. If I didn't know any better, I could have sworn the water started to boil.

33 GAVIN MILLS

"That bitch." I was pissed. Not only was my punk-ass father coming home, but Gina all but told me that I would not be welcome in their new house. This was going to put a serious monkey wrench in my plans. I was trying to stick around long enough for Merlin to go back to playing war games so I could get next to his hot wife. I still couldn't get the image of her round ass out of my mind as I banged her from behind.

I started pacing back and forth, trying to come up with a way to buy more time.

I needed to find a job, quick, fast, and in a hurry. I hoped my dad would be more compassionate if he saw that I was at least trying to do something with my life. As much as I hated to do it, I was going to have to put in work. Living off people was much easier. Problem was, I wasn't trained to do anything. I was twenty-five years old and had never held down a full-time job.

♥♥♥

After my shower, I went to the kitchen and fixed myself a bowl of cereal. My stomach yearned for a hot meal, but I didn't feel like fixing it myself. Since Gina had already left the house, I had to settle on what I could get. I started to leave the bowl in the sink just to piss her off, but I thought better of it since I was trying to buy myself some time.

As I was preparing to leave, I saw the keys that Merlin had given my mother. Without even stopping to think about it, I grabbed them and put them in my pocket. I drove to Auto Zone, which wasn't far from her apartment. I needed to get some keys made.

A slow smile spread across my face when the clerk handed me the keys. I paid my tab and doubled back to put the keys back where I found them. No one would be the wiser.

♥♥♥

"Bingo." I was feeling pretty good as I walked out of Tiffany's on Northside Drive. I managed to snag a job as a bartender/bouncer. I would work from ten to two as a bartender and from two to four as a bouncer. It was the perfect job. I don't know why I didn't think of it before. Tiffany's was a strip club that catered to both gay and straight patrons. I wasn't too thrilled about the gay guys, but I would take their money the same as I would take a chick's.

I was feeling pretty good. All in all, it was a productive morning, and I would start work later tonight. As I drove home, I was mentally searching my closet for something to wear that would have those faggots and bitches lining my pockets. Unfortunately, I couldn't think of a thing that would really set me apart from the other bartenders. Then I remembered the keys that I had made earlier. Since Merlin and his wife were still out of town, I decided to stop by his place and go shopping.

I walked with confidence into my brother's home. I wasn't afraid of anyone trying to stop me since we looked exactly alike. Merlin's neighbor tried to hold me up, but I told him that I was in a hurry and I would talk to him later. After I closed the door, I flipped the double bolt.

Memories of the last time that I was in their home flooded my brain. "Damn, this is me!" I could get comfortable in a place like this. It actually felt like a home, and I was eager to have one. Not just any home, but *this* one with the perfect wife beside me. I grabbed a beer from the refrigerator and went into the master bedroom. It was immaculate, as was the rest of the house. Gone was the chaos from the fight that had ensued the last time I was there. In fact, everything that was broken had been replaced as if it had never happened.

Their apartment was huge, unlike the one that I shared with my mother. In the master bedroom, they had his and her closets. I went into hers first. Her scent lingered in the air as if she'd just left the room. I breathed deeply as a small smile tugged at the corners of my mouth. My hand slipped down to my dick, and I gently tugged at it.

Her closet was filled with bright colors and business suits hanging neatly on plastic hangers. "No wire hangers for her." My baby had class. On the far left wall hung her dresses and pants; on the right, blouses and jeans. Her jeans had that dry cleaner look with deep creases. I fingered the blouses and my dick got harder.

The hamper was in the center of the closet. I flipped open the lid in search of a dirty pair of her underwear. It was almost empty, but I found a blue thong. I sniffed the tiny patch that covered her pussy, while lost in a fantasy world.

"Ah," a raucous sound coming from deep inside my throat escaped my lips. I unzipped my pants and grabbed my dick. I needed to get some relief. I went to the chest of drawers and found one of her sexy teddies and wrapped it around my dick as I stroked myself. I sucked the lining of the tiny underwear, and it was if she were sitting on my face all over again. I exploded in her teddy as I fell back on their bed.

"Shit." It wasn't as good as the real thing, but it was a close second. I lay there for a few minutes until the blood started going back to my head instead of my dick. I licked the lining one more time before I shoved both items into my back pocket.

"I'm keeping these." With a satisfied smile on my face, I stuck my dick back in my pants and went through my brother's closet. His clothes were just as organized as hers. Envy threatened to rip a hole in my heart. *All this shit should be mine.* I grabbed three pairs of jeans off the bottom rack and a couple of shirts. I kept them on the hangers so it wouldn't be noticeable that they were gone. I would have preferred a muscle shirt, but I didn't see any of those. I was about to grab his Stacy Adams but decided against it.

Nah, he might miss those. I spread his remaining jeans apart so that he wouldn't readily realize that some were gone. Satisfied that I had enough to get me started, I turned to leave. I stopped in the kitchen to get a large garbage bag to throw my loot in. I drained my beer and tossed the empty bottle into the trash. It clanked against what I assumed was another bottle.

I opened the door and was startled by the postman, who appeared to have been just about ready to ring the bell. I jumped back, and my heart began to pound harder. "C-can I help you?" I stuttered.

"Certified letter for Merlin Mills," the postman chimed.

"Sure, that's me." I took the envelope from him and signed my brother's name. I waited for the postman to get in his truck and leave the parking lot before I locked the door and went to my car.

That was close. Next time I come over here I was going to check the peephole before I opened that bitch. It probably wasn't such a good idea to sign for that letter, but I couldn't very well decline since I was standing right in front of the man.

"Oh well." I dismissed the thought and went home to take a nap.

Gina still wasn't there and that was just as well, because I didn't want her to ask me about the bag of clothing.

34 GINA MEADOWS

"Tabatha, I'm so glad you answered the phone."

"Hey girl, what's up?"

"I just need an ear. Are you going into work today?"

"Actually, I was planning on working from home."

"Can I come by?" I was already in the car headed to her house. I had so much on my mind, I just needed to talk to someone.

"Sure, see you in a few."

♥♥♥

I knocked on her door ten minutes later.

"Damn, that was quick," Tabatha said, opening the door.

"Yeah, I was already in the car when I called. I was hoping you would be at home instead of the office, but the way that I'm feeling I would even have driven down there."

"Wow, things must be deep because you hate my office."

"I don't hate your office. I just hate those fake-ass folks you work with." I walked right into the living room and sat down on her sofa. I didn't begin to speak right away because I was trying to figure out how much I was going to tell my longtime friend. She didn't rush me, and I appreciated it.

"Merlin came by today."

"Say what?" She paused. "Are you serious?"

"Yeah, I know. I still can't believe it myself."

"So what brought that on?"

"He came by to tell me what a lousy mother I was."

"Oh shit. I think I need a drink, do you want one?"

"Naw, I tied one on last night and my stomach still don't feel too good." My pussy didn't either, but I wasn't going to tell her that. I waited until she came back into the room before I continued talking.

"Okay, go ahead." She seemed too eager to hear the story, and I almost regretted even coming over here.

"Actually, I'm glad he said it because he forced me to really look at myself. He also said he forgave me."

"I'm speechless. I'm surprised you didn't slap him upside the head, and that he forgave you."

"I was horrible, wasn't I?" A tear slipped down my face.

"Yeah girl, you were, but now you can start over. Everyone doesn't get a second chance, so be grateful."

"Trust me, I am."

"What about his wife? How are you going to handle that?"

"I'm fine with that, too. She never was a bad girl, I just couldn't see it. Hell, she's about to have my son's baby."

"That's wonderful, congratulations. It's about time you let all that anger go. What about Gavin?" She sipped her drink as she eyed me.

"I'm not ready to let go with him yet. The jury is still out. I don't trust him. Gavin's so jealous of Merlin it scares me. He has so much anger pent-up it's not healthy."

"Hmm … sounds a lot like you."

If she had said that to me yesterday, I would've probably stormed out of her house and wrote her out of my life, but today I allowed the comment to slide.

"No snappy retort?" She sat back in the chair observing me.

"Nope, you speak the truth, but I feel like I'm healing."

Tabatha looked at me. "So when are we going shopping for your new grandchild?"

"As soon as I find out what it is. I'm going to love this one like it's my own." I had one more thing to get off my chest, but I decided to keep that information to myself. "Thanks for listening, girl. I'm going to get out of your hair so you can get some work done."

"Anytime, you know you and me are down like two flat tires."

I chuckled as I grabbed my purse and went out the door.

I knew I was less than honest with Tabatha when I didn't disclose that Ronald was coming home, but she would have given me a lecture about letting him into my life again. I think she assumed that I had let him go when I said I was healing, but that was furthest thing from the truth. I still loved that man regardless of all the pain that he had caused in all of our lives.

"I'm just going to have to wait and see."

35 GAVIN MILLS

I had only been working six days, but I was making mad money at the club. The sissies loved me, and the women kept begging me for dick. It was the perfect world. Things were finally looking up. I used some of the money that I made to buy a few muscle shirts and the shit was on and popping from there.

Nobody in the club, including the dancers, could touch me. I was easily the most handsome man in the club, and I had bank in my pocket to prove it. Management was pleased because bar sales were up, mostly due to the sissies who sat at the bar and stared me down rather than throwing dollars at the dancers. This kept more money in the club. The dancers weren't feeling me, but that was their problem.

I hadn't seen Gina all week because my work schedule was so completely different from hers, so I had no idea what was going on in her life. I didn't even know if my father had come back as promised, and I didn't care anymore. I had enough cash to get me a small, furnished apartment. As far as I was concerned, Gina could fuck herself. I didn't need her anymore.

I packed my meager possessions and carried them to the car. As I took one final look around the room, I noticed the letter that I had taken from Merlin's house. I ripped it open, surprised that I'd forgotten all about it. "Well, now looky here." The letter said that Merlin was scheduled to report for re-deployment to Iraq two days ago. This might be the break that I'd been waiting on. If he missed his date, he would be in hot shit. "Oh, well, fuck him." I couldn't worry about his ass right now. I hoped they fried his ass. I tossed the letter in the trash.

My new job was so time-consuming, I hadn't had much time to think about my brother or his wife. Right now, it was about stacking paper, fuck the bullshit. Although I hadn't forgotten the scent of Cojo's pussy, I had to come up before I could step to her.

If things kept going like they were, I would be ready for her in a few months. Hell, one bitch offered me $500 just to suck my dick. I almost took her up on the offer, but I figured if I made her sweat, she might offer me more, so I planned on making her wait. Last week, I let a bitch suck my dick for free. Those days were over, and things were looking better for a brother already.

♥♥♥

The club was packed when I strolled in. I felt all eyes on me as I stuck out my chest, as if I needed to do anything extra to draw attention to myself. My bald head gleamed like a beacon, turning all male and female eyes on me.

"Damn, when I think of all the years I wasted avoiding a job, I can kick myself," I muttered under my breath. I waved my hand at a few of the regulars as I made my way to the back of the club to clock in. I was early, but management didn't mind because I was a moneymaker. I came early so I could sit on the other side of the bar and talk to the customers. It was a win-win situation for me, and the house. As a result, I had a small box of phone numbers for pussy all over Atlanta. So far, I hadn't had time to call any of those numbers. Now that I was living by myself, I was sure that was going to change.

I was wearing a black muscle shirt, black jeans, and a pair of the new Jordan's that I bought with some of the money that I'd been making. I took a seat at the end of the bar and studied the crowd. It was still early, but there was an equal mixture of men and women vying for attention.

I noticed that the women came out early and were mostly gone by the time I started my shift. My guess was that they had to go home to their husbands. After midnight, the club was dominated by men, but there were a few exceptions to that rule.

"Can I buy you a drink?" a seductive-sounding female whispered in my ear.

I smiled before I turned around to see who was macking on me. The face that greeted me was pretty enough, but she had an Adam's apple bigger than mine. But hell, a free drink was a free drink.

"Sure, I'll take a shot of Remy Black." I turned away as if I wasn't interested in conversation. I didn't really like dealing with the shims. All they wanted was to be fucked, and there was no way I was putting my dick in someone's ass unless they were one hundred percent female.

"Are you new around here?" she asked as she pushed my glass toward me.

"Kind of, I've been working here for about a week."

"You work here?" She raised her nicely arched eyebrows at me.

"Yeah, I'm one of the bartenders."

"Well, hell, you should be buying me a drink then." She batted her false eyelashes at me.

"Look, I'm flattered and all, but I've got a wife at home, and she doesn't have to tape her dick to her ass."

"You son of a bitch," she hissed at me as she grabbed her drink and vacated the chair.

I threw back my head laughing. I normally didn't come off as rude because I was still about stacking paper, but I knew I wasn't going to get any from that shim. So I used her for what she was worth and kept it moving.

I turned my drink up and emptied my glass. I wanted it to be empty before someone else sat down next to me. I had no intentions of drinking a lot because I still had to function when I went on duty in an hour, but I wanted to get my buzz on as well so I could deal with all the flaming fags that would be hitting on me for the next several hours.

I didn't have long to wait for someone to be bold enough to sit next to me. This time the voice was all female.

"Hi, handsome, are you one of the dancers?"

I turned slightly in my seat to see who it was that was speaking to me. She was a good-looking woman, although she was a little short for my taste. I'd fuck her if I didn't have anything else to do. She was about five feet two with deep chestnut-brown-colored skin, deep brown eyes, and a short and sassy haircut.

"You flatter me but no, I'm not a dancer." I said with a smug grin on my face. If I had a dollar for every time someone asked me if I was one of the dancers, I would have been rich.

"You should be."

"Thanks, but if I'm going to shake my ass, it will be in private."

"Is that an offer?" She had a hopeful look in her eyes.

I glanced at her ring finger and saw that she was indeed married. "Sorry, I don't do married ladies." I was lying my ass off, but she didn't have to know that.

She tried to hide her hand from me, but it was too late. I'd already seen it. "Shame, I could make it worth your while."

She had my attention now. I looked her over again. I noticed the bling around her neck and wrist. She had to be stupid to come into a club such as this looking like a billboard for the rich, but it had the desired effect. She had engaged me.

"So what did you have in mind?"

"Everything that you can imagine. And trust and believe it will be worth your time." She never said how much, but I was pretty sure she could afford me. Any other time I would give it to her for free, but once again, I was about stacking paper.

She pulled her business card out of her clutch and handed it to me. "This is my private cell number. Call me during the day when you have some time."

I slid off the stool and seductively placed the card in my back pocket making sure she followed my hands as I slid them alongside my ass.

"Damn," she murmured under her breath. She waved her hand across her face as if she were getting hot or something.

"I'll call you." I turned and walked away fairly confident that she was studying my every move. I went into the back so I could put on my apron. As I reached the back door of the employees' lounge, I was approached by someone else. A familiar face— the same person who had offered me money for some of my time.

"Hey there," I said without breaking my stride.

"Can I talk to you for a second?"

Now that I had moved, getting money was my only motivation. Plus, I needed my dick sucked. I stopped and turned around. The woman was not at all my type, but I could close my eyes and pretend she was Cojo.

"Sure, what is it?" I glanced down at my watch because I didn't want to be late checking in for my shift.

"Can I taste that big, black dick of yours?"

"What's in a taste? Do you want to give it just a lick like a lollipop, or do you want to taste the center of a Tootsie Roll Pop?"

"I want the Tootsie Roll Pop."

"You know that shit ain't free."

"I understand that, Gavin; I'm willing to double my offer." She didn't have to say no more before I grabbed her arm and led her to the employee bathroom.

"Show me the money," I demanded as I started to unbuckle my pants. I watched as she counted out ten one-hundred-dollar bills and handed them to me. I folded the bills and put them in my pocket. I sat down on the toilet and the thirsty bitch dropped to her knees and went to work. I had to admit, home-girl knew her shit. I allowed my mind to think about Cojo as she worked my dick.

Either this sister had mad skills, or it was the thrill of the easy money that was being made. Either way, it didn't take long to get me off. I exploded in her mouth, and she swallowed every single bit of my precious cum.

"Umm, I knew it would taste good," she said, licking her lips.

"Thanks, baby. Nice doing business with you." I stood up and zipped up my pants.

She was still on the floor staring at me as if she wanted more, but I was done for the moment. If she wanted seconds, she was going to have to reach deeper into her purse. I reached out my hand to pull her to her feet. She looked like a little kid who had her toy stolen.

"I'd like to see you again."

"Get your money right and we'll see, but no promises." I was ready to get rid of her.

"I wasn't talking about inside this club. We could go out to dinner or something."

"Look, I enjoyed what just happened, but that's about as far as I'm willing to go. I'm strictly about the money." The chick paid me to suck my dick. What more should she expect from me?

"I understand." She ignored my outstretched hand and got to her feet on her own.

That was fine with me, because I would hate to have to bust this bitch in her face if she started to get out of hand. She walked out the door without even looking back. I went over to the sink and washed off my dick. If my luck held up, I might be able to get someone else to come off the money and wet my dick.

36 ANGIE SIMPSON

I woke up in the trauma unit of Grady Memorial Hospital. I recognized this place because I had to research its trauma center for a term paper last semester. Then it dawned on me: *Trauma center? What the fuck?* I tried to sit up, but the agonizing pain that shot through every inch of my body caused me to sit my ass still. I didn't even want to breathe too deep after that shit.

Little by little, I took in my surroundings. A morphine drip hung over my head to the left; an intravenous drip to the right. Then I remembered the fire, and I panicked. I really didn't want to do it, but I had to know. I peeked under my sheet and started to cry. Most of my body was covered with bandages.

A nurse came in the room carrying a bedpan. "Nice. You're back with us." She started checking my vitals, then noticed my tears and handed me a tissue.

"It hurts so badly."

"You can control your medications by pressing this button. If you're in pain, push the button." She pressed it for me before she handed me the controller. The pain started easing immediately.

I remembered asking for God's help as I ran through the fire. I don't remember anything after that. "How long have I been here?"

"Twenty-one days and counting. You're healing well. With some physical therapy, you'll get along just fine."

"My parents," I said. "I need to see my parents. The nurse checked her watch.

"It's two o'clock now. They have been here like clockwork every day at five o'clock since your accident."

Two men walked into my room. They both wore cheap suits and worn-down walking shoes.

"Oh no, you don't," the nurse said. "She just came out of a coma. She hasn't even seen the doctor yet."

The white man with a coffee stain on his Tasmanian-devil-printed tie stepped up. "Nurse Graham, we'll only be a minute."

I saw the bulge of guns under their suit jackets, and gold badges clipped to their belts.

Nurse Graham said, "Every time you come here you ask for a minute and take twenty, as if you have no concern for the patient. I'm going to get the doctor. When I get back, you two have to leave."

"Fair enough," the other guy said.

Nurse Graham left the room.

The guy with the Tasmanian Devil tie said, "I'm Detective Adams, and this is my partner Detective Lyle."

Detective Lyle waved. "Glad to see you pulled through."

"Thanks," I had the distinct impression that I was in trouble.

Detective Adams looked at my morphine drip. "You must be feeling pretty good, Ms. Simpson. They got you on the good stuff."

If he were attempting to be funny, I missed the damn joke.

Detective Lyle took a seat in the chair next to my bed. "Forgive me for getting right to the point. I have a feeling we won't have long to speak with you. We've been assigned to investigate what happened to you. Needless to say we have a lot of questions. There was an accelerant used to burn your house to the ground. My guess is gasoline, but we won't know that for sure until our lab results come back."

Detective Adams stroked his mustache. "I really don't think it was a suicide attempt on your part because you were found by Atlanta PD in your backyard; unless it was suicide-motivated, but you chickened out at the last minute."

Detective Lyle leaned forward. "But what's been keeping me awake at night is that you were naked. Why? My cop instincts tell me someone left you for dead."

"The doctors can't definitively say because of the severity of your burns, but they're pretty sure you were beaten," Detective Adams said.

Detective Lyle pointed at me. "How about you tell us what you know so we can stop guessing?"

I looked between the two as a dose of morphine hit me. If I wanted to lie to make myself look better in this ugly mess, the drugs wouldn't allow it. "I got in the car with this stranger on Cleveland Avenue. We went back to my place and had sex. We got a little aggressive with each other, and the last thing I remember was him choking me. I woke up and the house was on fire."

"So you got burned trying to get out?" Detective Adams started taking notes.

I nodded.

"What can you tell me about this stranger, Ms. Simpson?" Detective Lyle said. He too was writing on a notepad.

"His name is Merlin Mills. He's twenty-two, and he's stationed at Fort McPherson Army base. He's six-two, approximately 190 pounds. He drives a 2002 Malibu, brown, with a dent on the back door passenger side. License plate number is JE619."

The detectives looked at each other as if they were amazed.

"Well, I'll be damned," Detective Lyles said. "I've been in law enforcement going on twenty-two years, and I've never had anyone give me such a thorough description of a stranger."

I said, "Maybe because you've never asked for a suspect description from a criminal justice major. Would one of you mind getting Nurse Graham for me." I didn't like these condescending cops and I wanted them to leave.

37 GINA MEADOWS

Ronald started talking about coming home over a year ago. At the time, I didn't believe him. I thought he was just stringing me along again. However, things changed on his last visit almost six months ago. We actually went house shopping.

At first, we would visit neighboring subdivisions looking for a suitable house. I played along because I didn't think Ronald was serious. It wasn't until we started searching outside of Atlanta that I began to think he was.

We found a beautiful home in Alpharetta. It was everything that I had ever wanted and then some. After we toured the model, we sat down with the agent. When Ronald suggested we put down a deposit, I didn't hesitate to write the check for the last bit of money I had left from the sale of my mother's house. I was confident that Ronald wouldn't let me spend my last ten thousand dollars unless he was fully committed to coming home.

Now, the only thing left to do was close on our dream home. Although I was ninety percent sure it was going to happen, I didn't tell anyone, with the exception of Gavin, for fear of jinxing it.

♥♥♥

"Gina, I'm at the airport, can you pick me up?"

"Airport? I thought you were going to drive." My heart started racing faster. Already things weren't going as I planned them, but I tried not to let it bother me.

"Something came up and I couldn't. Are you on the way?"

"Yeah, I'm leaving now." Something didn't feel right about this. Why would he leave his car in Ohio if he intended to move here? What could have come up at the last moment? I tried to push all those dark thoughts to the back of my mind as I rushed to the car to go pick him up. Once I got in the car, I had to call him back because he didn't tell me which airline he flew in on.

"Why won't he pick up the fucking phone?" I'd called him three times, and it kept going straight to voicemail, which either meant he was on the phone, or he was ignoring me. Neither scenario left a good taste in my mouth.

Lord, don't let this motherfucker try to play me again. I knew I was wrong for saying motherfucker in the same sentence with the Lord's name, but I was tired of being taken for a ride like a broken-down pony at the fair. After several tense minutes, my phone finally rang.

"What's up, where you at?" Ronald asked, sounding upset.

"Which gate are you at? You know how big Hartsfield is, it will take me forever to check each terminal." I wanted to ask him so badly why he didn't answer the first three times, but I also didn't want to start this trip off with an argument.

"Delta, damn it. I only fly on Delta. I'm standing at the end of the platform at baggage claim."

I cringed. How could I have possibly known this? To my knowledge, he didn't fly much. "All right, already. I should be there in about fifteen minutes."

"Fine, hurry up." He hung up.

I tried to rationalize Ronald's apparent irritation. He was scared and was taking it out on me. Buying a home was a big step, so I cut him a little slack. It would have been nice if he had said something nice, like I can't wait to see you, or even better, I love you, babe, but it wasn't a deal breaker. For a second, I wanted to cry, but I sucked it up. I was going to ride this bike until the wheels fell off. If he tried to play me again, there would be no coming back from it. I was getting too old for this shit.

♥♥♥

"So what happened?" I was still apprehensive about what could have caused such a major change in plans. I moved over and allowed Ronald to drive my car.

"I told you, something came up. I had to be here for the closing, so I decided to fly in, handle the business, and drive back when I was finished things at home. Would you rather I blew off the walk-through?"

"No, of course not." As explanations went, his sucked. I would have been more reassured if he had at least offered a kiss or some other greeting when he got in the car.

Ronald did a dry settlement through the mail. Because of my terrible credit, I was unable to go on the loan documents. The last step in the process was the walk-through, sign-off and the exchange of keys. As we drove to the house, I could barely contain the butterflies in my stomach. The house was beautiful, and I couldn't wait to move in.

When the realtor gave Ronald the keys, I could have cried. My dreams were finally coming true.

"You satisfied now?" Ronald asked as we got back in the car. The whole process took a lot less time than I thought it would. I was so excited I didn't know what I wanted to do first.

We drove around the subdivision. There were only a few homes that were occupied which was a little creepy. I felt like we were sole survivors, and in a way, we were. Ronald and I had been through a lot and we were still standing.

"Yes, I'm satisfied. When can we move in?"

"We have the keys, so there is really no rush. I'm thinking about leaving them at the front gate so they can let the furniture people in when they deliver."

"Ugh, my stuff is going to look terrible in this house."

"We're not taking any of your furniture. You can pitch all of it in the trash as far as I'm concerned."

"Are you bringing your stuff from Ohio?"

"I'll bring most of it, but we should get something new for the bedrooms and the kitchen. If you want, we could go pick that out now before my flight back."

"You're leaving tonight?" I couldn't even hide my disappointment.

"Yeah. The sooner I get back, the quicker I can wrap things up. I still have some packing to do. If all goes well, we should be ready to move in two weeks from now."

I don't know about Ronald, but I was ready to move in today, but I wasn't about to say that to him. "Where to now?" I was all fired up and ready to discuss our plans for the future. Now that he had the keys, I wanted to tell him I could start moving right away and have the house all set up by the time that he got here.

"We need to pick out some furniture."

I clapped my hands excitedly. I assumed we would take the furniture that I already had, but I liked his idea better.

My stuff was old. We now had this fantastic house, so it was only fitting that we get new furniture too.

♥♥♥

We walked into the furniture store, and Ronald said, "Pick out whatever you want, babe."

It felt like when we first got together, and I was so happy. We ended up getting all the rooms furnished, and it would be delivered the following day.

The rest of the day passed by in a blur. Ronald transferred the utilities, arranged for cable and phone service and the next thing I knew, we were back at the airport. He didn't even bother to stop by the house for a quickie, which I was really ready for after the vivid dreams I'd been having, which subsequently had my pussy feeling used.

"Why do you have to leave so soon?" I tried to keep the whining out of my voice, but it wasn't working. We had spent so many hours acting like a couple, but never talked about anything concrete as it related to us.

"I told you I was on a tight schedule, baby. I'll be back in two weeks, and we can get everything straight then." He pulled up to the drop-off point and grabbed his carry-on from the back seat.

I don't even know why he bothered to bring a bag because he didn't open it one time. I got out of the car and went around to the driver's side. Ronald kissed me on the forehead and headed inside the terminal.

"What just happened here?" I had a real weird feeling in the pit of my stomach. Something just didn't feel right. Ronald and I hadn't seen each other in months, and all I got from him was a peck on the forehead? What the fuck?

I drove home in a semi-daze with thousands of questions running through my mind. I tried not to think too hard as I started packing up the things that I wanted to take with me like my clothing, pots and pans and linens.

As I was packing a sense of joy filled my spirit, and I forgot about all the misgivings I felt when I was with Ronald earlier. For the moment, I imagined everything was going to be okay. My apartment was already on a month to month lease. I just needed to make sure my place was clean before I left.

I was still a little apprehensive about what to do with Gavin. Even though I hadn't seen him in over a week, he still had my keys. If he'd moved, the least he could have done was let me know. I went into his room to inspect it for any damage, and his personal effects were gone. I breathed a sigh of relief. "Good, now I don't have to have that conversation with him."

I started to strip the linen from his bed. I had no intentions of taking them to my new house. Underneath his pillow, I found a blue thong and a red teddy. I didn't want to pick them up, so I just smashed them together with the soiled linen and dumped it all into a large trash bag.

I wasn't even going to guess about the identity of the owner of those items. I couldn't believe that Gavin had the nerve to bring one of his whores into my house. I finished clearing out his room and cleaning the bathroom. I was tired, but I still couldn't rest. I was full of nervous energy. I called the realtor who I'd been working with so closely for months.

"Hey Dan, it's Gina Mills." I loved how the last name Mills sounded coming out of my mouth.

"Hi, Gina. Congratulations."

"Thanks. Listen, I know we said we would move in two weeks from now, but I've packed up a lot of things from my old house and I can't see with all the boxes. Is there any way that I can start moving things tomorrow?"

"I'm out of it now. Whatever you decide is fine. That house is sold. Congratulations again."

I hung up the phone feeling satisfied that I could accomplish something while I was off from work. I would have felt better if I had my own set of keys to our new house, but I would rectify that soon. I finished packing the rest of my kitchen items and went to sleep, totally exhausted.

38 COJO MILLS

I was skipping work today and going to the doctor's for the first time without Merlin. It was imperative that I found out if the baby was actually my husband's. So far, Merlin hadn't mentioned his fears about raising a child who might belong to his brother, but I was sure he'd done the math in his head.

"Lord, please let this baby belong to my husband." I got up off my knees and started to get dressed. I hated to deceive Merlin, but my guilt and shame were killing me. Instead of gaining weight with the baby, I was losing it, and I attributed it all to stress.

Even though I knew Merlin knew it was a possibility that the child was not his, he never harped on it, and that made me love him more than ever. It wasn't my intention to cheat on him in the first place. I felt like I was tricked.

♥♥♥

"Cojo Mills?" the nurse called out.

I followed the nurse to the back, even though my nerves were wreaking havoc with me. I knew I was making the right decision by having a CVS test, but I hated that I didn't have the nerve to tell Merlin about it before I scheduled it. The correct medical terminology was Chorionic Villus Sampling. Typically, this test was performed to confirm the health of the baby, but it was also used for growth abnormalities on the fetus.

"Undress and put on this robe. The doctor will be in any moment." The nurse handed me the robe.

"Thank you." I waited until the door was closed and started taking off my clothes. Once again I started praying. *Sweet Jesus, please be with me through this process and make it all right. Please don't let me be carrying the son or daughter of my husband's brother. Amen.* I got up on the table and waited for the doctor.

"How are you doing, Mrs. Mills?" An Indian doctor came in the room. He was a small man.

"I would be better if I weren't spread-eagled on this table in front of you."

He chuckled. "I can't tell you how many times I've heard that before."

His nurse entered the room to assist him with the procedure.

With his strong accent, he said, "This isn't going to hurt, but it will be a little uncomfortable. I'm going to place a catheter through the cervix, and take a small tissue sample of the chorionic villa cells for biopsy. CVS is used to find genetic disorders, but it can also be used to determine the sex of the child. It should only take a minute, so please lie still."

"How long should it take to learn the results?"

"The results are usually available within seven to ten days. I will have preliminary results within forty-eight hours, but they will not be one hundred percent accurate. Would you like those preliminary results emailed to you?"

"Yes, I would."

"Okay, I'll make a note to the file. It is common for women to experience mild uterine cramping. This may be slightly uncomfortable, but it is usually not painful. If you experience pain, contact me immediately."

"Okay." I was feeling a lot better knowing that my mind would be at rest soon. Even if it weren't my husband's child, I just had to know. The unknown was killing my joy.

"You will be fine," the doctor said.

♥♥♥

"Are there any physical or sexual restrictions I should be worried about?" I asked this question as an afterthought. Since I felt no pain, I assumed there would be no worries.

"It is recommended that you refrain from strenuous physical activity, heavy lifting, sitting in water—such as bath or pool—and sexual intercourse for approximately twenty-four to forty-eight hours. In addition, you should avoid the insertion of anything vaginally, including suppositories, for twenty-four to forty-eight hours."

"Aye-aye, sir." I giggled. He spit out his orders to me as if he were a naval captain and I was on one of his ships, but I got it. I didn't plan on doing shit. Hell, I didn't have to. Merlin took care of everything around the house. I walked out of the doctor's office feeling better than when I went in, because I knew that I would have an answer soon.

♥♥♥

"So, whose baby is it? Mine or his?" Gavin stood beside my car with an evil sneer on his face.

Immediately, my heart started beating faster. He was the last person on God's green earth that I wanted to see, and I certainly didn't want to see him today.

"You need to get the hell away from me."

"Where's this animosity coming from, sis? I just want to know whose child you're carrying."

I didn't hate many people, but I could honestly say that I hated Gavin. "None of your fucking business."

"Oh, I beg to differ, because if it is my child—and I have the right to know if it is—I will not allow anyone else to raise it other than me. Let's be clear about that shit."

"Are you serious?" My heart started to beat even faster.

"Damn right I am."

This was crazy. How did he even know where to find me? "Wait, are you following me?" There was no way that he could know where I was—unless he did.

Gavin shrugged his shoulders, neither admitting nor denying that he'd followed me.

"I tell you what. If I find out that the child I'm carrying doesn't belong to my husband, you can follow me right back here while I abort the bastard." I got in the car and slammed the door.

Outside the car, Gavin was acting an ass. I ignored him and pulled out of the parking lot. It unnerved me to know that he was following me. Initially, I had no intention of telling Merlin about the test, but now that Gavin was sniffing around I realized I didn't have a choice.

I pulled over to the side of the road and sent Merlin a text message. *When you get a chance, I really need to speak with you. It's important.*

My phone rang almost immediately, and I used my Bluetooth to answer it.

He said, "What's wrong, baby?"

This was not the way that I wanted to have this conversation, but I felt it was better if it came from me rather than Gavin. "Honey, I went to the doctor's today to have a paternity test. I felt I owed it to you to make sure that I wasn't carrying your brother's child. I'm sorry I didn't tell you about it, but it wasn't because I was trying to deceive you; I wanted to relieve you." I started driving.

"Baby, I fully understand what you did. I would be lying if I said I didn't have my doubts, but I'd already made up my mind that regardless of the outcome, it will still be my child."

"You did?"

"Yes. You're my wife. I know you didn't cheat on me, and if anyone is to blame, it would be me and Gavin for not telling you."

"Oh my God! I've been so worried that you wouldn't love me anymore if you found out that I wasn't carrying your child."

"Sweetheart, hush. It's all a moot point."

"Wait baby, you have to hear this. When I came out of the doctor's office, Gavin was in the parking lot. I don't know how he knew that I was pregnant, but he asked if it was his. I think he's been following me."

Merlin didn't answer right away, and I could tell he was battling with his own emotions when he finally spoke. "I'll deal with Gavin. Go home and get some rest." His words had a bite to them that I was unfamiliar with.

I could tell he was mad. "Are you okay, baby?"

"Yeah, just go home. If he comes to the house call me back."

39 MERLIN MILLS

"Son of a bitch." The coffee cup that I'd been holding in my hands shattered all over the floor. It wasn't like me to lose control at work, but I felt as if I had been pushed over the very edge of the earth. "How dare the fucker follow my wife."

"Specialist Mills, are you all right?" my commander asked.

"No, I'm not all right. I need to take a personal day starting right now."

"You are going to have to take that up with the captain."

I had no doubt my request would be granted after the last army soldier went ballistic and shot up half his camp, but I didn't want to go out on a bad note. I went to find the captain. I found her to be completely human the last time I had to speak with her. Her door was open, so I knocked on it.

"Captain, I have a family emergency, and I'm requesting permission to leave to handle it."

"At ease. Shut the door."

I turned and closed the door behind me. I didn't want to take the time to explain the situation, but I also didn't want to fuck myself in my haste to get off the base.

Captain Jamison looked at me with genuine concern. "What's going on, Specialist?"

I thought about it for a minute before I divulged the darker circumstances of this new emergency. "Captain, you've been more than just an officer with me. You've shown me true compassion since I've been on base and I appreciate it. However, my brother is trying to make a move on my wife, and I can't let that happen. I thought he'd moved on, but I found out a few minutes ago that he hasn't. I need to check him." I couldn't bring myself to tell her about the baby.

"Go handle your business. If you need an extra day tomorrow, call me." She reached across her desk and gave me her personal card with her cell and house phone numbers on it.

"Thank you, Captain. You don't know how much this means to me."

"Yes, I do. I've been there, remember."

Our eyes locked for a second. She had told me her story, and I believed that she understood some of what I was going through.

♥♥♥

I rushed off the base intent upon setting Gavin in his place once and for all. He must have really lost his mind if he thought for one minute that I was going to allow him to come into our lives and ruin our marriage.

I didn't give a flying fuck if it was his child. He was going to leave my wife alone. I was so angry I almost ran my car into a truck in front of me which had stopped without warning. I stomped on the brake, propelling my chest forward against the steering wheel.

I drove over to my mother's house so that I could talk to my brother. I really didn't want to see him, but he wouldn't answer the cell phone I'd given him. When I pulled up to my mother's apartment complex, I didn't see his car or my mother's. I was so far removed from her life, I had no idea what shift she was working.

I sat in the car for several more minutes, hoping that one of them would show up, but it was to no avail. As a last-ditch effort, I wrote a note to my mother.

Mother, I'm trying to get in touch with Gavin. When he comes back, can you please have him give me a call on my cell? Better yet, if he shows up, could you please call me, and I'll come back over. What I have to say to him I need to say to his face and not on the phone. Thanks for your help.

Merlin.

I wasn't happy about this unexpected delay, but it was what it was. I would just have to wait and deal with my wayward brother later. Of course, this could have been a blessing in disguise, because I really didn't know how I would have reacted if I'd seen Gavin at this exact moment.

With no other options, I drove home to comfort my wife.

40 GINA MEADOWS

I packed as many boxes and bags that I could fit into my car. It was so loaded I could barely see out the windows. I almost wished Gavin were here so that he could help me and then I wouldn't have to make so many trips. This was what I got for trying to keep this a secret. I didn't even tell Tabatha that I was moving.

"Shit, I should have rented a U-Haul truck." As soon as the words left my mouth, I realized just how stupid it would have been because I had no idea how to drive a truck. *All right, Lord, I'm just going to do this the best way I know how.* I looked around for my purse. Once I found it, I locked the house up and took the long drive to Alpharetta. I started getting excited the farther I got away from the city. I was looking forward to the peace and quiet of the new neighborhood.

When I arrived at the gated community, the guard waved me in. He'd gotten used to seeing me during the construction phase of our home.

He leaned out the booth to speak with me. "Good afternoon. The door is open because some delivery men have already arrived with the furniture."

"Thanks, I'm just going to drop off some of my things and be out."

"No problem."

I was absolutely giddy when I pulled up in front of our new home. Leaving my purse in the car, I carried two boxes to the stoop before I tried the door. I walked into the foyer and marveled at how nicely the furniture that I picked out went in our living room.

I bent over and pushed my boxes over to the corner. As I was standing up, a lady walked out of the kitchen. She appeared to be in her late twenties or early thirties. She smiled at me in a welcoming manner, and I returned her smile.

"I'm just dropping off a few boxes," I said as I headed to the door.

She didn't say anything, and it didn't dawn on me to ask who she was. I went back to the car and grabbed a few more boxes. I was getting tired, and sure would have liked to have had some help with all this lifting and shit. I practically dumped my next box of household items all over the white carpeting.

"What company are you with?" she asked, still standing in the doorway of the kitchen.

I started to tell her that it was none of her business, but I decided to be nice. "I'm not with any company; I live here," I proudly announced.

"Excuse me?" Her eyebrows rose significantly as she placed her hands on her hips.

If I wasn't so tired, I might have noticed her defensive posture. "My husband and I are moving in over the next few weeks." I knew I didn't have to explain myself, but my exhaustion got my tongue to wagging. Plus, I was proud of our new accomplishment.

"What's your husband's name?" Her tone was even and held no hint of attitude.

"Ronald." I turned around to go get some more boxes.

"That's interesting."

I didn't know who this nosy bitch was, but she was starting to get on my nerves. "How so?"

"Because this is my house, and my husband just so happens to be named Ronald, too."

If the floor rose up and smacked me, I wouldn't have been more stunned than I was at that moment. My mouth gaped open as I tried to comprehend what she had just said to me. "There has to be a misunderstanding," I stuttered. Surely, Ronald hadn't played me like this. He wouldn't be that cruel.

"Oh yeah, there is a misunderstanding, and I think you made it."

I pushed myself into the corner trying to figure out what was really going on. Fear gripped my heart. "How long have you been married?" I asked in a whisper.

The woman practically glowed at the mention of her marriage. "Three months."

My shoulders slumped. Ronald had struck again; this time to the tune of ten thousand dollars. I needed to get out of that house before I did something that landed my ass in jail. I stumbled toward the door.

"What are you going to do about these boxes?" She was pretty calm given that I had just barged into her house claiming ownership of both her home and her husband.

"Keep them." There was no way I was going back into that house after learning that Ronald had duped me again. It was inconceivable that he would treat me this way. As I drove away, I was numb, operating the car on impulse alone. I was so void of emotions I couldn't even cry.

"This is crazy. I mean, *really* crazy." But I couldn't deny any longer what was placed right in my face. Ronald gave me his ass to kiss with a big bow on it. I tried to remember every conversation that we had over the last few months, and he never gave me any indication that I wouldn't be moving into the house with him. In fact, he kept saying we would be a happy family.

How the hell were we going to be a happy family when he had some other heifer living with him? Hell, he even married her, and that was something that he never did for me. I was having a hard time processing this information. It was all so bizarre.

Why would he let me pick out the furnishings to a house I wouldn't even be invited to? I was ready to call him and cuss his ass out, but I needed to pull myself together first. Over the years, Ronald had done his dirt, but he had never just thrown it in my face like he did today. I dealt with the cheating, the long-distance relationship, and the money he hoarded, but when it was all said and done, I felt confident that he loved me on some level. It hurt me more than anything to know that he married this woman after stringing me along for damn near twenty years.

Hell, as far as I was concerned, I was his wife. I thought he felt the same way. I was trying to get up the energy to go into the house, but I just didn't have the strength. I looked at all the boxes lining my car and felt like screaming.

"This is some Jerry Springer bullshit." I looked toward my door and saw a note attached to it. It had to be from Ronald. He's going to tell me it was a sick joke, and that we were all right. Suddenly energized, I quickly undid my seatbelt and rushed to the front door to get the note. My blood was rushing through my veins. I thought my heart was going to leap right out of my chest. I snatched the note from the door and read the opening line, hoping for the best.

It read: *Mother, I'm trying to get in touch with Gavin—*

I crumpled the note without reading anything further. I used my key to open the door before I started crying like a banshee. My hand was trembling so badly, I could barely get the key in the lock. I leaned against the door to keep from falling. When the lock did finally unlatch, I fell into the house and landed on the floor. I used my foot and kicked the door shut.

"I'm going to lie here until I feel better." The tears came, and I was happy that I was able to hold them back until I was alone.

41 GAVIN MILLS

Damn, things hadn't gone anything like the way I'd planned. I was back in my car speeding to my apartment to regroup. I couldn't believe I'd underestimated the effect it would have on Cojo when I showed up at her doctor's appointment.

Shit, I thought she would have been happy to see me, especially since her own husband hadn't taken the time to come with her. Women were such confusing creatures. I should have been getting some rest before my shift tonight. Instead, I took my precious time to let Cojo know I was there for her and our baby, but she acted like I had stepped in shit and tracked it all over her carpet.

I ducked into my apartment as quickly as I could. I didn't want to get too close to my neighbors. The less they saw of me the better. It wasn't my plan to live in this dingy one-room apartment for long. As soon as I could get Cojo to see I was the better man, I planned to move in with her. She needed a real man, and I was more than enough for the job.

Hell, I was even wearing the lucky polo shirt that I'd taken from Merlin's closet, and she didn't even notice. I said it was my lucky shirt because every time I wore it, the women and shims just threw panties at me. I couldn't understand why Cojo resisted her carnal instincts.

"She's gonna mess around and lose me if she doesn't change her attitude." I was talking shit and I knew it, but it made me feel better to say it out loud. I knew it was going to take some convincing to get Cojo over to my side of the bed, but I really was willing to put in the work, because I recognized her for the jewel she really was. I just had to convince her I was the better man, which wouldn't be hard to do since Merlin has always stood in my shadow.

My room was a mess. I hadn't fully unpacked, and I hadn't bothered to do any cleaning since the day I moved in. I had dirty dishes in the sink and clothes strewn all over the floors. Even as a child, housework was never my thing. But if I ever hoped to bring someone back to my place, I knew that I needed to clean up.

I scooped up all the dirty clothes from the floor and hid them in the tub. I didn't have a washer, so when I had worn my last piece of clean clothing, I would go over to my mother's house and wash. I didn't see the sense of paying a buck twenty-five a load to wash and dry my clothes when I could use her utilities for free.

I took off the clothes I was wearing and threw them into the tub and took a shower. I had just enough time to catch a couple of hours of sleep before I had to go to work.

42 ANGIE SIMPSON

The detectives were back, much to my chagrin. I had told them everything that I knew so I didn't know what else I could tell them.

Detective Adams said, "You're looking a lot better."

I was sitting up in bed sipping ice water. "I feel much better. I can even go to the bathroom on my own."

"You're making progress then. You'll be out of here in no time."

"I'm having a difficult time shaking the morphine, but they're weaning me off it with Demerol."

"The lesser of the two evils." He pulled up a chair and straddled it. "I need you to ID this guy, Ms. Simpson. Here's a pen." He gave me an expensive pen which probably cost more than his suit. "I'm going to show you a photo card with six pictures on it. If you see the guy who did this to you, I need you to sign your name right beneath his picture."

"Okay," I said.

He gave me the photo card, and I immediately recognized Merlin's face on the first card.

"This is Merlin Mills." I put a fingertip on picture number one. It was a mug shot when he was younger, probably around seventeen or eighteen, but it was him. "This is him." I signed my name under the picture of the self-satisfying piece of dick who had left me for dead.

Nurse Graham came into the room. Clearly, something was bothering her. Since she'd been caring for me, I'd learned that she wore her emotions on her face.

Now I was concerned. "What's wrong, Nurse Graham?"

She nodded at Detective Adams. "Do you mind giving us a few minutes?"

"It's okay," I said. "It can't be that bad. He can stay."

Ms. Graham shook her head as if she pitied me. "You're pregnant."

"Are you freaking kidding me?"

"Honey, I wish I was. I just looked at your labs."

I felt as if I couldn't breathe. This was the worst news ever. How was I supposed to deal with this latest atrocity? It was too much for my mind to handle. I blacked out.

43 MERLIN MILLS

My heart was heavy when I put my key in the door. For all my bravado, I'd accomplished nothing as it related to getting Gavin to leave my wife alone. I'd been by my mother's several times. Even though her car was back in the parking lot, she wasn't answering the door. I wanted Gavin's ass so bad, I could taste it.

"Any luck?" Cojo asked after I closed and bolted the door.

"Not yet. I couldn't get in touch with my mother, and Gavin isn't answering the cell. He's not stupid; he knows I'm looking for him. Gavin has always had a problem with boundaries." As soon as I said it, I realized that wasn't the best thing to say to my pregnant wife, who was being led around by raging hormones.

"What's that supposed to mean? Are you trying to justify his actions?" She was clearly agitated.

"No, sweetheart, that's not it at all. What I meant to say was Gavin's sense of right and wrong are different from the average person."

"Oh, is that supposed to make me feel better?" She burst into tears.

I rushed to her to take her in my arms.

I knew that I wasn't explaining myself well, but I was never good at discussing the enigma that was Gavin. "Let me run you a bath. Have you eaten yet?" I was trying to remain calm for her. Although my emotions were all over the place just like hers.

"No, I haven't eaten. I was too nervous. And I can't take a bath for forty-eight hours." She sniffed.

I led her to our bedroom. I turned on the shower and went to whip up a light snack for her. While she was in the bathroom, I continued trying to reach my mother. The bad thing for me was that I knew nothing of her life, so I didn't know any other number for her other than her home.

I had just heated up some soup and made a sandwich for Cojo when the doorbell rang. I wasn't expecting anyone, and the disruption really irritated me. Whoever it was on the other side of the bell was practically lying on it.

Don't tell me that bastard Gavin has the nerve to come over here after he's followed my wife, I thought. Putting my tray to the side, I strode to the door, ready to knock this fool's head off his shoulders. I snatched open the door ready to do battle.

"Merlin Mills?"

Facing me were two military police officers.

"Uh, yeah, what's this about?" For the life of me, I couldn't understand why two police officers would be standing outside my door.

The tallest of the two said, "You are under arrest."

They stepped forward, turned me around, and cuffed me.

"What in the hell are you talking about? What did I do?"

In the meantime, Cojo emerged from the bathroom in her robe. Her eyes were wide as saucers as she witnessed me being arrested.

"Specialist Mills, you have been listed as AWOL, absent without leave, and in violation of a direct order," the shortest officer said.

My eyes swung wildly between the two officers and my wife. "I'm sorry, there must be some mistake. I'm not AWOL. I was at work today. Call my captain, she can vouch for me."

"Merlin, what's going on?" Cojo's eyes were bucked as she clutched her robe around her neck.

"I don't know, sweetheart, but don't worry.

They were trying to drag me through the door, but I wanted to assure Cojo that I didn't do anything wrong, and I would be back by her side in no time.

"Call Captain Jamison. Let her know what happened and ask her to please help me." At this point, I was practically screaming this to Cojo as the other officer grabbed the door and shut it in my wife's face.

This day had turned into a nightmare, and I didn't know how to stop it from getting any worse. It was killing me to leave my wife at this emotionally vulnerable time, especially when my stupid-ass brother was running amuck and following her.

♥♥♥

"Where are you taking me?" I assumed they would take me back to the base so I could clear up any problems that they had, but we were traveling in the opposite direction.

"I suggest you put a lid on it, Specialist. We don't owe you any explanations," the officer said.

"No disrespect, sirs, but I'm telling you this is just a big misunderstanding. I've been to work every day. I was assigned a temporary job on base while awaiting my redeployment orders."

"Well, your orders called for you to head back to Iraq on June thirteenth. Obviously one of us is wrong, and I guarantee it's not us."

"Stop talking to the prisoner. You don't owe him shit." The taller officer commanded.

"Wait, hold up for a second. If I was going to go AWOL, why would I be at my house instead of held up somewhere else?" It was like I was talking to a wall. "Think about it, if I was going AWOL, why would I report to work every day as if things were normal? If I were truly AWOL, I would have left the state or even the country, but I didn't do that. And, if I tried to kill someone, would I still stick around? Come on, people—think."

"Maybe you're one of those crazy niggers!"

Since both of my arresting officers were white, I saw nothing funny about his remarks.

"Please, before you put me on a plane and waste taxpayer money, please just look into this. If I'm wrong, then I should be punished, but I promise you that I did nothing wrong."

"Shut your pie hole, Specialist."

44 GINA MEADOWS

I was not believing this shit. And the worst part about it was I couldn't even call Tabatha and tell her about the shit that had just gone down, because she warned me, and my hardheaded ass wouldn't listen."

Everywhere I looked I saw boxes. It seemed as if it had taken forever to pack them, and now I'd need to spend the next week unpacking them. But before I could even start that daunting task, I had to make sure my apartment was still available. If not, I would be out there pounding the pavement, trying to find an apartment that I could afford.

This whole situation was a nightmare that I couldn't believe I was living. Part of me wanted to start unpacking immediately just in case someone dropped by and I had to explain to them why all my shit was in boxes, but I just didn't have the energy.

I went into the kitchen and fixed a drink. If I ever deserved a drink, it was now. I had never been so humiliated in my life. Ronald had been giving me the shaft for years, but no one outside of us knew what was going on.

I embarrassed myself in front of a total stranger. I wanted to get mad at the woman and go back out there and kick her ass. The reality was I couldn't get mad at her for the shit Ronald had been doing to me for years. Knowing him, she probably didn't know jack shit about me.

Ronald was the motherfucker at the root of all this shit. If she knew anything about me, things might have gone differently.

Hell, she could have shot me for walking up in her spot like I owned it. I had no idea what was in the boxes that I left at their house. I figured it was just a matter of time before Ronald showed up and dropped them off. Seeing that he was a coward, I wouldn't have been surprised if he waited until I was at work and then dropped them off.

That bastard really didn't want to see me. Just thinking about Ronald made my blood pressure rise. I planned to get my money back from him, too. I was a good woman to him, and he treated me like shit. When he started talking about coming home this time, I didn't pressure him to do it. It was his idea. If he were going to do me like this, I don't know why he even bothered to tell me he was coming. He could have just shown up, and I wouldn't have been the wiser. It wasn't like I traveled to Alpharetta on the regular. He could have lived his life to the ripe old age of one hundred, and I would have never known the difference. Shit just wasn't adding up. I lie down on the sofa, too tired to think anymore.

I was going to have to find a way to get past this hurt and move on with my life. I wanted to call Tabatha so badly, but I couldn't hear 'I told you so'. Not tonight. I was whupping up on myself already. I didn't need any more help in that regard.

45 MERLIN MILLS

I wasn't able to speak to Captain Jamison when I saw her come through the door, but I immediately began to relax knowing that I had someone on my side who would stand up for me. I could tell by her stride that she was pissed. She went into the commander general's office and closed the door.

"Yes!" I screamed and fist pumped the air.

She didn't take too well to people fucking with her folks; however, she didn't appear as confident when she came out of the office. My heart sank. I knew this had to be some type of mistake, but I didn't know who was culpable for it. She came into the room they were holding me in with a confused expression on her face.

"Specialist, I'm trying to fight this, but I have to know why you signed for these orders and ignored them."

"Orders? I haven't received any orders."

She slid some papers across the table for me to see. I could tell from her demeanor that she was struggling to remain calm.

"Captain, I've never seen these papers before. Do you really believe I would sign something of this magnitude without speaking with you? This makes no sense." I picked up the papers to look at them more closely. They were sent

Certified Mail, and someone signed for them the day Cojo and I had left for the mountains.

"Captain Jamison, remember I told you I was taking my wife to the mountains because I had just found out she was pregnant?"

"Yeah."

"These papers were signed after I left. There is no way I could have signed them!" I could see a small glimmer of light at the end of the tunnel.

"Well, someone signed for those papers, or else we wouldn't be here."

"But I didn't do it. Can't they compare the signatures?" The only other person that knew I had orders coming was my mother, and I didn't want to believe that she had thrown away our newfound understanding and fucked me. I just didn't want to believe that, so I couldn't throw her under the bus.

"That might be enough to get you out of here tonight, but we have got to get some answers. I've gone out of my way to make concessions for you. Don't let this bite me in my ass!"

♥♥♥

It took another few hours before I was finally able to go home. Thankfully, Captain Jamison agreed to drop me. She started speaking after we got into the car. "They were gunning for you for some reason. Is there anything else that I should be aware of?"

"I promise you, Captain; I'm as squeaky clean as they come. I don't have any surprises in my closet that will come back to bite you in the butt."

"I hope you're telling the truth because I take objection to folks chewing on my ass."

I wanted to laugh because it was a funny comment, but the severity of the situation made it impossible for me to laugh. "Do you really believe that I would have traumatized my wife over some bullshit? Oops, I'm sorry, Captain, but this has really pissed me off. First, my sick ass brother running around trying to hit on my wife, and now this."

"That's crazy your brother would do something like that."

"Tell me about it. We look just alike. He tricked my wife into thinking he was me and had sex with her. Lord, I can't believe that I'm telling you all this."

"Go ahead, I think I need to hear this."

"It wasn't the first time he did this shit either. He pulled this shit when we were kids and ended up doing time for it too. But this last time, he got my wife, so it's personal. I never told my wife about him."

"Why not?"

"He was in prison so I wanted to forget he even existed. He just showed up when he got out; the sad part about it was I hadn't made it home from my tour. She thought he was me, and well, what can I say. I made it home right after they finished. Now he's trying to say that the baby is his. This is some bullshit."

"Oh damn."

Hearing Captain Jamison cuss somehow made her seem more human to me. "I know, it's jacked up. I left today because my wife went to the doctor's to take a paternity test because she was afraid that it might be my brother's. She didn't tell me because she didn't want to stir up some shit, but my brother showed up at the doctor's. My guess is that he's been following her."

"Wow, who does that? This is some reality television mess."

"Yeah, tell me about it. I'd just gotten home when they came to arrest me. I didn't even have a chance to deal with my brother. Talk about bad timing."

"You know if your brother was following her, there is a chance he might have gotten to your mail. Do you think he would stoop that low?"

"With my brother, yeah. He would do something like that."

"Have you spoken with your wife yet to let her know you're safe?"

"No, I didn't bring my phone with me, and they weren't offering me one at the lockup."

She fished around in her purse and handed me her phone. I was grateful for the chance to put Cojo's mind at ease, but I didn't feel all that comfortable speaking to my wife in front of my captain.

Despite my misgivings, I called Cojo. "Hey, babe."

"Merlin? Whose phone are you calling from, and what in the hell is going on?"

"Hold on, baby, calm down. I'm with my captain, and she's bringing me home. I told her what we've been dealing with, and she let me use her phone to call you and put your fears to rest." I heard her exhale.

"Thank God."

"Is everything okay at the house?"

"Yeah, just been waiting to hear from you."

"I'll be there soon. Love you."

"I love you too."

I handed the phone back to Captain Jamison. "Thanks, I really needed to do that."

"Don't mention it. I shared a lot of my story with you, so I understand what you're going through. I only wish that someone would have taken an interest in me when I was going through similar situations after I enlisted. The biggest problem that I see, is when people get these positions in the military and they forget that they were people first, and with that comes life's problems. My CO didn't care about anything unless it was connected with the army."

"I'm glad I didn't enlist back then, because I probably would have gone AWOL."

"I understand what you're saying, but don't even joke about that. My ass is on the line for this. They really wanted to ship you out tonight. I had to call my direct supervisor to get it stopped. I don't want to have the brass all up in my business again."

"You won't have to. As I said, I'm squeaky clean. Once I get my sick ass brother under control, you'll probably never hear about me again."

"I'm gonna hold you to that!"

46 COJO MILLS

Merlin was on the way home, so I rushed around the bedroom to get dressed. I swept my hair into an updo to get it out of the way. I didn't know if his captain would come in, so I wanted to make a favorable impression on her. I didn't even know his captain was a woman until I had to call her for Merlin, so I was anxious to see what she looked like.

I had a red teddy that would be perfect for an after party with Merlin once the captain had left. I was very meticulous about my clothing and knew where every item was placed, but I couldn't find this red teddy to save my soul. I pulled out every drawer and sorted through each item in them, but I couldn't find it.

"That's so strange." After wasting a good fifteen minutes, I decided on a white teddy. I liked the way my chocolate skin looked against the white backdrop. I pulled on a pair of jeans over the teddy and put on a shirt to cover it. I decided against a bra. My boobs were feeling extra heavy, and wearing a bra for eight hours was enough for me.

I was in the living room when Merlin came through the door. I launched my body toward him and damn near knocked him down.

"Damn, baby, I haven't been gone that long."

"I know, but when you left it scared me so bad, I didn't know when I was going to see you again."

"I feel you, I was scared too. Those jokers were serious." He gently pulled me from his chest and turned toward the door. "Babe, let me introduce you to the person who is responsible for getting me out."

I didn't even wait until he finished his introduction before I was rushing forward to greet and thank his captain for her help. "Thank you so much for your help. I don't know what I would do without him."

Captain Jamison said, "You are very welcome. He's a good guy, and I can tell he loves you."

My heart swelled with her comment. It was one thing for him to tell me that, but it was something entirely different when a stranger said it. Without warning, I burst out in tears.

"Sweetheart, why are you crying?" Merlin had a horrified look on his face, but I couldn't make him feel better when I was raging out of control.

"I don't know," I wailed. I walked toward my husband and wrapped my arms around his neck. I needed him to hold me and reassure me that everything was going to be all right.

"It's going to be okay, baby. There is no need for you to be crying." He stroked my back, and I began to feel better.

I suddenly remembered his captain. I pulled away from his arms to face her. "I'm so sorry. I didn't mean to carry on this way in front of you."

"Honey, hush. I was pregnant, too. I know what you are going through. Up one minute and down the next." She patted me on the shoulder reassuringly.

There was a heavy knock at the door.

"I'll get it." Merlin went to the door and opened it while still looking over his shoulder at us.

Two white men wearing the cheapest suits I had ever seen were standing there with their guns trained on Merlin. I gasped, and my knees buckled.

"What?" Merlin said, trying to make sense of my expression, and turned toward the door.

"Merlin Mills?" the taller of the two white men barked.

Merlin's head swung around with his mouth gaping open. "What the fuck?"

The man who was wearing a tie with Looney Tunes printed on it said, "Get on the ground and place your hands behind your back."

That's when I noticed the badges clipped to their waist.

Merlin laughed nervously. "Oh wow. We just got that little situation taken care of."

The guy with the tie charged Merlin and knocked him to the ground. The other guy kept his gun pointed at my husband.

"I said get on the ground." He put his knee in Merlin's back and pulled out a set of handcuffs.

"My captain is standing right there," Merlin said. "Ask her."

"Merlin Mills," the man said while cuffing him, "you're under arrest for attempted murder and arson."

My eyes damn near jumped out of my head. Just when I thought things could get no worse, they did.

47 GAVIN MILLS

"You ready to go?"

"Damn, don't be rushing me." I was aggravated. I never should have promised to meet up with the trick. Now I was mad at him and myself.

"I ain't rushing you, boo."

My stomach turned a little. I started to check him right there at the club, but I didn't want to draw any attention to us. "What's your name?" I was stalling, trying to figure out exactly what I was going to do.

"It's Wayne." He didn't ask for my name, and if he had, I would have most definitely told him a lie.

"All right, Wayne, let's bounce." I followed him out of the club.

"My car is right across the street." He walked off, and I got in my car to follow him. His arrogance reminded me of Merlin, and it made hotter than fish grease.

I followed him to his house, which wasn't too far from the club.

♥♥♥

"Do you want a drink?" Wayne asked as he left the living room and went into the kitchen.

"I could use a beer." I looked around his upscale apartment. From the looks of things, Wayne did okay for himself. His apartment didn't have that rundown look that mine had and that only made me madder. "I like your crib."

"Thanks," Wayne said as he handed me a beer. He took the top off his bottle and took a generous gulp. He appeared to be nervous as he walked over to the television and turned it on. I took a seat on the sofa. "So what do you do?"

"I'm a pharmacist."

I didn't expect that. I thought he was going to tell me that he was into interior decorating or some other gay shit like that. "Oh yeah, that's good."

He sat next to me on the sofa. I got nervous.

"You are really cute. Do you dance?" Wayne said as he scooted over closer to me.

"No, my talents are limited to pouring liquor."

"I wouldn't say that," Wayne said suggestively. He ran his finger up my thigh, and I had to suppress the urge to punch him in his fucking face.

"Hey, I've got to use your bathroom." I jumped up from the sofa.

"It's down the hall on the right, sweetie."

I took my time in the bathroom, looking through his medicine cabinet and underneath the sink. I was surprised to find a bottle of Rohypnol.

Rohypnol was the date rape drug. I flipped open the top and poured out two tablets into my hand. I was formulating a plan in my mind. When I agreed to go out with Wayne, I had every intention of letting him suck my dick for money. However, I didn't think I could even get my dick up for him, and that was a problem. I casually walked back into the living room. I needed to find a way to get the pills that I had stolen from the bathroom into his beer. "Can I get a glass of water?" I asked.

"Why you trying to kill your high with water?"

"Damn, can't a brother drink a little water just because he wants some?"

Wayne went into the kitchen and got my water, and I was able to slip the pills into his open bottle of beer.

I sipped at the water and drowned the beer waiting for the pills to take effect on Wayne.

"Can I go and get comfortable?" Wayne asked.

"Sure, do your thing. I'm going to go into the kitchen and make me a drink."

"That's cool, I'll be out in a minute." He was shaking his hips as if he were enticing me. Little did he know I had no interest in what he had to offer. I just wanted to roll his pockets and get the fuck out of there.

♥♥♥

I had settled onto the couch and was watching the news when Wayne came out of the bedroom. He was naked and appeared to be very proud of his tiny dick. I almost laughed when I saw him posed in the doorway.

"Where are your clothes, bro?"

"We both know what you're here for. Just tell me how much it's going to cost me."

"I don't get down like that. Put a towel around your ass. I get with men who I can connect with mentally," I lied.

"Ah, shit. I'm sorry. I just thought you were one of the fuck them and leave them type of brothers." He turned around and went back into the bathroom to get a towel.

I stifled a laugh. Poor fella was about to learn a valuable lesson in trust.

Wayne walked back into the room looking slightly embarrassed.

"Don't worry about it, man; I get this all the time. I like to know who I'm sleeping with so I take my time."

He picked up his beer and drank the rest of it. He did exactly what I wanted him to do. All I had to do was wait. He sat on the sofa with me, and we watched the news. However, I couldn't sit still when I heard the top story. My brother Merlin had been arrested for attempted arson. Under normal circumstances, I would have been happy that he was out of the way. I found it laughable that he would be charged for a crime that I'd committed.

The news was unexpected, but it came right on time. I needed to get to Cojo. This was my opportunity to get close to her, and I was going to seize the moment.

"Uh, Wayne, thanks for the beer. I've got to get going." I patted my pocket for my keys.

Wayne's face looked stricken. "So soon? What did I do?" His eyes were starting to droop, either from the effects of all the drinks he'd consumed in the club or the drugs in his beer. Either way, he was a winner. This little news excerpt saved him some money and a possible ass whipping at the same time.

"You're fine. I just realized I don't roll that way."

"Fuck you mean you don't roll that way." Wayne attempted to stand up but swayed on his feet.

"You don't want to do that, buddy. Sit your ass down and consider yourself lucky. Don't fuck with me again. Better yet, keep you and your little dick out of my club. You can't hang with the big dogs."

I pushed Wayne out of the way as I left his apartment laughing all the way. I had to get to Cojo—she needed me.

48 GINA MEADOWS

Whoever coined the phrase 'when it rains, it pours,' never lied. First the debacle with Ronald's wife, and now my son's arrest. It was too much to take. It had been over a week since it happened, and I still couldn't get my shit together. I called my job and took off another week. I was still having a hard time understanding why things were unraveling so fast.

The only thing I accomplished during the week was unpacking my shit. I didn't want Gavin coming in and seeing the boxes and asking me a bunch of questions. But strangely enough, I hadn't seen him. This only confirmed my suspicions that he'd moved. I was fine with that since I didn't want him living with me in the first place, but still…I wondered. I started to cry again. My heart felt as if it had a hole in it that would never heal, and I didn't know how I would be able to go on with my life.

The doorbell rang. This wasn't the first time that I ignored it, but it was the first time that I was standing near it when it rang.

"Gina, answer the motherfucking door," Ronald screamed. He pounded on the door like he meant to come through it.

I wasn't ready to see his sorry ass, so I went back into my bedroom, hoping he would go away.

"I'm not leaving, so you might as well open the fucking door."

I wondered what happened to the keys that I made sure he always had, but I guessed he got rid of them when he took on his new keys to his Alpharetta palace that I helped him to get. As far as I was concerned, he could kiss my ass.

There was silence on the other side of the door for a few minutes before I heard him fumbling with the lock.

When he finally got it opened, he pushed against the door like a superhero. In his arms, he had the boxes I had left at his house. "What the fuck is your problem? I've been trying to get in touch with you for days."

"What the fuck is *my* problem? Nigga, please. My problem is the wife whom you have posted up in a house that I paid the down payment on."

"I never told you that you would be living in that house."

As if that shit made it better. I wanted to beat his head in with an iron skillet. "You never said I wouldn't. Why the fuck do you think I gave you that money? You think I had it like that? Or you didn't care and you just wanted to fuck me one more time? You son of a bitch! You said that we were going to be a big, happy family." I started making my way to the kitchen. I was on the verge of tears, and I refused to let him see me cry.

"I never said I was going to marry you."

I talked louder so he could hear me from the kitchen. "I see. I just had it all wrong then?"

"Yeah, it was a big misunderstanding." He had the nerve to chuckle like it was a big-ass joke.

That was when I snapped. I grabbed the biggest knife that I had left in the kitchen. "So let me make sure I understand what you're telling me. You married a woman nearly half your age and moved her into a home that I helped you get, picked out the furniture, and did all the planning for. Is that what you came over here to talk to me about?"

"Well…I guess so, and to bring you these boxes you left at my house."

I'd heard enough. I rushed toward Ronald with the knife. I wanted him to hurt as bad as I did. I stabbed him as hard as I could. I was aiming for his heart, but only managed to cut him on the shoulder. I tried to hack it off.

"Bitch, are you crazy?" Ronald pushed me off of him clutching his arm.

He had hurt me for so long it was time he knew what it felt like.

"Yes, I'm crazy. You made me this way. How dare you treat me like a jump-off and move some other bitch into your house instead of me? Why would you marry her when I put in the work?" I tried to get close to him to cut him again. I realized that I was going to go to jail along with Merlin, but I didn't fucking care. Ronald had trampled on my feelings for the last time, and I felt like this was the only option.

"I can't help who I love."

No, he didn't just say that shit to me. I hit rewind in my mind, but I heard the same words. I let the knife hit the floor because it wouldn't matter how many times I stuck him, he would always come back with the same response. It was over, and the fat lady was singing.

I crumpled to the floor. My wails were so loud, I didn't even realize they were coming from me. I felt as if my heart had been broken into pieces. It wasn't the first time that Ronald had hurt me, but this was the ultimate. I now knew that all my years of work were in vain. And I didn't know if I could go on with that knowledge.

I got up from the floor and went into the bathroom. He was still in the kitchen trying to stop the blood flowing from his arm. I went straight to the medicine cabinet. I was done with this life that refused to treat me fair.

I wasn't a bad person. In fact, I had spent so many years in service to others, if this was the thanks that I got, I was past done. I didn't have anything else to live for. His children were grown, and I was going to wind up old and alone thanks to Ronald's trifling ass.

Ronald was still in the kitchen cussing, but he wasn't running up behind me to get even. I guessed that was a blessing. I wanted to leave this world, but I wanted to do it on my terms. I went through the cabinet looking for the most lethal combination I could find.

The best thing I could come up with was some bleach. As much as I hated myself, I wasn't trying to die this horrible death, writhing in pain. I wanted my death to be easier than my life had been. "Ain't this a bitch."

Dejected, I walked back into the living room. My front door was open and Ronald was nowhere in sight. I followed his trail of blood all the way out to the parking lot. He was gone. I went back inside.

Fear set in. I was going to jail. "Lord, I'm sorry, but he made me do it," I wailed as I once again fell to my knees on the floor.

"I talk a lot of shit, Lord, but I'm a coward." Once I realized that I didn't have anything in the house that would allow me to leave this world painlessly, other ideas started floating in my head. I was quite sure that Ronald was on his way to the hospital and with that, the police would probably be en route to my house. I picked up the phone.

"Tabatha, I need to come over; are you busy?"

"No, I'm just chilling. Do you want to order some pizza and veg out?"

"That sounds good to me; I'm on my way." I wasn't the least bit hungry, but I needed to get away from this house if only for a moment. Eventually, I knew I would have to face the music, but I wasn't ready to do so right now.

Tabatha said, "Stop and get some beer too."

I almost told her what was really going on, but I didn't want to admit to it over the phone. I had stuck Ronald pretty good. "I've got to get the fuck out of here." I rushed into my room and grabbed several outfits that would hold me for a couple of days. I wasn't sure if Ronald knew where Tabatha lived, but I wasn't taking any chances. If I were going to jail, I was going to go on my terms with my own lawyer and bond practically set before I got there.

I don't know what made me make the call, but I decided to call my daughter-in-law as I was leaving the house. "Hello, can I speak to Cojo, please?"

"Who is this?" Cojo asked.

"Gina."

"I'm sorry, Ms. Meadows; I didn't recognize your voice."

"It's okay, sweetie; we don't talk often."

I held the phone away from my face, shocked that she was being nice, but I realized Merlin must have told her about our talk. "I know I've been a real bitch to you, and I would like a second chance. Do you think we could try that?" I knew my time was running out, but I wanted to at least put that shit behind me.

"Are you serious? I would like nothing more. I could use another mother in my life."

"Mother? Wow, I would like to try if that's okay." I laughed.

"I would like to try, too."

♥♥♥

Tabatha looked me up and down and turned up her nose. "Girl, what the hell is the matter? You look like shit."

I pushed past Tabatha into her apartment. I didn't need her to remind me about how bad I looked. I was on the run and looking good was the least of my concerns.

"Shut the door, you're letting out all this air conditioning." I was trying to decide how much of the drama I was going to mention. I took a seat on the sofa as she shut and locked the door.

"You still haven't answered me. What the hell is going on?"

"Uh ..." I was still shaking and nervous as hell.

"Uh, hell. Spill it, girl. You know you can't keep shit to yourself for long."

She was wrong there. I had kept a lot of stuff from her over the years, and if I told her any of it, I would have to tell it all.

"It's all good. I just had to leave the house before I went stir crazy."

"Stop bullshitting me and tell me what's really going on."

I started to cry again, and she came over and wrapped her arms around me. She didn't pressure me to talk. I just rocked in her arms until I got my tears under control.

"It's kind of a long story," I said.

"Can I get the short abbreviated version?"

I pushed away and moved over to the other side of the sofa. She was watching Jerry Springer on television and for a second, I got caught up in all the drama on the set.

"Ronald finally agreed to move home. I've been meeting with builders to design a house for us, and we did the final walk-through last week. He said we were going to move in next week and be a happy family."

"Oh, wow. I know I should be happy for you, but you know how I feel about that man."

"I know. And as much as I hate to admit it, you were right."

"Say what?" She raised a brow.

"Yeah, he was lying to me all along."

"Oh, Lord. What did he do?" Her voice was concerned and angry at the same time.

"He said it was me. I jumped the gun. I was so excited about the new house and the new furniture that he let me pick out, that I went home right after the walk-through and started packing. I didn't realize that I'd accumulated so much shit. I had so many boxes, I couldn't even walk through my apartment. So I had the bright idea of taking some of the boxes to the house and dropping them off."

"Okay, that sounds reasonable."

"It sounded good to me, too. I went to the house, and the guard let me in because he knew me."

"Let me guess – the house is in his name only."

"Yeah, but Ronald said it was because of my credit. I put down the initial deposit, but that was it. Anyway, I get to the house and the door is unlocked because the furniture people were still delivering furniture. I go in and start dropping boxes, and this heifer I had never seen before comes out of the kitchen. I thought she was someone whom Ronald hired to decorate."

"Oh, shit."

"You can say that again. I asked who she was, and she told me she was Ronald's wife."

"Double shit."

"I've never been so embarrassed in my life. I hightailed it out of there. I didn't even have the strength to get back my boxes. I told her to keep the shit."

"Shit."

"You said that."

"Damn, I don't know what to say. I knew the motherfucker was lowdown, but even I didn't think he was that low."

"Well, go on and say it," I said.

"Say what?"

"I told you so."

"Sweetie, I'm not that insensitive."

She surprised me. She always said she would be the first person to say I told you so when Ronald tired of me, and that was why I hesitated to even tell her about it. She moved closer to me.

I said, "Thanks. Needless to say I've been pretty much a basket case all week."

"That is one dirty son of a bitch. Have you spoken with the bastard?"

"He showed up at my house today with my boxes and let me tell you, it wasn't pretty."

"I'll bet. If it were me, I would have chopped off his dick," she said, laughing.

"I didn't get his dick, but I wore the fuck out of his arm."

Tabatha pushed me away. "What did you say?" She looked at me real strangely as if she just noticed the blood splatter on my shoulder and arm.

I could see tears welling up in her eyes. "You heard me. I asked him why, and he started telling me some lame-ass shit, and I grabbed the biggest knife I could find, and I swung at him."

"Oh God!" She fell back against the sofa as if I had stabbed her too.

"I got his ass good, too, but now I'm afraid that I'll go to jail."

"Oh no, boo. This can't be happening. Why did you even let his sorry ass in?"

"I didn't let him in; he still had the key. Besides, I wanted him to look me in my face and tell me what he'd done. If he didn't want me, why wouldn't he just let me go?"
Why would he take me shopping to furnish a house for the next bitch?"

"That is so crazy. He can't just play with your heart like that." She shook her head.

"He doesn't care. You've told me that for years, but I was too much in love to listen to you. I always thought that I would be the one he married, and I just snapped."

"Sweetie, you have to go home. If Ronald went to the cops, and you've left the scene, it will only make you look more guilty. If you go home and the police come, plead temporary insanity. Once you tell them all the shit he's put you through, I'm sure no jury will convict you."

"I can't go to jail! I'm not about to fight off some butch-ass bitch and wind up spending the rest of my life behind bars."

"Relax, honey; they'll just arrest you, and then you get arraigned. Since you have no priors, they will give you bail. I'll be waiting to post bail, then we get you the best lawyer whom we can afford to go to court with you."

"We?"

"Girl, you're like a sister to me. Do you think I would let you go through this by yourself?"

"Thanks, Tabatha. I know I don't deserve it, but I'm glad you're my friend."

"Go home and call me when you get your first phone call." Tabatha made a lot of sense.

As much as I didn't want to, I drove home.

49 COJO MILLS

I hadn't heard much from Merlin since his arrest the week before, and it was taking its toll on me. I knew that he was trying to protect me, but the lack of information was driving me insane. I needed to know what was going on, but the cops refused to speak with me about his case. I hired an attorney, but thus far, he hadn't returned my calls.

I called his attorney once again to get an update.

"Mosby Law Group."

"Yes, I would like to speak with Attorney Ricardo Mosby."

"Ma'am, he's not in the office at the moment, but I do expect him. Would you like to leave a message?"

"Yes, would you please tell him that Cojo Mills called again. I really would like an update on my husband's case."

"I'll give him the message."

I hung up the phone, frustrated. I felt a pain deep down in my soul, and I knew that the only way to fix it was to have my husband home with me.

The phone had been ringing off the hook since the news started broadcasting his arrest, but none of the calls were from my husband.

I knew this stress wasn't good for our baby, but I didn't know what else to do but worry and cry. This wasn't like the first time that he was led out of the house in handcuffs—this was serious. The officers said murder and arson!

For the life of me, I couldn't understand why they would accuse my mild-mannered husband of such heinous crimes. I was thankful my mother was out of the country, or I would suspect she'd be calling too. The most surprising phone call was from Gina. I couldn't tell her anything about Merlin, but she offered to be my support system while he was gone.

I was pacing the living room floor crying when the doorbell rang. I rushed to it and yanked open the door. I was so distraught I didn't even bother to check to see who was on the other side of the door. I gasped when I saw who was standing there. "Merlin?"

"Try again, sweetheart." Gavin wore a sickening grin on his face.

He was the last person that I wanted to see, especially since I was in such a vulnerable state of mind.

"What are you doing here? Didn't Merlin tell you to stay the fuck away from us?" I was mad, but I couldn't deny the sexual attraction that I felt just looking at his wonderful body.

"I know, and under normal circumstances I would have stayed away, but I was concerned about how you were holding up."

I stepped back from the door. I didn't expect Gavin to even care about his brother after all the things that Merlin had told me.

Gavin stepped into the apartment and closed the door behind him. I looked at him suspiciously. Today, he was different. He didn't have the arrogant swagger. He actually acted as if he cared about me and Merlin. Ever since he'd come into our lives, it had been nothing but turmoil. I needed my life to get back on an even keel.

"When I first saw this on the news, I wanted to rush over here to make sure you were okay, but I wasn't sure how you would react. I certainly didn't want you to think I was stalking you or something crazy like that."

"Oh God." Fresh tears rolled down my face. I didn't like the fact that our dirty laundry was being viewed on television.

Gavin rushed toward me and took me in his arms. Instinctively, I tensed up, but I couldn't hold on to that because it felt good to be in his arms. As much as I wanted to deny it, I was sexually attracted to Gavin. He continued to hold me in his arms and, for a minute, I relaxed and allowed him to comfort me. His hot breath against my neck excited me. It took me several minutes to remember that he wasn't my husband, and his arms should not be around me.

I pulled away. "I appreciate your stopping by but Gavin, you need to leave. When Merlin comes home, he won't be happy to know you've been here."

"Cojo, he may not be coming home."

A low moan escaped my lips. "Merlin is innocent," I tried saying it with conviction but my delivery was weak.

"Are you sure? The police wouldn't have arrested him if they didn't feel as if they had a good case against him. Besides, he's still in there. That has to mean something."

I was pacing the floor. Gavin was saying the things that I'd been thinking but was too afraid to say out loud. What would I do if they actually kept my husband in jail?

"Why are you here?" I demanded.

"I came for you. Regardless of whether or not you're ready to accept this, we connected. I don't want my brother to spoil another relationship for me."

I looked at him as if he'd lost his ignorant ass mind. "What are you talking about?"

"This is not the first relationship that I've had that my brother ruined. He killed my first girlfriend and fingered me in the scheme, and I wound up doing time?"

"Huh?" I was so confused.

"My first girlfriend. He killed her and managed to blame me. Thanks to him and Gina I did seven years, but I still have mad love for my brother."

"Wait, I don't understand. He said that you blamed him, and he got arrested." I was feeling dizzy, so I sat down on the sofa.

"Of course he would tell you that. It wasn't me; it was really him. He has a violent temper. Of course, you know that, don't you?"

"He had every right to be mad—I slept with you!"

"So why did he take it out on you and not me?" He sat back on the sofa with a smug smirk on his face.

I was so confused I didn't know what to think. Suddenly, I wasn't so sure of my convictions that Merlin was innocent. I remembered the night when he left the house in the middle of the night and came home with blood on his clothes and refused to speak about it.

Gavin scooted over next to me. "Every story has two sides. He got to tell you his; it's about time you heard mine."

He planted a seed, and I had enough water at my disposal to make it grow.

"Cojo, I think we belong together, and this might be God's way of making sure it happens."

I jumped up off the sofa. Gavin was talking some bullshit. How in the world was I going to abandon my relationship with Merlin and take up with his brother?

Gavin was relentless. "Merlin has lied to you, Cojo. I know my brother. He probably tried to blame me for all the shit he's done over the years, but it isn't true."

"I need to lie down." I left the living room and went into the master bedroom. My mind was on overload, and I didn't know what to believe. I just needed to be by myself so I could think.

"I don't think that you should be alone. Can I stay here until we know more about Merlin's case?"

"I don't care." I wasn't thinking straight. Gavin had me thinking that I didn't know my husband at all.

"I'm going to go and get us something to eat. I'll be back." He followed me into the bedroom and kissed me on the forehead. There was nothing sexual in the kiss.

"Let me hold your key so I won't have to disturb you when I come back." Robotically, I reached into my bag and pulled out my key. Technically, the lights were on, but I wasn't home. I passed the key to Gavin and climbed into the bed with my clothes still on.

"Okay." My mind had taken a vacation while I thought about my relationship with my husband. Who was this man who I married? At this point, I was having second thoughts about having a child at all.

♥♥♥

I'm not sure when Gavin came back. I had been sleeping off and on since he left, but I felt him when he climbed into the bed with me. At first, I thought he was Merlin, but I recognized Gavin's distinctive smell. My body tensed as Gavin eased up behind me.

"Gavin, stop." I didn't have the energy, or if I were honest, the desire to fight him.

"I just want to comfort you."

"This is wrong. The first time was a mistake, but if we do it again, it's intentional," I said.

"Well, I'm going to keep it one hundred with you. Getting with you again is definitely intentional with me. I know we're destined to be together so I'm not even going to lie." His words shocked me, and I turned around in his embrace.

"What do you mean?" I asked.

"My life is not worth living without you in it."

Part of me was flattered, but the rest of me was scared as hell. His lips dipped dangerously close to mine, and for a second or two, I allowed myself to dwell in the fantasy.

I was tired and didn't try to fight him. Truth be told, I wanted another opportunity to be with Gavin, but I didn't know how to admit it. Merlin's arrest offered the perfect opportunity.

As Gavin peeled off my clothes, I tried to pretend as if I were asleep, but I was aware of everything that was going on around me. I stifled a moan when he took my extended nipple into his mouth.

"I want you so badly," Gavin whispered as he positioned himself to enter me. I kept my eyes closed, as if this would absolve me of committing adultery a second time with my husband's brother. I knew that I was dead wrong, but I couldn't stop myself. Gavin was right; we did connect in a way that Merlin and I never did.

He spread my legs and aligned his body with mine. Without fanfare, he inserted his dick into my vagina, and I couldn't believe the intensity of the feeling that I felt when he gently rocked his dick into me. The feeling was intense. There was no need for words. I was already into the moment the second he had taken off my clothes. I never felt so close to a man in my entire life. We rocked this way for twenty minutes before he busted a nut inside of me.

"Damn, that was amazing," the words spilled out of my mouth without my permission, but I could tell by Gavin's smile it was what he wanted to hear.

50 COJO MILLS

My phone rang. "Cojo, I really need to speak with you. Are you alone?" Braxton, my husband's closest friend, said from the other end of the line.

"Hey, Braxton," I was trying to wake up. Gavin and I had sex so many times, I was still feeling the afterglow.

"I drove by your house a while ago. I thought I saw Gavin's car. Has he been over there?"

Immediately, I began to feel nervous. This was not how I expected our conversation to go.

"Uh…he came over to see if he could do anything while Merlin was locked up." I knew this was a piss poor excuse, but I couldn't think that fast.

"Cojo, be careful; there is a lot about Gavin that you probably don't even know about."

How would he know? I thought to myself.

"Well, according to Gavin, there are a lot of things that I don't know about Merlin."

I heard Gavin draw in a sharp breath, and I felt as if I were incriminating myself.

"Don't get caught up in his lies; he is a born con-man. He's good at deceiving folks."

I was tired of the lies, and since I couldn't speak to Merlin directly, I needed to have some answers. I crawled out of bed and walked out of the bedroom. Gavin didn't even move.

"Braxton, if you know so much, could you please tell me what's going on?"

"Cojo, normally I would mind my fucking business, but this shit is scaring me. A couple of months ago, I saw Merlin's car and followed it. He had this girl in the car so I took off. I didn't want to get caught up in no shit if you know what I mean. Well, that house he went in was the same house as the girl who was killed. Of course, I freaked when I realized it. I called Merlin and asked him what the fuck was going on. He told me it was Gavin driving the car and not him. I didn't even know Gavin was back. I'm telling you that dude is bad news."

I was nervous as hell. I can't believe I let him trick me twice. "Braxton, you have to go to the police and tell them what you told me. This might be what we need to get Merlin out of jail."

"Okay, I'll go by the station now. Don't forget what I said about Gavin; believe me when I say it—he's dangerous."

I was shaking with both fear and anger when I hung up the phone. I had to get Gavin out of my apartment, and I had to do it without him being the wiser about my telephone call. I walked back into the bedroom and shook Gavin's leg.

"Huh?"

"You have to get up and get dressed," I hissed as I started grabbing my clothes off the floor and putting them on. I felt ashamed of my nakedness.

"Why, what's going on?"

I thought fast. "Gina just called. She's on her way over here."

Gavin jumped up. "Shit, what does she want?" He swung his legs over the side of the bed and started looking for his clothes.

"I forgot I told her she could go to the doctor's with me, and then we're going shopping." I was trying to buy myself some time.

Gavin stopped dressing and my heart practically stopped.

"Ain't that special. Since when did you two become so close?"

I bit my lip to keep from screaming in frustration. I didn't want to talk to him. I wanted him out of my house. "I think it's the baby and Merlin being away and all…"

"Away? That nigger ain't away, sweetheart. He's in jail," Gavin said, laughing.

I wanted to punch him in his nut sack, but I started making the bed while he still sat on it.

"Gavin, please. I don't want no shit with Gina right now. Can we have this discussion later?"

"All right. I just want you to know I'm not going to tolerate her meddling in our affairs. I have firsthand knowledge of her childrearing capabilities, and she won't be using them on no child of mine."

My heart was beating so loudly I was afraid he was going to hear it. I had made the worst mistake ever, and it was going to take a miracle to fix it.

Gavin finished getting dressed and I ushered him to the door.

"I'll be back later," he promised as he leaned in to kiss me.

I turned my head and allowed him to kiss me on the cheek. Instead of the magnetic pull that I'd experienced the night before, I felt revulsion at both him and myself.

"Call first, okay?" I pushed him out the door and shut it. I breathed a sigh of relief, but immediately sucked it back in as I yanked open the door and ran outside.

"Gavin, wait!"

He turned around. "Changed your mind, beautiful?"

"My keys. I need my keys."

"Oh, yeah. I forgot all about those. I left them on the coffee table next to the phone."

I backed up just in case he wanted to give me another kiss in broad daylight.

"Great, thanks." I hurried back inside and closed the door. I felt like I had dodged a bullet for the moment, but I wasn't so sure I could do it again.

I went back into the bedroom and stripped the sheets off the bed with tears streaming down my face. I had betrayed the man I loved for some bullshit. I didn't deserve his love. I tore at my clothes and threw them in a heap on the floor. I couldn't wait to wash the stench of Gavin off my body.

♥♥♥

The waiting room at the doctor's office was crowded. If I didn't want to know the results as bad as I did, I might have left, but I took a seat and pulled a novel from my purse and started to read. I was really trying not to dwell on what Braxton said to me. I just hoped that he followed through and went to the police, and was discreet when he spoke to Merlin about it. Braxton didn't owe me a thing. He was more Merlin's friend than mine, but I hoped that he had enough sense to know that telling him about seeing Gavin at my house would destroy Merlin.

"Cojo Mills?" I looked up, surprised to have been called so quickly.

"I'm here." I looked around the waiting room and cringed from the hateful glares I received. I wanted to explain that I was only there to get results and that I wouldn't be long, but in reality, I didn't owe them nothing. It was just my conscience eating at me.

"Come this way," a nurse instructed.

"Can I go to the bathroom first?" I had to go the moment I stood up.

The nurse glanced at her watch. "Of course." She smiled at me as she directed me to the bathroom. "The doctor will see you in his office."

My nerves started to get the best of me again. Part of me wanted to walk right out of the office and let the chips fall where they may. Regardless of the outcome, I wasn't going to abort the baby, so what difference does it make?

"Because you owe it to Merlin," I said softly.

He deserved to know, and so did our unborn child. As much as I hated to think about Gavin as the father, I would tell him if the results indicated that he was the dad. I would even allow him to have a small portion of my child's life, but I would fight him like a banshee if he attempted to get any form of custody.

I finished up in the bathroom and went into the doctor's office to wait for him. "I wish doctors cared enough about our time as we have to care about theirs." I started to read my book again and before I knew it, I was asleep.

"Mrs. Mills?" This time it was a male voice that was interrupting my nap.

I wiped the drool that had seeped out of my mouth and sat up in my seat. "I'm sorry," I offered the apology, but what I really wanted to say was that I wouldn't have fallen asleep if he'd scheduled his time better and not had me wait so long.

"There's no need to apologize. I'm sorry for the delay, but we've had a couple of emergencies today."

He must have been reading my mind, because I had half a mind to tell him he couldn't just let a pregnant woman sit.

"Can I go to the bathroom?"

"Sure, there is one right through that door. I'll be here waiting for you."

I was feeling a little self-conscious because he knew the results of my test and I didn't.

Does he think I'm a whore because I had to get a test to find out who my baby's daddy was? I dismissed the thought as I flushed the toilet. He would get paid regardless of who the father of my child was. I finished using the bathroom and hurried back to the office.

"Your husband won't be joining you today?" I couldn't tell if he were being condescending, and it made me nervous all over again. Had he seen Merlin on the news?

"No, he couldn't get away from work. Can we do this before I have to go to the bathroom again?"

He nodded his head and opened the file that he had on his desk. After a moment of study, he said, "Your husband...is the father." He paused for dramatic effect. I could have done without his Maury-like delivery.

"Are you sure?"

"As sure as we can be with identical twins."

I jumped up and ran to the door. I couldn't wait to see Merlin and tell him the good news. "Are you done with me?"

"Yes, I will see you next month. Take care of yourself and don't overdo it."

"I won't, Doctor, and thanks." I snatched open the door and practically danced all the way to the parking lot. I rummaged through my purse to find my keys and my phone, but I kept pulling up everything else.

I was going to call Braxton to see if he had any luck in talking with Detective Adams. I was doing my happy dance, and all the stress that I'd been carrying on my shoulders felt as if it had been lifted.

"Shit." A hand was placed rudely over my mouth, and I was dragged away from my car kicking and struggling to scream.

51 MERLIN MILLS

"Man, I can't thank you enough for speaking up on my behalf. Those cops are a trip. I kept telling them I didn't do anything, and they just weren't listening."

"Don't sweat it, man. You know how we roll," Braxton said as he gave me dap and a hug.

I was so happy and grateful to be free, but I was also angry as hell at my brother. Finding out that I spent the last week in jail because of something my brother may have done sapped the last bit of love I had for him right out of my heart. "Can I use your phone? I want to call Cojo."

Braxton handed me his phone, and I tried her four times in a row but it kept going to voicemail. Cojo didn't normally turn her phone off, so I was beginning to get worried. I sent her a text just in case she didn't recognize Braxton's number.

"Did you get her?"

"No, it's going straight to voicemail, and she's not picking up the house phone either."

"Maybe she went to the doctors," Braxton said hopefully.

"Yeah, maybe she did. Can you drop me off at the house just in case she's there?"

"Sure thing."

I dialed my mother. I needed to know if she knew where Gavin was. The police wanted to question him, and I intended to help them as much as I could to find him.

"Hey, Mom. Just wanted to let you know I'm out. My boy Braxton saved me."

Gina said, "Are you okay? I was sick with worry."

"I'm fine. It was a big misunderstanding. I'm on my way home, but I can't get in touch with Cojo. Have you heard from her?"

"Yes, we had a nice conversation, and I'm looking forward to spending time with her. I have something to tell you; do you think you could drop by my house?"

I was torn. I wanted to find out what was up with Cojo, but I was also curious as to why my mother wanted to see me. Since we were just rebuilding our relationship, I thought it was important that I go over there.

"Okay, I can come over there, but I can't stay long. I want to see Cojo."

"It won't take long." She sounded strange, but I quickly dismissed the thought. We hadn't been close in years and I didn't know her like I used to know her.

"I'm on my way."

"If you get here and the police are here, keep on going. I don't want you to get in any more trouble."

"Police? What are you talking about?" I paused. "It's Gavin, isn't it? He's done it again."

"I'll explain when you get here." She hung up the phone without giving me any more details.

"Everything okay?" Braxton asked.

"I have to go by my mom's house before I go home. Can you drop me off? She was talking all crazy. I hope she ain't drunk."

"Sure, I'll swing by there. Do you want me to wait on you?"

"Nah, I'll get her to drop me off if I need to, or get Cojo to pick me up when I find her." I tried to call Cojo again to let her know I needed to stop by my mother's house, but her phone was still going straight to voicemail. I was having a very bad feeling.

"Damn, where is she?"

52 GINA MEADOWS

I was getting my affairs in order, and seeing Merlin was the last thing I needed to do before I went to jail. His knock on the door frightened me. I snuck up to the door and peered through the peephole. When I saw it was Merlin, I released the breath I was holding.

"Hey," he said when I opened the door.

"Hi, come on in." I was trying to think of the best way to tell him all that had happened with his father. I needed for him to know the truth before he read about it in the papers or saw it on television. Since I had been excluded from Merlin's life for so long, I didn't know how he felt about his father and how he would react.

"Did you get the note I left you about Gavin? I left it on your door but never heard back from you."

"Son, I got it, but things have been a little crazy for me. I haven't seen Gavin in a while. I think he moved out."

"Shit. Figures."

"What do you want with that fool?"

"Trust and believe, I could care less about Gavin, but several things have happened that I'm sure you're not aware of. Gavin is the reason I was in jail. He tried to set me up again."

Gina's eyes widened. "Please tell me he isn't responsible for that girl getting hurt in the fire? I knew you couldn't have anything to do with that."

"If he didn't do it, he knows more about that girl than I do. I never met her. The police are going to want to question him."

"I want to hear about this. I really do, but I need to tell you something else first. It's about your father…"

There was an urgent knock on the door. It startled both of us. Merlin started toward the door.

"Merlin, wait!"

He peered through the peephole. "It's the police." There were two officers, one black and one white.

"Merlin, wait before you answer the door; there is something that I have to tell you."

The police knocked again, this time more violently.

"What is it?" Merlin asked.

"I stabbed your father and that's probably the police here to arrest me."

He staggered, and I lunged to catch him.

"You did what?"

I pushed Merlin aside and opened the door. I was ready to face my consequences.

"Yes," I said as I unlocked the door. Part of me was relieved that I could get this behind me, but the other half was scared as shit that I was going to spend the rest of my life behind bars.

53 MERLIN MILLS

My mind was melting down. I had just received too much information in too short an amount of time. First, I learned that Gavin set me up again, and that my mother stabbed my dad. "What the fuck?"

I watched my mother open the door and two armed officers enter her apartment. My heart sank. Instinctively, I wanted to protect Gina, but I didn't know how.

"Can I help you?" my mother asked.

Even if she had been a bitch over the last ten years, she was still the only one who showed me love as I was growing up, and the thought of her going to jail made my head hurt. I thought I was going to die in jail; it would be worse for Gina.

"Good afternoon. We are here looking for Gavin Mills."

She inhaled deeply, and we both visibly relaxed. Gina made eye contact, and I nodded back to her.

I could not wait to hear why she stabbed my father and if he were still alive.

"He doesn't stay here anymore. I haven't seen him in a couple of weeks."

"Do you have any idea where we can find him?" the black cop asked.

"His moving in was a temporary situation that neither of us was happy about, so I don't know where he would be."

"I see. Do you have any way to contact him?"

The black officer was busy looking around my mother's apartment, and didn't appear to be following the conversation. He kept staring at me. Finally, he pulled out a picture. "You look very much like the person we're looking for."

Shit, the last thing I needed was to be dragged into Gavin's bullshit again. I reached into my back pocket to pull out my wallet, and the officer immediately pulled out his gun. "Wait, hold up. I was just reaching for my wallet. Gavin is my twin brother. I think I know why you're here, and I'm not the one you're looking for. I can show you my license if you want to see it."

"Show me, nice and easy."

He didn't lower his gun until he'd read my name off my license. He gave it back to me slowly. "Do you know where your brother is?"

"I actually came over here today to ask my mother where he was." That wasn't the only reason that I was here, but it worked so I was sticking to it.

My mother said, "Could somebody tell me what's really going on with Gavin?"

The black officer said, "We're not at liberty to discuss it with you, but we need to speak to him as soon as possible."

"Mom, I can explain everything once they're gone."

All eyes turned to me.

"Oh really?" the white cop said.

"Yeah." I retold the story that Braxton told to me and the detectives, and I didn't feel bad.

The black cop turned to my mother. "Mind if I use your phone to call the station to confirm this?"

♥♥♥

When he hung up, he said, "You were right. We did get eyewitness confirmation from your friend. Detectives Adams and Lyle are investigating, and since this isn't the first time that Gavin has been charged with violent crimes against women, the department has given the matter high priority."

I said, "I think you should. I don't think my brother is stable. Recently, he seems to have become obsessed with my wife. He tricked her into believing he was me, and they had sex. Since then, he's been hanging around our house stalking her." It pained me to admit this in front of the officers and my mother.

"Merlin, no! Please tell me that isn't true," Gina cried.

"Sorry, Mom. That's why I've been trying to get in touch with Gavin since the day I left you the note."

Gina hung her head and said, "He's been asking me questions about your wife. I feel so bad for talking to him about her."

The officers looked confused as if we had given them more information than they came to collect.

"Where is your wife now? Do you think she knows where we can find him?"

"I don't know where she is. I haven't been able to reach her since I was released from jail. I just hope Gavin doesn't have something to do with it."

"We have a description of his car. Do you happen to remember the license plate?"

"He's driving my old car. It's a 2002 Malibu. Brown, with a dent on the passenger side. The plate number is JE619."

"I'll call in the APB," the white cop said.

"Wait, there may be another way to find him. I have OnStar in that car. All we need to do is call them, and they will tell us where the car is. As long as he's near the car, we'll find him. Officer, I'm so afraid that he may have my wife. She always answers her phone and–"

"Calm down, Mr. Mills. If he has her, we'll find him."

Gina said, "I just don't understand that boy. Merlin, I'm so sorry for not doing more to protect you from him."

"It's not your fault, Mother. Perhaps if our dad had been around more, things would have been different."

It appeared as if my mother went into a trance or something because her eyes got this blank stare. She swayed before me, and I moved closer to support her.

"We found the car," the black officer said after getting off the phone with OnStar.

"Can we come with you? My wife is expecting a baby."

He nodded. "That is totally against regulations, but if you just happened to follow us, well, there's no law against that." He smiled.

I quickly grabbed my mother's hand and followed the officers out the door.

As we were buckling up our seatbelts, I said a prayer. "Lord, if he has her, please make sure she is all right."

"Amen," my mother replied and looked at me. "Why am I feeling like I did when I was pregnant?"

"What do you mean?"

"I'm feeling..." she rolled her window down "...morning sickness. I feel like I'm about to throw up."

I shrugged. "Probably because you've been doing the nasty. Imagine you being pregnant at your age."

"Yeah, imagine that. I'm fucking forty years old and now this!" She held her stomach. "And I haven't been doing the nasty with anyone in a long time."

"Then, you're not having morning sickness. It's probably just stress."

She threw up in my lap.

54 GAVIN MILLS

Cojo came out of the doctor's office practically dancing. That could only mean one thing. I wasn't the father. I knew she was up to something when she shooed me out of the house so fast. The giveaway was when she mentioned Gina. I knew for a fact that they didn't roll like that, so I followed her.

I watched as she danced her way to her car as if she didn't have a care in the world. I wanted to teach the bitch a lesson. I leaped from my car and snuck up behind her.

After making sure no one was looking, I put my hand over her mouth and dragged her, kicking ferociously, to my car. I didn't know what I was going to do once I got her there, but I knew that I needed to speak with her and plead my case. Roughly, I pushed her into the back seat and climbed in behind her.

Cojo clutched her stomach protectively. "What the hell do you think you're doing?" she yelled. "You had better let me the fuck go."

I locked the doors. "Not until I've had a chance to talk to you."

She came at me like a banshee, scratching and kicking. I wasn't prepared for her attack. She was punching me like a man. I punched her back and knocked her out. I instantly regretted hitting her so hard.

"Damn, baby, I didn't mean to hit you," I whispered in her ear before I got into the front seat and took off. I didn't know how long she was going to be out so I drove to the nearest motel, the Alamo, and got a room.

I carried her into the room after I secured the key. She was still out as I laid her on the bed. While she dozed, I got some duct tape from my trunk and taped her wrists to the wrought iron headboard. For good measure, I placed a piece across her mouth to keep her quiet.

Her eye was swelling up. I went into the bathroom and looked at my reflection. I had a railroad track type scratch down both sides of my face. It immediately made me mad. Part of me wanted to go back into the bedroom, strip her clothes off, and fuck her into compliance. But I wasn't trying to make her madder. I only wanted to talk some sense into her about the baby, and to tell her how much I loved her. I would tell her about the strip club and how much I was making, and even offer to give it up if she would agree to be my wife. I was going to remind her about how incredible the sex was and promise more of it. My eyes wandered again to my face, and something inside me snapped.

"How dare she do this to me?" I rushed back into the bedroom and began to hit her repeatedly. I was in a zone. Each time I swung my hand, I wasn't seeing Cojo's face. Instead, I saw the faces of my father, Merlin and Gina.

Cojo woke up and started to fight back as best she could with her hands bound. I was out of control, but could do nothing to rein myself back in.

"Settle down, bitch," I snarled. I was still mad at her, but I remembered the baby.

She was crying profusely. Her eyes looked like two pee holes in the snow. She continued bucking against the bed despite my warnings to calm down.

"Are you trying to hurt our baby?" I demanded.

A tranquil feeling came over me. I was ready to convince her that I was a better man than my brother. She stopped bucking immediately.

I reached over and rubbed the slight bulge that she was developing. "Pregnant women are so sexy in the early months." I was trying to let her know that I would be supportive of her gaining weight. I unbuttoned the first two buttons of her blouse. She started to cry again, and this made me upset.

With an open hand, I smacked her across the face. "What the hell you crying for?" This was so unlike earlier when I held her. She didn't pull away then so she shouldn't be pulling away now. She continued to cry. I didn't understand why she was acting so strangely.

"Hell, if anyone should be mad, it should be me. Look what you did to my face. How am I going to explain this shit?"

Her tears stopped. She followed my every move with dilated eyes.

"Did I scare you? Is that what's wrong with you?"

She didn't acknowledge me right away, but after a few seconds, she nodded her head, and something in her demure movement softened my heart, and my anger dissipated. I removed the tape from her mouth.

"I didn't mean to scare you and I'm sorry you made me hit you, but you confused me when you attacked me. I just needed to speak with you alone. I went back by the house and you weren't there. Do you know how badly I want to touch you, taste you, feel you?"

Her eyes got wider.

"You know I heard you on the phone talking shit to Braxton. You thought I was asleep, but I got you. You ain't the only one who can pretend and shit. Braxton don't know shit about me. I should have fucked his ass up a long time ago."

"I...uh..."

"Gina said you were a witch. Did you cast a spell on me? I think you did, you little bitch. I haven't been able to get you outta my mind since the first time I fucked you. Then last night, you just gave it to me like it was government cheese. Can't fault a nigger for taking free shit, can you?"

"You're crazy," Cojo said as she spat at me.

I slapped her again. "I think you like it rough. Is that what turns you on, Cojo? A punch or two get you feeling slushy inside? Is that what I got to do to make you mine?"

Cojo moaned loudly swinging her head from side to side. "I'm already married," she whispered.

This was not what I wanted to hear from her. I slapped myself upside the head several times. "Stop saying that. My brother is gone, don't you get it? He won't be coming back for a long time."

"That's not true."

"How do you know?" I yelled. I was so close to her nose, I could have bitten it off. I didn't know why she was still fighting with me when we could have been making sweet love.

"I want to let you go, but you've got to promise me that you're going to behave."

She just looked at me as if I were speaking a different language.

"Did you hear what I just said?" I raised my voice because I was getting tired of this whole episode. I wasn't used to having to woo women. Normally, women flocked to me. This was the first time that I actually cared enough to put my best foot forward. Cojo shook her head, and I took that to mean she would cooperate. I removed the tape from one wrist.

"Ouch," she yelled.

"I done told you, you need to be quiet."

She nodded her head again. I was about to release her other hand, but she hadn't proven to me that she was going to fully cooperate with me yet.

Cojo said, "What do you want?"

"That's easy. I want you, and if you're honest with yourself, you would realize that you want me too. I want to wake up to you every day. After last night, I know you love me." I was prepared for her initial denial, but it didn't come.

"What about your brother? Are we gonna just let him rot away in jail, pretend like he doesn't exist?"

"My brother? Fuck my brother. This isn't about him and me—it's about us. We connected, and you know we did."

She really pissed me off when she brought my brother in the room. I was sick and tired of people bringing my brother into my life. I had spent the last seven years without a care in the world for him, and now, all of a sudden, he was in practically every conversation that I had, and I was done. I had half a mind to beat her ass to death just for mentioning him.

"So what did the doctor say?" I needed to change the subject so I could figure out a way to convince her that I was the man of her dreams and not my brother.

She switched gears on me catching me off guard. "How do you intend to support me and a baby?"

I started to get mad all over again. Everyone, including my mother, was focused on me working a nine-to-five. Why couldn't they understand that a nine-to-five job wasn't for me?

"There are other ways to support a family beside a nine-to-five."

"Oh really? Name one."

"I could go into business for myself." I just pulled that answer out my ass. She was not ready for the strip club.

"Doing what?" She had me there.

When I mentioned going into business, I was talking about going back to my old ways of robbing and stealing. "That ain't none of your business. I just want to know if you want to be with me or my brother?"

"I know the truth now; I want to be with my husband."

I jumped up from the bed as my blood pressure rose. This was just another slap in the face. As much as I loved her, I couldn't allow my brother to walk into the sunshine with the love of his life. That just wasn't going to happen.

As I approached the bed to put Ms. Smarty Pants out of her misery, the door to my hotel room burst open. The noise startled both of us. Cojo started screaming as I backed up against the wall trying to find out what I was dealing with.

"Police, get down on the floor."

Son of a bitch, how did they find me? I slowly lowered myself onto the floor as my mind started thinking of a plausible excuse for being in a hotel room with my brother's wife bound to the bed.

"What's going on here? What seems to be the problem?" I asked as my hands were yanked hard behind my back and handcuffs were applied. Another officer rushed over to Cojo, who was crying again.

"Gavin Mills, you are under arrest. You have the…"

I tuned the officer out. I knew my rights, so I didn't have to hear them again. I was more concerned about how Cojo was going to spin this. She had the ability to hang my ass out to dry.

"Cojo, tell them we was just playing, baby," I pleaded, but she wouldn't even look at me.

I was hauled to my feet and led outside. I tried to hold my head up like it was just another day at the office, until I saw my brother and Gina standing next to the police car. Gina appeared to be holding Merlin back. I faltered, but the officer pushed me forward.

"It's not what it looks like, man. She wanted it. She was begging for it."

"What about my wife, is she in there?" Merlin avoided looking at me.

The officer replied, "Yeah, she's inside."

He tried to break free, but the officer stopped him.

"You can't go in there yet. We'll bring her out when the paramedics get here."

"What did he do to her? Oh my God, she's pregnant."

They were talking all around me as if I weren't even there.

"It's my baby, motherfucker. I can't help it if she likes my dick better than yours."

Merlin lunged forward, his face twisted in a scowl. The officer used my cuffs to spin me out of the way, cutting off my circulation.

"Watch these fucking cuffs!"

"I would watch my mouth if I were you. If there weren't cameras here, I would let him get you, you sick son of a bitch," the officer growled in my ear.

"What is wrong with you?" Gina shouted.

I heard the loathing in her tone, and it hurt. I wanted to hurt her as badly as she hurt me. "Oh, come on, Mother. You above anyone else knows what it's like to be in love with someone who doesn't love you. Don't you?"

If she responded, I didn't get to hear it as I was rudely shoved into the back seat of the police car.

Gina rushed to the car and pounded on the window. "I'm ashamed of you. I can't believe that you could be this lowdown."

"Shut up, woman; you don't know anything about me."

"You're right, I don't know you. And if you want to take it a step further, I don't want to know you. You're an animal, and completely out of your mind. I would like to blame this on your father. But truth be told, it probably came from your hood-rat mother. I'm done with you. Do not, I repeat, do *not* call me again—ever!"

"Oh, you're that type of bitch that would kick a brother when he's down? No wonder my father left you. Your pussy ain't that good, either."

"You lucky I can't get to you like I want to. But that's okay; you're about to get yours. I've done everything that I could and should do for you. You're a grown man now, and it's time to face the music for the things that you've done. And you don't have a clue what my pussy is like."

"Whatever, bitch." I turned my back on her, but not before I saw Merlin rush to his wife who was being wheeled out of the hotel room. My heart ached. Merlin won again.

55 MERLIN MILLS

"Sweetheart, are you okay?" I held Cojo's hand as I climbed into the ambulance with her. Her face was badly bruised. Her right eye darkened and shut, and her hair was all over her head. I attempted to smooth it down for her.

"How did you find us?"

"We can talk about that later. I just want to know if you and the baby are okay?"

"We're fine. He hit me in the face, but other than that he didn't touch me."

I breathed a sigh of relief. I don't know if I would have been able to handle it if my brother had sexed my wife twice. It was bad enough the first time. I was still trying to get those images from my mind. "Thank God! When I got out of jail I started calling you right away. I got worried because I know that you never turn your phone off and it went straight to voicemail."

"Gavin must have turned my phone off. He was waiting for me when I got out of the doctor's office. He kidnapped me and brought me to that nasty motel. I can't wait to have a shower. I feel dirty just lying on that bed."

My heart started beating faster. Why did she have to even mention lying in the bed? My imagination had them doing more than just talking. But I couldn't afford to entertain those types of thoughts. She was battered, but safe. The ambulance arrived at the hospital, and I suffered for a few moments while they checked her in and I filled out the necessary paperwork. Gina came in as I finished filling out the forms.

"How is she?"

"She seemed to be okay. I can't believe he beat her like he did. If he wasn't in jail, I swear before God, I would kill him."

"I just don't know about that boy. Sometimes I don't think he's wrapped too tight. I honestly thought he was getting on with his life when he wasn't around. I had no idea he was smelling after your wife."

"I just didn't know how to tell you. It's been difficult, especially since she did get pregnant around the same time this all happened."

"Are you okay with that?" Gina asked as a look of concern crossed her face.

"Regardless of who fathered the child, this will be my baby. What happened with my brother wasn't her fault, and I refuse to punish her or my child because of it."

"You truly are an amazing man, and I am so proud of you."

"I'm not that special. I just try to be a better man than my father. Speaking of him, what did you do?"

Gina gave me this uncomfortable laugh as she pulled me over to the side of the waiting room. "I did a very bad thing, but I don't regret it. Your father played me for the very last time and I stabbed him. I didn't kill him, but he might be left-handed from now on." She chuckled.

"When did all this happen? Do you think I should go check on him?"

"Do you really care about him?"

287

"Not really. I don't even know him, but I was thinking I might be able to talk him out of pressing charges against you."

"Don't worry about me. If he was going to do something, I think it would be done by now. If he does, I'll cross that bridge when I get there."

"Well, I'm glad you're taking this so well. I think I would be a basket case."

"For a minute, I was completely outdone, but I'm tired. I'm too old to be dealing with this foolishness."

"Good. I guess I'd better go see if I can find out what's going on with Cojo. Can you stick around; we're going to need a ride home afterwards."

"I'll be here."

♥♥♥

Cojo was smiling when I walked into the examination room they had taken her into. "There you are. I was beginning to think you left me."

"Sweetheart, I would never leave you. I was talking to Gina trying to bring her up to speed."

"The doctor said I could leave as soon as they take this IV out."

"And the baby, is everything all right with it?"

"The baby is fine. I've got some good news though."

"What's that?"

"It's your baby. The test results are ninety-nine percent accurate. I'd just gotten the results when your brother snatched me."

"Sweetheart, that's wonderful but I already told you, it will be my child regardless of who the dad is."

"I know you did, but I feel better about it now. I didn't want that hanging over our heads."

I was happy about the news, but I still worried about what happened during the time that she was alone with

Gavin. I couldn't shake the feeling that there was something more between them. Although I vowed to love the child, regardless of who the father was, I knew I might eventually have a problem with it that could jeopardize our relationship.

"I'm ready to take you home."

"Not as ready as I am to get there. They need to hurry the hell up – I have to pee."

56 MERLIN MILLS

Two Weeks Later

Cojo and I have been going through counseling and things were better between us. When I looked at her, I wasn't seeing my brother's tramp stamp etched in her skin. It was difficult at first because it meant talking about the emotions that we had stuffed inside. I was finally embracing our marriage and our child with all my heart.

"I can understand now how you wanted to forget your brother. He's one piece of work."

"Yes, he is. I'm not going to lie; it still hurts to think about him and his hatred toward me. I never did a damn thing to him but he kept a hard-on for me."

"I'm convinced he was jealous of you and that he wanted everything that you had. I think that's why he was so drawn to me because I was your wife."

"I know that's right. He always wanted what I had, and most of the time, I gave it to him. I'm ashamed to admit this, but I'm glad that he's in jail. I hope they throw the book at him too. I'm almost positive it was him that signed my orders as well. He didn't give a fuck about me."

"Well, I forgive you for not telling me about him. I might not have married you if I knew he was floating around in your gene pool."

"Are you serious?"

"Yeah, because crazy doesn't fall far from the tree."

"That's not fair. I am nothing like my brother. As far as our parents go, we don't even know them."

"My point exactly. They could be loopy as hell for all you know. But look on the bright side. Who would have thought that Gina and I could become friends?" Cojo started laughing as she wrapped her arms around me. I laughed with her.

"I know that's right. The other good thing is that my transfer has been put on hold, at least until after Gavin's trial. They can't send me out of the country just in case I'm needed to testify at his trial."

"If that's the case, I hope he never goes to trial. I want you here when the baby is born."

"I want to be here too. But in the event he does go to trial sooner, we should really talk about what we're going to do if I do have to leave."

Cojo sighed. "I don't want to think about that." She pulled away from me and walked into the bathroom.

"Captain Jameson said I should think about taking you with me." I heard the toilet flush and the water running in the bathroom sink.

When Cojo came out of the bathroom, there were tears in her eyes. I rushed to her. "What's wrong? Are you in any pain?"

She shook her head no and pulled me down on the bed. "Merlin, you know I love you, right?"

"Of course I do."

"If you have to leave, I want to stay here. I've lived that life before with my parents. I can't do it again. If it was just me, I would consider it, but I don't want to subject our baby to it. It's too hard."

My heart skipped a beat. My first instinct was she didn't want to be with me, but I had to listen to what she was really saying. As hard as it might be, I had to put my feelings to the side. There was still a chance I wouldn't be deployed or that she would change her mind.

"I understand, sweetheart. I won't pressure you to do it if you don't want to. I want what is best for you and our child. The only reason why I mentioned it was because of Captain Jameson. She confided in me that her marriage didn't survive the forced separation. She told me not to make the same mistake she did."

"Hopefully, it won't come to that. If it does, I think we can survive it. We've made it this far."

I wasn't as optimistic as Cojo was, but I didn't admit it out loud. Our last separation almost did us in, but that was different because of my brother.

"What are you going to do today? I have to go to the base."

"Believe it or not, I'm meeting with your mother. We're going to have lunch. I think she's benefiting from the therapy too."

"I think you're right. I haven't heard her say one thing about my dad in a couple of weeks. But I am worried about her. Every time I talk to her she's sick. I still ain't forgot about how she threw up in my lap that day at the hospital."

Cojo giggled. "That was bad, but you should have seen your face – it was classic."

"I'm glad you thought that was funny. Just wait till your water breaks and we'll see who's laughing then."

We both shared a laugh as I kissed her goodbye. "Tell Gina to call me and I'll see you tonight."

"Love you," Cojo mouthed.

I closed the door with a smile on my face and hope in my heart. I wasn't sure what tomorrow would bring, but for today, I was happy.

ABOUT THE AUTHOR

Tina Brooks McKinney began her writing career as a dare. As an avid reader, writing was the next step for her. Armed with a very active imagination and a story to tell, Tina penned her first novel All That Drama. Readers fell in love with Tina's no-nonsense characters and her comedic style of weaving a story. Since then, Tina has written ten novels and two novellas. Her titles include, All That Drama, Lawd, Mo' Drama, Fool, Stop Trippin', Dubious, Deep Deception, Snapped, Got Me Twisted, Deep Deception 2, Snapped 2: The Redemption, Betta Not Tell and Catch Fire and Catch Fire 2 and Outdone. The next installment, Done should be available in the summer months.

A wife and mother of two, Tina uses real life situations to both entertain and inspire her readers. You can find out more information about her by visiting her website www.tinamckinney.com or drop her an email at tybrooks2@yahoo.com. She would love to hear from you.

CPSIA information can be obtained at www.ICGtesting.com
Printed in the USA
LVOW04s2115290115

424898LV00032B/1948/P